BY CHARLOTTE PAINTER
. . . .

The Fortunes of Laurie Breaux
Who Made the Lamb
Confession from the Malaga Madhouse
Revelations: Diaries of Women
(co-editor with Mary Jane Moffat)
Seeing Things

SEEING THINGS

Charlotte Painter

PHOTOGRAPHY BY LLOYD PATRICK BAKER

RANDOM HOUSE NEW YORK

SEEING THINGS

ST. PHILIP'S COLLEGE LIBRARY

Copyright © 1976 by Charlotte Painter
Photographs copyright © 1976 by Lloyd Patrick Baker
All rights reserved under International and Pan-American Copyright Conventions. Published in the United States by Random House, Inc., New York, and simultaneously in Canada by Random House of Canada Limited, Toronto.

Grateful acknowledgment is made to NASA and Nova I Gallery for their cooperation with the photographer.

Designed by Antonina Krass

Library of Congress Cataloging in Publication Data
Painter, Charlotte.
Seeing things.
I. Title.
PZ4.P148Se [PS3566.A346] 813'.5'4 75-31501
ISBN 0-394-49739-2
Manufactured in the United States of America
9 8 7 6 5 4 3 2
First Edition

To
ALICE GEARY KILHAM

"The secret protects itself . . ."
　　　　　　　　　Old Saying

SEEING THINGS

Authentic Beings

I am a spirit guide, called Philomen. Today I have an express assignment, to report to the sincere student of life about an extraordinary ceremony involving three wise men and an especially endowed virgin. Many humans call upon my skills often, for my more general assignments are in the broad areas of nourishment and demon expulsion. One of my favorites, who will help me in today's task, has just sent a summons.

She is Selena Crum, sixty-five, whose signal comes to me as she rides on her bicycle. Before I can respond, however, Selena sees a being she actually prefers communicating with, through the window of the Berkeley Black and White Liquor Store. He is one of the three wise men of this report.

They have been lovers for seven hundred years. The moment she met him, Selena saw the spiral of their experience whirling through ages of high-intensity illumination. He is the Tibetan monk Tsinghai Yana, and is capable not only of visiting his past lives but of empowering others to see theirs. The sight of Tsinghai Yana makes Selena feel feathery and tender, like a young goose.

She gets off her bike to say good morning. Her Birkenstock sandal catches in a pedal, but Selena recovers her balance and pulls down her ankle-length skirt, which she keeps hiked up to her knees when cycling. Her auburn-gray hair, reflected in the display window, receives a fluff, and she goes inside.

"*Rinpoche,*" she says, using the Tibetan term of respect to her lover and nodding to Tsinghai's chauffeur, also a friend, who is at the counter purchasing three bottles of Black Velvet bourbon.

The holy man is at that moment gazing at the liquor store's burglar-alarm system beside the entrance, a video scanner. But at the sound of Selena's voice, he turns in delight, for he shares her tender featheriness and walks toward her with even a somewhat ganderlike sway. Some of his critics say he cannot walk a straight line, but such cynics are not our concern.

Like many of his countrymen, Tsinghai is homeless now, he and several from his monastic order having fled the Communists together, but Tsinghai is at home in the world wherever he is. All of it is familiar ground to him from past lives. Many times incarnated as a lama, he has also frequently found his way into other countries. The holy man is now about Selena's age. In this lifetime they have known one another since his arrival in the United States. It is she who gave him the Peter Max tie he wears today; she is pleased by his adoption of Western dress, usually of a quite conservative turn. He takes her in his arms and gives her an enthusiastic hug.

The monk listens attentively as Selena tells him that she is on her way up to the Claremont Hotel to prepare for a ceremony in which they both will take part that evening. Although he elicits information from her with little nods of encouragement, little frowns of incomplete comprehension, even occasional finger gestures to draw further words from her, he makes no utterance himself at all. For forty-two years, Tsinghai Yana has been under a vow of silence.

Remarkable as this long speechlessness may be, there is something even more remarkable about Tsinghai Yana. Scarcely anyone is aware that he does not speak, so adept is he at thought transference.

For example, although she had never before known any facts at all about her past lives, when they met he placed a series of thoughts into Selena's mind. She spoke to him of things which he confirmed with smiles and nods of remembered joy: that once they helped one another overcome the weakness of false pride, and that together they learned to love fools while discouraging their folly, and that they accomplished these important lessons while living as servants to the Druids.

Often people receive Tsinghai's thoughts without realizing it. Selena is now skilled at understanding him.

She says, "I hope you'll be free for the little extra ceremony we're having this afternoon, Tsinghai."

He thinks: What ceremony?

She says, "The Immersions. It's a kind of baptism."

He thinks: I shall become master of a water cult before very long.

She says, "Who knows, you might become master of a water cult someday!"

He thinks: Anyway, you will need me this afternoon. As you have throughout the ages.

She says, "Besides, I've a feeling I'm going to need some of your reliable help. This is a most peculiar day and things could pile up."

He thinks: It's only Karma.

She says, "Except that what goes wrong has to be right for some reason, doesn't it?"

The chauffeur, also a monk, named Suclong Rumpa, goes past them with the liquor purchases and places them discreetly in the car outside. A Tibetan more tradition-bound than Tsinghai, he wears black robes and a shaved head.

Tsinghai carefully watches the video scanner when the other monk passes it. As the camera turns on its support, Tsinghai gazes directly through the lens, examining the camera's insides.

Selena remarks, "It is the All-Seeing Eye."

Tsinghai thinks: Except that it isn't.

Selena looks more closely at the camera and asks, "It isn't seeing anything?"

The liquor-store owner looks up. "What do you mean?" he says. A burly man with high color, he is inclined to leap to conclusions. He does not have Selena's gift for receiving unspoken thoughts and feels attacked by her remark.

Tsinghai thinks: It can't see a thing.

"You see, it isn't seeing," Selena says to the liquor-store owner.

"What makes you think it isn't seeing things? I pay a hundred a month for this alarm system. It damn well better see." Annoyed by her skeptical look, he decides to demonstrate. "Look, I just push this button here below the register and it takes a few frames of film. I can get a picture of whoever has held up the place."

Tsinghai thinks: No one has tried yet.

Selena says, "You haven't needed to use it yet, have you?"

"So what?" the man says. "Five minutes from now I might."

"Except that it wouldn't work," Selena says.

"Come on," he says. "What are you—salesmen from Bay Alarm? It takes the picture, I ring for the cops, they get out their mug shots and pick him up."

Tsinghai thinks: Some film would help.

Selena smiles appreciatively at her lover and waits to see if the man he is trying to help can possibly receive the message. Who but Tsinghai would have troubled to look into the camera with his own all-seeing eye?

The liquor-store proprietor looks at them apprehensively now. "This is Berkeley after all," he mutters. "You can't do without protection around here."

He realizes the two people are just standing there with a certain calm patience looking at him, even though they have completed their business in the store. He shifts his weight. He says, "You two are acting pretty strange, as a matter of fact. I think I'll take a few frames right now." He presses the button.

The store owner muses, half to himself, "It'd be a funny thing if that security systems expert, that fat know-it-all, forgot to put film in the camera, wouldn't it?"

Selena and Tsinghai smile at one another, agreeably pleased that their experiment has worked. Investigation will prove the proprietor's surmise correct. He, however, will not know whom to thank for his insight. A burglary will occur that very afternoon, but the culprits will be photographed and apprehended. The store owner will tell his friends that he might not have checked the camera except that a nosy old pair started asking suspicious questions. Such is the path of secret altruism followed by Tsinghai Yana.

The gentle monk leads his love of seven hundred years outside. There he and Selena bring their hands together at their hearts and bow one another farewell.

Selena's remark that today is peculiar falls well into the realm of understatement. Today is the day of Selena's death. A surgeon is treating her for a disorder of the uterus, but she will die of something totally different. A sudden lesion in a large visceral vein will cause a fatal hemorrhage this evening. Today is also a day of unusual insights among all who know Selena and many who do not. It is also chosen as the day for my special assignment, because a high event may occur, among many nonevents.

You can imagine how far-spread my activity must be, in that nourishment is a world-wide concern, falling generally under the female principle. Demon expulsion, which has been my other general concern, is more narrowly focused, usually conceived as part of the male principle. That is why, when humans who contact me ask my sex, they may feel they don't get a straight answer. I am simply neither male nor female.

It is no longer unusual for spirit guides to make reports. They occur with rising frequency. Unlike many other such messages, my task is to report about the conduct of earthly life, no other, and it is an opportunity not only for humans but also for me in self-development.

I am told that my attitude is at fault, unbalanced, toward my dual assignments. It appears that I have leaned toward a preference for the heroics of demon expulsion. That I enjoy excitements of conflict too much. If so, that is certainly reprehensible in a spirit guide. I am told that I must find ways to bring public vitality to the sustaining activities of nourishment. What a job! Healing, peacekeeping, house-holding—humans have a historical prejudice against such low-key dynamics. But there is now something in the air . . . and anyway I may never neglect a given task.

A problem I have known as a human may help me to begin. I have been held in Karmic thralldom for many lifetimes as a woman, and sometimes as a man, by a certain petty vice, gossip. I have a theory, from my present perspective, that gossip is a vestigial root in the shape of consciousness. Not the scandal-mongering sort of gossip, but the kind that inquires into conduct, that wonders about the nature of injustice, abuse, iniquity. Two heads together asking something like this: "How could *who* have done *that* to *whomever?*" at least pose a moral question. That sort of gossip, if not based upon principles too rigid, may possibly lead to some slightly higher insight into human behavior, such as that practiced, for example, in psychiatric offices. I put this forth as a theory, nothing more. As I prepare my report, I may come upon a form of consciousness even I cannot yet see.

Many mediums advertise the earth as a training ground and life as a lesson or a series of lessons, but education does not stop there. Although it isn't generally confessed, almost all guides, like humans, are in need of improvement. Sometimes I think there is no end to it.

And so, to begin with a bit of gossip: Sages are moving about this planet. They come out of caves, hermitages, nunneries, and respond to invitations to speak, or if under vows of silence like Tsinghai Yana, merely to appear. They travel by jet. Masonic temples, Unitarian churches, and Astrodomes seating tens of thousands are engaged for them.

It is no wonder to these humans when they are asked to meet together, for they have foreseen everything. And it is no wonder at all to those who have arranged this evening's meeting that it should happen in Berkeley, precipitous shelter of seekers, called by some the valley of the gurus, resting as it does on the Hayward Earthquake Fault, a city whose 120,000 know what it is to wake to shudderings in their upper stories or groanings in the basement of knowledge hidden underground.

They are already beginning to arrive this morning, the many visitors to the Claremont Hotel, which is a vast wooden Victorian structure and country club spa. They will come from all over, in ankle-length robes, in costumes of the East—Near, Far and Middle. And also of Peru. A young black-haired girl clad in blue chiffon is being released now by a limousine, and something is glowing above her head—a gold ring, a *halo*? You may have heard of the Sisterhood grown up about this child, many members related to her by blood but others by adoption, a society of women whose power has now permeated its native Incan land, has proved impervious to national borders, and has penetrated the heartland of America, spreading beneficently in the manner of power centers of contemplatives in the Hindu Kush, which through the force of meditative union hold the world together. Vulgarizers, simplifiers, sexists, and those crazed by inept readings of Robert Graves suggest that the triumphs of popular women's movements may be surface manifestations of the power of the Little Mother, whose deeper mysteries may never be quite plumbed.

I have a great deal to tell about the Little Mother, of her home in the Andes, of the capture of a portion of the astral plane where she resides, all relevant to that general task I have of bolstering the female principle.

But for now, Selena Crum is calling me.

As she pushes her bike off, her pedal makes a click, which reminds her that she and I had been in communion before she met the monk. Her mantra makes a clicking sound.

Most people know that a mantra is a special saying, usually obtained from a personal teacher, a guru. Under certain circumstances the teacher privately will give this saying to an individual, who tells it to no one else. Or a person may use a traditional saying, such as *Om*, or one that an aide of Tsinghai taught Selena, *Om Hum* . . . *Om Hum*.

Selena began to feel the need of a mantra before she ever heard the word or knew about teaching gurus, and so she filled the vacuum herself. Later, she told Tsinghai that she had tried going *Om Hum* . . . *Om Hum* repeatedly, but it didn't do a thing for her, and when he realized that what she had been using was more American than apple pie, he flew into a state of sheer delight. We have seen how he favors

Western style. Her device is a teletype machine. She simply turns on her machine in her mind and she is in touch with me. Cltickaclicktictlic— Well, that inimitable type cannot be reproduced here, but who is not familiar with the sound of its advance, hesitation, pauses, rapid fire, with the ticker tape's fits and starts, its wondrous randomness, its inexplicable mystery, its powerful control over lives? Somehow, it meets Selena's needs perfectly. She slips a thought into the machine, which turns it into clatter, where its meaning is scrapped and she is becalmed by that symbol of American abundance and shredded paper parades.

She is now on Claremont Avenue, where she enjoys meditating, because parts of it are a dividing line. It separates for many who live in Berkeley the states of being somewhere and of being nowhere. On one side of that avenue lies Oakland, dismissed by Gertrude Stein with "There is no there there," yet often invaded by those who live in Berkeley, who raid its Genova delicatessens, dine at Love's Pagan Den, haggle at its Oriental groceries, invade its parks when acres of spring dahlias bloom, or riot in its street at appropriate political moments. However, for many on the Berkeley side, Oakland is a land of dark conservatism and chaos, a mini-Chicago, a smogbog San Francisco thrust across the Bay at the feet of the garden that is the World's Greatest University.

The town provides the same homing center that in happier times people found in Paris. Back to it they come again and again, elated by its simple disharmonies. Paris it is not, but also it is not foreign. Or Godforsaken like New York. Some say rather that it is God-infested.

Confirmation of the superiority of the Berkeley side crosses Selena's path. A pack of dogs stops with her at a red light, waiting for it to turn green. At the change, the dogs stroll as orderly as a group of street people into the crosswalk and to safety. Selena is so fond of this habit in Berkeley dogs that at times she will round some of them up for a run on the beach.

"Philomen," she says to me, "where else would there be no need to enforce a leash law?"

Selena often speaks to me when she rides her bike. Some people see only an old woman cycling along talking to herself, but it is not that simple. Selena has a lot to tell me (just as children have to tell their parents). Sometimes I think she has more to tell me than I have to tell her.

When she reaches the Claremont Hotel, her meditation ends, and I realize I must leave her for a time. I am not yet ready for the psychic tug of the scene in preparation. I must impose the caution of the sages, turn back from the hotel door to the oblique path where the dust of human destiny rises, seek greater readiness, deeper expectation.

I leave Selena for now to her tasks.

We move down the street. We must move with care so as not to fall into the one hundred twenty thousand Berkeley seekers at once. They are even a more massive hazard to me than the exotic personages arriving at the hotel.

It happens that one of Selena's friends over whom I also watch, Carrie Moon, lives in the appropriate place, neither above the hotel in the hills, nor down too close to the San Francisco Bay. The magnetic pull of either extreme might distort the balance I have been told to find. Cities built on hills always attract wealth to the top into buttery clusters, and slum dwellers are left in the churn of skimpy flats below. Carrie Moon's garden is a good place for me, midway, in relatively modest quarters, down from the grand hotel.

Carrie, a sculptor and painter in middle life, is one of my favorites, but I see at once that she is not the one who has drawn me there today. Instead, a glance through the high windows of her studio shows me who has—a medium!

The medium, a young man named Jim Smith, is sitting with the sunlight on his face. He is speaking to another of my favorites, Luna Newcome. "You have quite a lot of trouble with men," he is telling Luna.

She shifts in her chair and lifts her hand to adjust a comb in her cascading blond chignon, gazing at him, a handsome young man with remarkably unswerving, yet gentle, eyes. Her bracelets jangle about the sleeves of her Bedouin dress.

Luna knows that she has quite a lot of trouble with men. It has been her life-theme for all its twenty-nine years, she reflects, and so she says nothing, merely waits as the man falls silent, clicks off the remote microphone he is holding and closes his eyes.

Jim is making a tape of his reading as a matter of routine. Luna, however, has not let it rest there. Behind her own chair is a videotape camera, and she is putting the session on film. She plans to edit it later, with other taped readings, to make a video pilot.

Needing an attractive setting, she has brought him to the studio of Carrie Moon, for whom he has just finished a psychic reading. Carrie's work surrounds them in the studio: sculpture and painting, much of it of one figure, Selena Crum, who has modeled for Carrie for quite some time. From the high-vaulted glass ceilings, early-morning sunlight streams down onto the round oak table between the two people. Jim has told Luna that nowadays mediums seldom require darkness because the collective mind has moved into an age of light. She has liked that. She has liked a lot of things about Jim Smith.

He doesn't look the way most people expect a medium to look, but instead resembles a tennis player. In fact, he put his tennis racket in the corner of the studio when he came in, having met a friend for a set in Willard Park in the early-morning hours. Jim is of a strong, athletic build, dark-haired and clean-shaven, and his gaze is calm and penetrating, yet not overly intense. With nothing bizarre about him, no flowing guru robes, no beard or long hair, Luna sees him as an ideal vehicle for her videotape. He has just received a license to practice family therapy but incorporates into his work techniques for contacting the invisible world he says he has known since childhood. As Luna has remarked to Carrie, he is at neither extreme, neither shrouded in the occult nor straight and cornball like many practicing psychics she has seen, and is therefore perfect for her "statement about human consciousness and evolution." In one cranny of her mind not yet accessible to herself, he is also perfect for certain other designs Luna can't help having. His phrase "trouble with men" reverberates in that cranny, but those cells are dozing and she doesn't wake up yet to what is happening.

Another agreeable thing about Jim is his age, the same as her own, twenty-nine—an age of lingering idealism, in which experience has not yet eroded enthusiasm for more of the same, in which judgment has made only elementary gnawings upon hope and promise, and when youth's flash of beauty bears its highest luster.

Jim flips on the microphone. "I've just flashed on something," he says. "You're not in a stable situation today. I'm not sure what it is, but somebody could draw you into something really evil today. Does that make any sense to you?"

Luna gives an ambivalent, good-humored shake of her head. He closes his eyes. "Well, just watch where you go and what you do," he says. He shuts off the mike again for a few moments and waits.

"I am receiving a bridge. Are you planning to go over to San Francisco today?"

Luna shakes her head, then remembering they are taping, says, "No." Then he delights her by launching into an explanation of psychic symbols. "You probably know that we receive visual symbols in our readings—boxes, flags, jewels, water, and so on. We have so many bridges around the Bay Area I'm tempted to take it literally, but we have to look for a character sign. A bridge also means a challenge of some kind, crossing the great water, reaching out to something not easily available." A pause, eyes closed. "The bridge is swaying in a high wind. This means you have a difficulty ahead, turbulence, and the water is a problem with your female sexuality." A longer pause. Jim, open-eyed now, looks Luna over carefully after that term "female sexuality" comes out. He turns off the switch and takes a deep breath.

He flips the switch on again. "Does the concept 'Authentic Man' mean something to you?"

Luna gives a start. She leans forward excitedly. "Why, that's another way you have of receiving information, isn't it? Old-fashioned mind-reading, telepathy."

He looks at her with that quiet, unswerving gaze. "You were thinking that?"

Actually at this moment Luna wasn't thinking that. But Authentic Man is her term. For the sake of her tape, she says, "Yes! You've read my mind. I was thinking that phrase. So you've shown us two techniques clairvoyants use—the symbols a person arouses in your own mind and what you receive from theirs by telepathy."

Jim glances at the camera to which she is obviously playing, then closes his eyes. Luna thinks things are going wonderfully well. And hadn't she used that phrase "Authentic Man" only yesterday, in telling Carrie what she wanted in a psychic for her tape? Hadn't she expressed the hope that Jim might be not only psychic but an *authentic man*—competent, adventurous, responsible to the world, responsive to women, insightful as well as clairvoyant, perceptive as well as a channel for knowledge? That *is* a lot to ask, but Luna expects her videotape to launch her at last into Meaningful Work, and so she is insisting upon high standards. She is not concerned, for instance, with run-of-the-mill psychics, who might be able to read through sealed envelopes, receive the symbolism and aura of an individual on sight, see around corners and into the future. All that is not particularly interesting to her. What does interest her is something much more subtle, more scientific, too, and she intends to maintain a stance poised between sympathetic receptivity and investigatory skepticism.

Jim says, "Actually, I didn't receive the phrase through telepathy, but from a guide. A guide I haven't heard before."

Luna's delight rises. This will be a marvelous pilot, combining spontaneity, surprise, explanation—and Jim, too. "You *heard* a spirit guide?" she asks.

"Yes. The guide wants me to explain something that isn't generally understood." He listens closely, then laughs. "The guide says that some people in consultation with mediums ask imponderable questions that place a strain on the etheric web." Jim looks at her, apparently quite pleased with this message, which I have sent myself, thinking it would be useful for Luna's tape.

"But what about the Akashic Records?" Luna asks in some surprise. Luna actually does not believe Akashic Records exist, or at least tries by her expression to indicate skepticism. "My understanding of the Records," she says, "is that they give a guide access to every event that has ever occurred on earth."

Jim listens to me, then says, "Not always." His voice expresses disappointment; mediums do not like hearing about our limitations. But I urge him to go on. The fact is that sometimes the Records are not easy to get at. Imagine the red tape, the cross-indexing, the computer breakdowns! And there are often difficulties in linguistics and translation. It's a definite strain to go to the Source. He tells her, "The spirit says that while a guide has certain gifts humans do not, such as the ability to be neuter—that is, neither male nor female in the spirit state—they do not know everything . . ." A pause while he assimilates this. Then: "They are only ex-persons."

He smiles. "That's a nice insight," he remarks appreciatively.

But I have given myself away to Luna. She says, "Neither male nor female! That would be Phil, Selena's guide."

"Phil? This is a woman's voice I'm receiving," says Jim.

"Philomen is either sex, or neither, or both. Sometimes Phil will use a man's voice or a woman's. Sometimes I get a feeling I hear Phil myself, speaking in Selena's voice or Carrie's!"

Remembering her tape, Luna says, "Let's go back to that term 'Authentic Man.' It's interesting to me that you picked up on that." She is a little too interested, in fact. She stands up to move her camera closer, believing his description of an authentic man warrants a close-up of his thoughtful brown eyes. Her excitement disturbs the camera on its tripod and it jerks. "Machinery!" she cries. Luna has had some difficulty getting video technology under control, and the "spaghetti of electronics" is her main complaint about the Meaningful Work she has chosen. She is confident she can master the basics of the medium but is constantly disturbed by its cumbersomeness, complaining it is as outmoded as Alcatraz Island.

Jim leaps up to help her shift the camera, setting his microphone on the table. It happens that his hands can't help touching hers on the lever that adjusts the angle of vision. She says, "I want to get a close-up."

Actually, he is very close up to her at that moment, his thoughtful gaze bent upon her wide gray eyes. He murmurs, "I'm not sure I can handle this."

"What do you mean?" she asks. "You were doing so well. Authentic Man is perfect!" She is smiling at him a shade too brightly.

She receives a message from me herself: Watch yourself, Luna.

He draws away from her so that he may look at more than her eyes. He says, "You're so damned gorgeous."

That at last alerts Luna to her own slumbering motives. She says,

"Oh, no!" She turns away, thinking: *This again!* And she remembers a dream in which she is in a phone booth with practically nothing on, under the Marine billboard, "Looking for a Few Good Men."

She says weakly, "What about the authentic man?"

He reaches out for the sleeve of her Bedouin dress, then lets his touch sink gently through to her arm, pulling her back toward him. "Luna, there is no such thing." His hand moves down to her wrist, then finds her warm hand, which it takes possession of.

"Let go," she says unconvincingly. "You'll wreck the tape."

"Turn it off."

"Damn it, Jim—"

"Turn off the camera."

She turns it off. "What do you mean, there's no such thing as an authentic man?"

He sighs, draws her other hand to him and comes closer. With a mock Svengali gaze, he asks, "Is there an authentic woman at home in there?"

"Jim, let's get on with the reading!"

"Luna, I can't do a reading for you."

"You started off fine."

He nods and moves in closer. "A lot of trouble with men, sure. And a lot of trouble *to* them too, I'll bet." But he is smiling and now has his hands upon the Bedouin dress, at the round curve where it fits as no other Bedouin dress fits. Unlike other Berkeley women who wear ethnic dress, Luna takes hers to a dressmaker to have them redesigned. Jim's hand caresses the darts and tucks that have cleverly revealed the shape of Luna's earthly breasts. Even though her astral body is also available to him, he has completely lost interest in it. It might as well take an astral trip.

"Cut it out," Luna says. "This will ruin the project. It's important to me! You know how I'm trying to get things together, I—"

"You'll have to get another psychic. I'm not right for it. My sexual energy gets in the way, impedes the flow."

She pushes him away, laughing indignantly, and stalks to the other side of the room. Sexual energy! Impedes the flow! Maddening! How could she have been so obtuse? She must have led him on in some unconscious way. She tells him it's not what she had in mind at all. She wants a working relationship. She wants a friendly, easy understanding, not sexual involvement. Here she makes an open-armed gesture, her wide sleeves flowing out gracefully. She wants mutual respect, sincerity, the highest affection; she wants for once in her life to achieve a lofty intimacy, to attain androgyny!

Jim nods sympathetically. "And I just want to go to bed with you," he says. Then he decides to make a more energetic appeal. "This androgyny boom! It's as popular as the baby boom after World War Two! You know, it has its dangers. Sexual aloofness can turn into a problem. Detachment may be okay for an older woman like your friend Carrie, but it's not healthy for someone like you. You need a different configuration. You need to become centered and grounded rather than aloof." However she might have reacted to that, he then makes a mistake. He says, "Why can't you look on this as a random experience? Don't be so uptight about it."

Luna wants to fly into a rage. She can't bear fluxy Berkeley any more, with its hit-and-run sex, she says. She is trying to change her life. There must be some other way to get it together! It's not fair!

"Life is never fair," Jim observes, a bit platitudinously. "Some women would probably think it's unfair for you to be so beautiful."

Luna cries, "I even set this session up here instead of my place. I must have suspected somehow. Come on, Jim, you can do it. Sit down; let's try again."

His eyes are fixed on the bosom of the Bedouin dress. He says, "You'd better come spend the day with me. I can keep whatever it is that may happen from happening."

"Really! You don't think of yourself as a pitfall?"

"Look, the warning came. I didn't invent it," he says. "But I'll protect you."

But Luna is ready now to lose her temper altogether. "What a travesty!"

"I'm sorry," Jim says meekly. This has an infuriating effect.

"Well, go then. You've really blown it! Get out of here! I can't stand any more of it."

He opens the door and says he'll call her to suggest a substitute when she cools down. "I'll try to find somebody you can't turn on. But don't expect him to be the authentic man either."

Her cheeks burn; her eyes flash. She reaches for a small bronze sculpture of Selena Crum as if she would pitch it at him. He grabs his tennis racket but then stops with a complete change of attitude.

"Wait a minute, Luna. This could be a critical thing." His face is serious, almost grave. "Something could really fuck you up today. Be careful *today*, will you?"

She glowers. "Get out, damn it! I don't even believe in psychics."

As soon as the door closes behind him, she carefully replaces the sculpture. It has been the wrong gesture, she knows, childish and transparent, enough to show Jim that she shares his sense of being impeded by their attraction to one another. But what a setback, a nuisance, a disappointment, and, she has to admit, at last following my advice to watch herself, what a familiar pattern!

She turns to the mirror on the studio wall and sees her own image there, a blond beauty richly endowed to undergo the trials of the flesh in this life. Why couldn't she be more like the other image she sees in the mirror, Carrie, whom she glimpses reflected outside in the garden? Carrie, whose middle-aged composure speaks of already having dealt with some of those trials. Carrie, whose art is abundant enough to fill a whole studio and is enjoyed in many houses and museums. Carrie, who is successful in her work, *un*impeded by sexual conflicts, whose life has attained a serenity and peacefulness!

Jim Smith and Carrie have become engaged in conversation in the garden, which Luna cannot hear. They speak together calmly, easily. Carrie lifts a cotton glove in which she holds a trowel, to push back a wisp of her gray-brown hair. No man could ever disrupt Carrie's work, thinks Luna, for she meets all persons equally without impediments. Luna sighs and turns to gather up her video equipment.

As Jim turns to go, Selena Crum swings open the gate, wheeling in her bicycle. She has finished her errand at the Claremont and is here to model for Carrie. Were Luna still looking into the mirror or out the window, she would see Selena embrace Jim Smith with almost as much affection as we have seen her lavish upon Tsinghai Yana. Jim is another of Selena's loves, but in this particular Karma it was many years ago. Their reunion is brief, with promises to meet again soon. Jim, with a last backward look, in the vain hope of glimpsing Luna at the window, goes out through the gate.

Luna opens the door and sees that Selena has arrived. Now she wishes she might be more like Selena, even further than Carrie beyond the range of fleeting sexual impulses of men, or her own.

There is a freedom about Selena that Luna has never known. Did one have to grow old to attain that? Luna glances at the work in the studio, the Crums (as they have become known) which Carrie has worked on for years. She has painted Selena in many attitudes—at the Safeway talking to a checker, at the seashore, in yoga postures, chatting in the coffeehouses of Berkeley with others on the Path. Then came the sculptures which suggest that the range and capacities of Selena Crum defy definition—on ice skates on a Möbius strip, on her bicycle in a hypnagogic trance, in the bathtub under her pyramid. Carrie has even toyed with the notion, Luna recalls, of some life-sized Crums made of upholstery fabric, but decided against it when a gallery owner wanted to do a show in which the upholstered Selenas would move about with dancers zipped into them.

These three people, Luna, Carrie and Selena, a three-generational triad, are the primary reasons and resources for my report to the earth. They are the means by which I may be enabled to make the rare and unusual events to take place today at the Claremont Hotel available to earthly understanding.

Carrie sees that Luna has opened the door and comes toward her with a laugh. "What a delightful person Jim is!" Carrie says.

Luna seethes. She wants to tell Carrie and Selena what has happened between them, but she feels she handled it badly.

Carrie says, "I was just now telling Jim about a dream I forgot to mention during my reading." She sighs. "He seems more interested in character reading than most psychics. I suppose he's right."

"What was the dream?" Selena asks.

"Mercifully short," says Carrie. "I was living inside a triangle, which itself was inside an elephant. Jim says it is another example of how I've closed up my female sexuality. That I've got it hidden away underneath the thickest skin I could find."

Luna explodes. "That term of his! Female sexuality! He's so simplistic, so utterly sex-oriented. Listen, anybody who knows you could give a better interpretation of that dream." And she proceeds vigorously, applying her anger to the task. "The triangle is a female symbol, true, but it predates Jim's sexual fixation, going back at least as far as Paleolithic art. It also signifies the third eye and the pubic patch, two chakras. It is also a pyramid, the sign of psychic expansion. And *he* claims to receive psychic symbols! The elephant is not only thick-skinned, it is a hundred things; lumbering havoc-maker in china shops and forests, it is also lord of mystery, immense, looming, maternal. The female bears the process of gestation for two years within her gigantic form; the male is tusked with ivory—pure, white, hunted, precious. Yes! If you see only a thick skin in an elephant, you cannot imagine its force! For isn't the elephant, because of its immensity, a magical creature, capable of fooling us about its very identity —or so the ancient tale of the blind men goes—and isn't that the wonder of the dream, that within a massive, bewildering world, where our senses betray us by their constant misjudgment of the whole because of their incapacity to receive all at once the entire meaning of what happens to us, by their quickness to judge, by their telegraphic insistence upon opposing the slowness, the seeming ponderousness with which wisdom is acquired, that within such a vast, elephantine world, you, Carrie, survive, endure, expand, within this symbol of royal splendor! That fool—he blew it!"

Carrie and Selena smile at one another. Luna does run on! Carrie turns her trowel as if sifting Luna's alluvia of words. Occasionally she finds them glinting with gold dust from a hidden vein of some mountain stream. Of all the young women Carrie knows, Luna has the most striking problem because her beauty—which can make her appear vacuous, something to fill up like an alabaster bowl—is accompanied by a mind so jammed with information, true and false, with opinions worthy and illiterate, with all those *words*, that men frequently flee on sight. Sometimes even Carrie, who does her best to encourage Luna, sees her as a beautiful vessel whose cargo causes her to list dangerously.

Luna says, "I'm *so* disappointed! Selena, I'll play the tape for you.

You'll see he's not what I need." And to Carrie she says, "I'm coming to some definite decisions about my life, too!"

Carrie is gazing at her herb bed. Marjoram has crept into thyme, and it is only June. Her gaze shifts slightly to an adjacent rock, and she loses herself in it.

Selena says, "If you want Carrie to listen, you'll have to get her out of that nick."

Luna sees that Carrie has fallen into a state Selena calls a "nick of time." Carrie is given to visions. Actually they take very little earth-time at all, but a great deal goes on in them.

A nick, according to Selena, is a notched-out-piece of salvation, time-free. A quickie meditation.

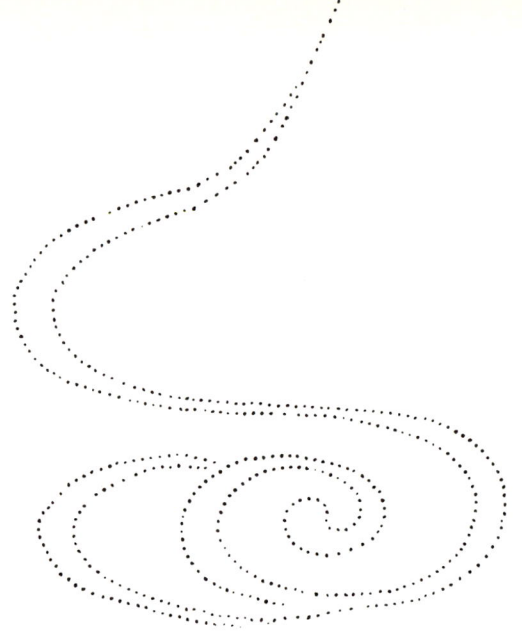

DU and ICH

"To go further, back up." I am quoting a *Sayso*, which is a term coined by yet another of Selena's lovers, an American elder statesman among psychiatrists, Emil Jewels. A *Sayso* is an enigmatic nugget of wisdom, a wise saw, a *given* to meditate upon, a saying with remarkably hidden layers.

This particular *Sayso* occurs to me now because I must back up to Selena's morning errand at the Claremont to go further with my own task.

In the hotel lobby, where she telephones one of the rooms, she notices a letter board of the day's events beside the elevator bank. Among other attractions, Turk Murphy and his Dixieland band are playing there today. At the bottom she reads: "Psychic Reality Ceremony ... Under the auspices of DU and ICH, also ICH and DU."

The repetition of the name of the two sponsoring organizations does not surprise her. It appears also on the invitations to the ceremony: after "Psychic Reality" there is an asterisk which is like the head of a pin over which great minds debate, not about dancing angels but about mortal strife. Two rival organizations make up the Psychic Reality core, and the footnote to the invitation about the dual sponsorship only hints at some of the tensions between these two groups.

In these days of acronyms and public relations, DU has not wished to cheapen its image by the use of the initials PR for Psychic Reality. However, the leader of ICH, himself a former PR man, has a deep-seated craving for publicity. ICH itself is an acronym—for Intergalactic Cosmic Hookup.

Much of ICH's teaching originated when Tsinghai Yana, in an occult ceremony somewhere outside Tibet, handed the rod of power to ICH's leader, Strong Elkhart. This enabled him to create a doctrine from the spacey writings of an Israeli prophet and psychic named Ira Omensetter, whose manual of the beyond is called *DU and ICH* (in the American edition, *You and Me*, published by Stonebooks). Elkhart's ICH synthesis also borrows from teachings of Tsinghai Yana and other sources of illumination.

Selena, a DU-by, enjoys the hope that mankind's strongest and most elusive attribute, cooperation, may prevail between the two groups. She telephones the room of the tacit leader of DU, Bubba Burr, to tell him she has arrived. In theory, DU has no leaders, but Bubba started it and, Selena sometimes thinks, ought to finish it.

She speaks into the phone, saying she will be at the swimming pool, and goes out the rear entrance. She has come to make sure of the preparations for the afternoon ceremony she has mentioned to Tsinghai Yana. Selena herself will be the tacit leader for that service, which she herself invented—the Immersions into DU, a kind of initiation rite. She goes into the bathhouse to change into a swimsuit, thinking she may have time for a quick swim. However, as soon as she reaches the pool, she is met with an unexpected challenge, a reporter from the Berkeley *Gazette*.

A white-mouse-faced girl, wearing stockings and a Kimberly knit dress, corners her. "What is the purpose of the baptism, Ms. Crum?"

Selena glances with mild suspicion at the several young girls in bikinis who are setting up for the pool ceremony. One of them must have let word slip to the *Gazette*, possibly the novice who is trying to balance a large earthenware jug filled with tules. But all the girls are innocent-hearted, she reflects, and don't know of the wrongful interpretations of DU that have previously reached the press. They have been ridiculous enough to cause Bubba Burr to forbid interviews. Selena cannot reproach the new and earnest students, who are so happily and efficiently placing the props they will need—the tules and cattails and the small tray of plastic reeds—beside the steaming Jacuzzi whirlpool.

"Is that where it's going to take place? In the hot pool?" the reporter inquires.

Selena sighs. "We really don't want any publicity."

"But we cover all local weddings, baptisms and funerals," says the girl, a sly twitch of secret mockery pursing her rodent lips. "I understand you usually do the baptisms at the baths in Calistoga Hot Springs, but that you're using this less bucolic setting because of the wedding this evening."

Selena is trying to decide how to deal with this insistent person, probably a Mills College graduate sent by the *Gazette* on a mistaken errand. She understands Bubba Burr's paranoid mistrust of publicity. She knows that she herself looks ridiculous, wearing a bikini like the novices, which reveals the varicose veins she earned while working on an assembly line during World War II. She knows that anything she says will probably go into print as an absurdity. She sits down on a flowered vinyl mattress that covers a redwood chair, a move which the reporter chooses to see as an invitation. Sitting next to Selena, the girl pursues her story.

"Actually weddings and baptisms are two very separate rites in most churches, aren't they? I mean, you *are* a church, aren't you?"

Here at least is a question Selena feels it is safe to answer, if briefly. "No, I am not a church."

"I mean, DU is a church," the reporter insists, writing furtively. Selena is about to say no, but realizes the Internal Revenue Service might be interested to hear that DU no longer considers itself a church. The girl goes on writing, doubtless a description of Selena herself, like the one the *Examiner* ran some months ago: "An ageless gnome, perky-faced, with bright blue eyes and long salt-and-red pepper hair . . . a familiar Berkeley figure, known to have once danced with the Isadora cult in the hills, to have lived among San Francisco's beats and hips, a mixed bag—no pun intended . . . forever a follower of the avant-garde." Such is the mixture of metaphor available in the local press. There is really nothing Selena can safely say about DU to this avid young woman, who urges her: "Please go on. For example, how might I describe the wedding this evening? What will the bride wear?"

At that a harsh male voice speaks over their shoulders, a voice intentionally softening itself. It is ICH's leader, Strong Elkhart, running his large hand over his clean-shaven chin. Elkhart is always running his hands over something, Selena thinks. "I can explain that," he says, pronouncing "I" almost like "Ich."

He stands behind them in his swim trunks and has apparently been listening in. "Everyone will wear the color of their aura," he says, ready to seize this opportunity to get into print.

The girl squeals delightedly. "Oh, you must be the one they call Mr. ICH!"

"Strong Elkhart," he says, extending his large hand. Leaning toward Selena, he whispers, "Buzz off. I can handle this."

Selena neither buzzes nor budges; rather, she seems to the reporter to go into a trance. Actually, she puts Elkhart's order into her teletype machine and rises above it, listening to all he says, and at the same time having a brief exchange with me:

"*Philomen?*"
"*Yes, Selena.*"
"*Get rid of him.*"
No reply.
"*Please?*"
No reply.
"*Do I have to do it?*"
"*Yes, Selena.*"

Selena is surprised at this change in me, for now I am obliging her to use her own resources in my effort to restrain my love of demon expulsion.

Her first effort at getting rid of Elkhart has been unsuccessful. When he first came to the Coast after a trip to the Andes, she warned Bubba against him. But he was already committed. Selena had never met a man more disdainful of women than Elkhart, or more successful with young ones. It is a sore point between herself and Bubba, for Bubba is not entirely clear of male arrogance himself and cannot take Elkhart's contempt seriously. He has merely laughed off Selena's misgivings. "You're just bugged by his weakness for young chicks," Bubba has said. But Selena is not one to confuse narcissism and Don Juanism, which Elkhart undoubtedly is plagued by, with the more sinister quality she senses in him. She knows ICH has its roots in sales techniques Elkhart picked up as ad manager for GM in New York. She also knows that his work has often been a front for jobs for the CIA. What he is saying now to the reporter is colored by that secret past, even though veneered with a worldly humor. "ICH has come out from its New York base for this occasion, to foment reconciliation," he tells the reporter.

Who else, Selena wonders, would have happened upon the choice of that word "foment," and who else would be so insensitive to the Berkeley *Gazette*'s unreadiness as to hand the reporter a copy of the Psychic Reality wedding invitation while explaining to her the meaning of each color in the aura spectrum?

As for Elkhart, his own opinion of Selena is based on his first encounter with her, when under the influence of a certain Andean drug, he saw her body undergo a change and grow from one side—the left—an enormous, disproportionate, milky breast, like a lopsided madonna from a Rubens painting. That this distortion of vision was his own, he never considered; he was instantly convinced he had been given an insight into Selena's character beyond question: a mother-oriented female of the worst sort, the kind he feels dedicated to combating. Elkhart cannot conceive of any worse organ of intrusion than a distended nipple, for reasons we need not consider, and has it in for motherhood.

The reporter quickly scans the invitation, which she will print in its entirety in the *Gazette*. Here it is:

Psychic Reality* will inaugurate an annual marriage ceremony on the first Sunday in June. It is an occasion not only of solemnity but of divine laughter, open to those who have been married during the year, whatever the form, or who wish to be married within the Psychic Reality core. The wedding will be devoted to the emergence of the Female Principle in Man. This initial group wedding will be honored by an unusual gathering of presences, who will endow the solemnities with a higher grace and magnificence than the common earthly marriage.

Officiating by special arrangement will be:

Tsinghai Yana. This august monk, whose vow of silence has been in force for forty-two years, will make his first public appearance, having bestowed the rod of power of his order upon an American.

Ali Pshaw. We in the West owe a great debt to this scholar of esoteric secrets, all of which he has divulged, each disclosure yielding the certainty of deeper unknowns. Thanks to Ali Pshaw, we can renounce the Secret Society and embrace Multiplex Transmission.

Emil Jewels. There are some who have yet to receive the instruction of our own beloved American teacher, psychiatrist and friend, disciple of Gurdjieff, Freud and Reich. But there is surely no one alive who has not yet appreciated the great Jewels *Sayso*: "Wake up and come."

Mamacita. The Little Mother of Peru, sacred among the Incans for more than fifteen incarnations since the Conquest, is now inhabiting the body of an eleven-year-old virgin. She is making her first visit outside her own nunnery, although some of us have been privileged to visit her retreat in the Andes, on a section of the astral plane homesteaded by the human mind and inhabited by her high sisterhood. Her visit among us is an auspicious event, and her officiating, together with the Three Wise Men, at our initiatory marriage, an honor of the highest order.

The crowning moment of the ceremony will occur when Mamacita's powers are manifest to all present and the marriage party enabled, by dint of her spirit, to see her halo. This halo is pro-

---

* Under the auspices of ICH and DU, DU and ICH.

duced through the natural alchemy of chlorophyll, ether and love, all available to Mamacita because of her singular gifts. The halo symbolizes universal joy, the unbroken circle of being.

It must be clearly understood that no one will be admitted without this embossed invitation, for which you have signed a blank check. Your gift signifies surrender of the bonds of material life and devotion to the *Sayso* of the eternal marriage: "Every Mind a Blank."

The reporter does not miss the asterisk after Psychic Reality. She asks, "Why does it repeat both names like that? Trouble about who gets top billing?"

Bubba Burr arrives at the poolside just in time to hear this pointed question and steps in, clapping Strong Elkhart on the back. Bubba flashes a smile through his heavy beard, obviously pained that Elkhart has given the reporter an invitation. She is sure to come and write something unfavorable.

Bubba moves in on her, telling her his name, which she recognizes. Bubba Burr has once enjoyed local fame as champion of the oppressed on the Berkeley-UC campus in the days of the Free Speech Movement. Bubba, too, shrinks from an imaginary newsnote: "After getting his Ph.D., this existentialist-turned-parapsychologist—"

"Do me a favor, Ms.—" he draws out the Ms., waiting for her to supply her last name. "Yes, Ms. Barnes. Will you please come to the wedding before you write anything about it? Make use of that invitation?" He explains that Psychic Reality is something that cannot be understood until it has been experienced.

Elkhart agrees enthusiastically, sensing no reproach. "Look, sweetie," he croons, running his hand along her arm, "whatever your deadline is, forget it. If you'll excuse the corn, our ceremony is a *life*line. ICH may be what you've been waiting for all your life."

Ms. Barnes smiles. "Just one thing. This Female Principle in man —would that be in woman too?"

Bubba winces. "Printer's error. It's supposed to be Human*kind*." He maneuvers Ms. Barnes toward the exit gate. "We'll be happy to see you this evening. But please," he says, "no pictures."

"Tsinghai Yana wouldn't mind," Elkhart says.

"Oh, yes, he would," Selena objects, feeling she has a better line on Tsinghai than Elkhart.

"I *know* Mamacita would object," says Bubba irritably.

This dispute intrigues Ms. Barnes enough that she decides she wouldn't miss the wedding for the world. She tucks the invitation away and obliges Bubba by taking her leave. Selena, you'll observe, did not get rid of the girl or of Elkhart. My attitude is new toward her. She has a lot to learn all in one day, and it her last, too!

"Damn it, Strong!" Bubba says. "We agreed—"

Elkhart raises his hands. "I know. I got carried away. I dug her style, refreshingly straight."

"Is there any style you don't dig?" Bubba is quite exasperated, but he realizes the damage is done. "We can't have publicity, Strong. This is *power*. Playing with power is dangerous. I don't have to tell you that."

Strong Elkhart doesn't have to be told anything about power, in his opinion. Even the word starts his mind spinning. He reels away and takes a dive into the swimming pool, leaving Bubba to meet Selena's gaze.

The plunge into the pool removes Elkhart's consciousness from the people around him. He has many such techniques of detaching himself from consciousness, abrupt and sometimes peculiar disconnections, most of them less innocent than a dive into the pool. The dive registers as a division of reality in his mind that might alarm an ordinary mortal. But not Elkhart. Inside his head he sees another plunge, that of an enormous log bolting down a large metal chute toward a piece of grinding machinery. He hears the shrill scream of moving steel and a splintering crash. It is only a flash vision, but it has begun to occur repeatedly inside Elkhart's mind, the great log, the chute, the scream of metal and the splintering of fiber.

He rises to the surface, smiling with a look of deeply secretive satisfaction. He is glad to see that both Bubba and Selena have gone. Now he can move back into this present moment, where the girls arranging cushions beside the pool draw him like nectar.

. . .

Selena is biking toward Carrie's now. Her ticker tape is shredding the unpleasantness of the encounter with Elkhart, so that by the time she arrives she is refreshed and ready to be of service.

The line Selena slips into her teletype machine has come from me. "Today is my last." It is a thought that flows out of Selena into her machine without a twinge, so quickly and lightly that she does not even realize its source. It has occurred to her that she will die soon, and if today is the day, then she is willing. She pedals carefully along the avenue, however, determined that no accident will claim her.

The Nick of Time

Luna's words about Carrie's dream flow into the garden like sand. They drift onto Carrie's bed of thyme and marjoram, pile up against a rock, a whole sand bar of words. Carrie is listening but also reflects with some whimsicality that perhaps sand is what words *are*, not meant to glitter in faceted isolation like gemstones, but little fragments worn against each other for human use. Carrie herself is more taciturn than most of her friends, having been in her youth an inarticulate painter and over the years having developed a healthy respect for the power of words to make images and action. But the end of words—Carrie receives glimmers of not only their use but their end—is even more interesting to her.

And now as she kneels beside the rock a surge of exhilaration possesses her. Carrie has to put both hands on the ground to maintain her balance.

Luna, who has been standing in the studio doorway beside the strawberry arbutus tree, disappears in mid-utterance. Blond hair, gray eyes, spangled bracelets, Bedouin dress—Luna and her entire get-up telescope and vanish into a clear white space. Selena (who has gone inside to change into a costume Carrie wants for a sculpture) vanishes too; the studio disappears as well. Everything in Carrie's world goes, reappearing in—was it in the pause between breaths? What has caused it? Luna's words, "the process of gestation," reverberate as a number of stories, happenings, visions swarm before Carrie's eyes. She is in what Selena has called a "nick in time."

Anything can happen in such a nick. Carrie might be standing beside the bay, for instance, and see under it the rubble and ruin of lost continents, or cities in their original splendor, gleaming, white, inhabited by magical, authentic beings, people familiar to her life; she herself might even be there.

Carrie knows there are names other than Selena's for such flooded states; she even has her own name. She calls it "layering," a term used by an artist she knows to describe superimposed images, but Carrie takes comfort in it as a gardening term, likening these spells to the layering a conscientious gardener will make of shoots and plants, bending them and covering them with earth until they are rooted and create new plants. Such as that row of elderberry trees beside the studio which her gardener Ginseng has layered, so that the lean trunks make a latticelike screen extending the length of a bed of irises. Gardeners may become eccentric, but they seldom go insane.

The world about her is extremely vivid, as are the layers of images. Carrie gazes at the rock beside her trowel. It happens to have a shape to it like the face of a man she once knew. Nothing unusual there, in that rocks easily remind sculptors of faces. Carrie often sees faces in flowers too.

But now her own face appears upon the rock, together with the man's, and with a little surge, again, she is there with the man, *inside* the rock. But then he is gone, and Carrie is there alone in her garden, as she has been for years. Who was the man, so fleetingly recognized? Her former husband? An earlier love?

Then she sees what has scattered the image—two shiny, brown-specked ladybugs who have come to eat the aphids off the rosebushes in her garden and have settled upon the rock. Their tails are engaged together, one mounting the other, their wings fluttering. Ladybugs? Carrie wonders: would Luna, who could be so derisive sometimes about the members of her female commune, to whom she nevertheless gave intense if divided support, would Luna call them *woman* bugs? Was one of them a *man* bug? Carrie watches these benign insects, who have imposed themselves over the young man's face, displacing it. Then, both in and out of the nick momentarily, she remembers Selena has told her that Harrison is coming today, is going to leave some of his machinery at her house while he goes for a meeting in the city. And Harrison's face is there; under the fluttering wings of the mating bugs she can see his large, wide-set eyes.

Selena has introduced Carrie to Harrison, an eccentric inventor from Calistoga Hot Springs, only a week ago, briefly, yet in this swirling layer of images he is her lover, has been her lover for some time. And she also realizes that although she has not seen him for weeks, her anticipatory emotion is not joyful. It is instead gnawingly unpleasant to her. Harrison is someone she does not want to resent or to have any problem with, now that in this layer he is her lover, because he is tender, creative, funny, sensitive, vulnerable, unique, appreciative of her, warm, engaging, good in bed, gifted, ironic, an inventor of genius; but he is also childlike, dependent, needing, a large consumer, an eater, a wanter of nurture, an occupant of space. Of course! She has seen these less appealing traits when they met but suppressed them, and now, inside the rock, there he is, attached to her, banging into her living room with his invention, dumping a mass of machinery onto the Oriental rug, a gigantic man with hair growing down behind his ears, wearing a rumpled hunting jacket and boots and Levis, his work clothes, and looking as if he might be found on Telegraph Avenue asking for spare change except that he is beardless, or emerging from underneath the body of a Porsche or a VW, grease permanently embedded beneath his fingernails, except that unlike the normal garageman fostering a mystique to keep his customers coming, Harrison will discuss, at length and lucidly for those who will attend, the workings of the internal combustion engine, will disclose (now that he has a patent) the solution he has created to the engine's greatest weakness, its thirst for and drunken dependency upon the demon tetraethyl lead. Harrison, down from Calistoga Hot Springs, into the smog belt, which he avoids except for money and—though reluctant to admit it—for love, now that he has formed this mysterious attachment with Carrie, and also to attend one of the conferences with the industrialists who have contracted for his patent.

No greeting. Just "I've got a couple of retorts with me and a still. I'm working out a last kink in the process. Open the garden gate, and I'll bring them around. This engine I don't want to leave outside. Maybe it can go into the studio; it's got to be watched closely."

Watched? Guarded? Or does he mean safeguarded against rain, burglars, patent plagiarists? Carrie sighs. Enter the classic male animal, taking over not only her house but her garden and now her work space, her sacrosanct studio—move it over, woman, move over your easels, your clay, your Crums. Here comes Harry, the man with his big grand engine!

Carrie says, "Harrison, hello," and wonders at the tremor the sight of him causes, when only weeks ago, before she had ever seen him at all, such a tremor seemed impossible, forever undesirable even, no longer a sensation of her existence, a condition Selena has inquired into, aware of Carrie's history and, since her divorce, distaste for man-hunting or indulgence in current sexual vogues.

Having found early in life an art unique to herself she could practice, having had occasion and need to practice it, Carrie has become something of a model among younger women who, like Luna, search for meaningful work. How many women have looked to Carrie's friendship, hoping to unlock the secret whereby they too might become more independent, less frightened of individual action, not imprisoned by some unsatisfactory matrimonial scheme! Corrine Castle, stopping by to report on the disappointments in her latest couples' swap; Louise Lever, her voice a sponge on the telephone, soaking up hope, asking advice about her husband whose fifteen-year occupation has been to play jazz of the fifties at home on the piano until he formed a group with a miniskirted flutist, now pregnant; Clarissa Marvel, there to explode under the pressure of communal living and open marriage; Ginger Beacon, undone by her venture into bisexuality with a woman whose three preschool children she has recklessly agreed to care for every day. Raking through the small events of sexual salvationism, they have swept through Carrie's garden, while Carrie, continuing to work, has given her sympathy but not her participation in any of it. The women have gone back to their conflicts with a deeper admiration for Carrie, tinged by the suspicion that there may be something missing in the life of a woman who eludes conflict.

Even Selena has questioned her. "You want nothing, desire no one?"

Carrie has replied with a poem from Sappho:

> The moon is down
> and the Pleiades;
> it is the middle of the night,
> time passes, time passes,
> And I lie alone.

Its cosmic reverberations aside, Carrie thought that expressed quite well her belief that lying alone is better than the consequences of not lying alone.

And Selena immediately has remembered having met a certain inventor while taking a walk to escape a tedious Psychic Reality seminar. Strange spurts of steam from behind a fence, swearing, exclamations of delight, have drawn her to investigate and discover that rare person. Remembering his own talk about freedom from sexual attachment, Selena has decided they are both ready to be tested. "I am a monk, an ascetic, a hermit by choice," Harrison has boasted.

Harrison is stomping into Carrie's layered vision with all that machinery, dragging his portable distillery out to the garden. Ginseng rushes to help him, to wonder and to marvel: "What's that, a retort, and that?" Harrison lifting Selena in an effusive hug, then seizing Carrie, lifting her in his huge arms, hugging her until she thinks her ribs will crack, then releasing her suddenly with only a peck on the cheek, walking into the kitchen, flinging open the refrigerator door, demanding food, cursing the heat of the drive down, needing, wanting, hungry.

Damn! Carrie wants to go on with her work, is torn, angry.

She simply doesn't want a big clumsy elephant child around now. Curtailing her activity, demanding care. He would want, want, bellowing through his trunk, knocking over statuary, stampeding the garden, gobbling up all the peanuts, sucking from a milk bottle. "It's the psychic space a man takes up—I don't want it filled," she has said once to Selena, explaining her reluctance to let any man into her life, to which Selena has replied, "An elephant can be trained to dance on a drum." But Carrie, groaning, has not been amused. "I've already raised my children, haven't I?" But in the following silence they both have considered the unendingness of nurture, of the lifetimes it might take before motherhood is rightly attained, before the perfect child is enabled to grow into a more perfect adult than anyone has yet seen. And so, within the rock of her vision, Carrie is lured into the kitchen, yields, takes out the sandwich makings, pours a glass of milk for Harrison (a tall glass of milk), feeds him, feeds him. Watches him eat, acknowledges her own hunger, touches his cheek, cares for him, loves.

The ladybugs flutter, undulating upon the garden rock. The female will lay her eggs and teach her children where the aphids are on the rosebushes growing near the rock.

And then a rose appears on the rock beneath their tiny bodies, and Carrie is watching Selena in the Berkeley Rose Garden.

I might mention how much I myself enjoy these layers of Carrie's, which take me above the distressing sequential human state and also allow me to pursue my own work in female consciousness. Not only is Carrie seeing herself and Harrison in her own garden but simultaneously Selena with another man. Selena, never troubled with the loneliness that any solitary worker like Carrie knows, is being courted, too, after a fashion.

She and the man, Peter Delgado, sit surrounded by every variety of western rose. He is trying to persuade Selena to go away with him.

Peter is only a few years younger than Selena. His slimness, the weary elegance in his glance, the slight Latin accent, all contribute, he well knows, to his talent for having women under thirty cling to him. Yet Peter has singled out Selena for the fulfillment of his life, and has brought her up to the Berkeley Rose Garden. They have had tea together—Peter, three brandies—and now in the setting sun, which they can see below the San Francisco skyline as a muggy, withering rose, he urges her to consent.

"You're worth it, Selena, believe me."

To his astonishment and dismay, she replies, "Peter, *I* may be worth it, but is *it* worth doing?"

In his practice in psychotherapy (more recently sex therapy), Peter has seen everything and does not like to be astonished. He has a studied patience he brings to bear upon the situation, realizing perhaps that Selena may not understand her days are numbered, nor grasp the quantity of young women who would snap at the chance to dash with him in his Porsche down to Mexico, or fly down for the particular adventure he has in mind.

Peter imagines he will have to explain aging to her. "Selena, I have a patient," he begins, "recently moved here from New York, a man older than myself . . ." Peter clears a tight throat. "He told me a story so terrible that I resolved to lose no more time. He was with a lady friend of his, a woman younger than he, in the Plaza Hotel, overlooking Central Park one hot summer day. It was so hot, he said, that one of the horses standing there below his window hitched to a hansom cab, fell down. You know those cabs that ride you around the park? Well, he couldn't get over that horse. Falling down in the hot sun, too old to be of any use, worn out, an anachronism, dying on the pavement. People stared at it for a long time before a policeman thought to call the ASPCA wagon, which came and hosed the horse with water in a futile effort to revive it. My patient watched it all from his hotel window . . ."

Peter's voice has an emotion in it which betrays to Selena, almost from the start, that he is telling about his own experience, is merely shielding himself with the older-patient fiction. "The man began to have fainting spells, my patient, and every time he blacked out, he'd believe he *was* that horse in front of the Plaza Hotel at Central Park. And the girl with him at the time, who had gone through a sexual disappointment with him—after all, he was older than I—the girl would just look on, making no effort to help him. And finally when he was totally unconscious, he believed she would go call for the ASPCA wagon to come and hose him down. He felt he was that old, tired horse, who had stood waiting all his life in inclement weather doing a job of work that was essentially fatuous. No wonder he fell down." Peter looks at Selena, expecting that she might also see herself in that horse.

But Selena only says, "You really want to be young again."

At first Peter does not grasp that she in no way shares his ambition. He reaches for her hand beside him on the bench. "Look at your hand, Selena. Imagine it without those veins, that crepiness"—he rumples her skin so that it is even crepier and rubs her finger joints—"those arthritic burrs. Imagine no numbness, no stiffness—"

Selena merely laughs. "You sound like a television commercial."

But Peter hangs onto her hand, and as he talks, he gazes not into her bright blue eyes but at the hideous wrinkles around them, letting his attention rove to the fold underneath her chin, to the earlobe elongated by the years of gravitational pull and possibly by the gold dangles hanging from them, to Selena's neck, becoming crepy too, blotched by pigment loss. He murmurs, "We need only go to the Hacienda once a month—fly down together—and take the injections. Then if you like we could go over to Tijuana to the bullfights afterward, or fly on further to Rio if you like. It is painless and, I promise you, feasible. Eventually the FDA will have to allow its use here, but we, you and I, don't have time enough to wait for that."

"Why me, Peter?" Selena asks with a neutrality Peter chooses to understand as coyness.

"I admire the fact that you do nothing to hide your age. You wear no make-up, have never had a face lift. You don't color your hair or wear a wig, or wear clothes that are too girlish for you—your costumes, in fact, are ageless." That is true. Selena has a certain knack for dressing (and costumes was the appropriate word) in a manner that is distinctly her own, not of the period of the end of her youth (as older women have a curious habit of doing, as if trying to freeze time at their own peak) nor of any current fashion either. Her clothes come from thrift shops, pieces from all periods, the color of her aura, yellow-gold shading to white. This evening she has on a gold wool jacket with a full-length skirt. When she found it in the Turnabout

Shop, it had a hole in one elbow, which she has patched with a deeper shade of gold leather.

Peter says, "I might take along a younger woman. But they all are inexperienced. I want someone who has lived with a point of reference I can relate to. Who, except nostalgia freaks, really knows the World War II songs, for instance? I was a medic in the Battle of the Bulge, just about the time your husband was dying over there. A young girl might be amused to see me growing younger, but it wouldn't be a mutually shared recreation of life. Also you, being mature, would make no demand upon me until I was ready."

Some of Peter's longing has touched Selena, and although she does not revise her perception of him as kinky and his Mexican medicine man (actually a German doctor pursuing illegal researches into reversal of endocrine and cellular function) as a deranged and misguided quack, she begins to be moved by Peter's peculiar desire to see the gray disappear from his temples, to experience the lightness, the resilience of young tissue in a body not yet ravaged by the uses of cigarettes, alcohol, fat, caffeine, smog—in short, by breathing, eating, sleeping, loving, trying to love . . .

Selena casts about for some encouragement for him. "Is it anything like chelating?" she asks. She knows a doctor practicing in California who, after doing a chemical analysis, can chelate human cells in a process that removes chemical impurities from the air and water of this nuclear age, and who is being opposed by the AMA, an organization resistant to preventive medicine—that is, medicine that could prevent the accumulation of wealth by the medical profession.

I might explain here that Selena's interest in chelating is my doing. I sent her to the lecture where that doctor spoke, and now she always urges any pregnant woman she knows to go for an analysis and chelation. This is part of the long-range program I share with throngs of other guides to amplify the voice of those who bear and nourish the human body. If I were allowed to practice demon expulsion, poison falling from upper space into the marrow of the unborn could be more speedily dispatched—indeed, might never get up there in the first place! But here is an example of the slower, less exciting mode of handling disturbances in this assignment devoted to the female principle.

Peter says, "Selena, chelating does nothing to slow aging. Not even as much as HBO, the oxygen treatment. Think of it, month by month we would lose a year, twelve years for every one. Next year, you would be fifty-three, the year after forty-one, and in another year twenty-nine. You must have been gorgeous then, auburn-haired, ripe. I want us to be twenty-nine together, knowing what we know now. We would not touch one another until we were twenty-nine. What tender constraint that would place upon us during the year we were in our thirties! That is what I need—a woman of constraint!"

"Do you stop the therapy then? Or do you just keep on going another two years until you disappear?"

She *was* being difficult. "Of course we stop. When we terminate the injections, we begin to age normally again. Oh, Selena," he clasps her hands, "you would become the romance of my life. We could back up whenever we liked, move forward, say, to thirty-nine, and then—" He puts his hands up to his temple, seeing that Selena is looking at him closely there. She is noticing how he works at hiding his age. She has never before seen how abruptly that gray at his temple stops, but now she can see in the fading light of the rose garden that Peter wears a wig, which he has tousled at the top so there is no part where the fabric might show through. His yellow teeth—as the word "romance" causes him to lift his lips—are, she realizes, false.

Selena looks about the garden. How curious, how touching, that he has brought her to that lovely bower of spring blossoms, to make this dismal proposition. There they sit on a bench—perhaps the tennis players in the adjacent courts imagine they are aging lovers, or an old married pair on a reminiscent stroll. What thoughts pass through the minds of visitors to the Berkeley Rose Garden? Selena has come there from time to time and talked to the gardener, a sensible, well-informed man who gave her some good advice about mites. *Thonk, thonk* go the tennis balls at intervals, punctuating Peter's speech. As he talks, Peter's eyes linger on Selena's wrinkles, her trophies of experience, as if he longs to snatch them from her. She points to a late-blooming bush, a Bella Abzug, only just beginning to reach bud-set and asks, "Peter, what do you notice about that bush?" He says, "Thorns, of course," and the thorns do stand out strongly on a branch that arches above their head. When Selena laughs, he says, "Well, look at those thorns—gigantic, like hanging claws."

Selena points to the buds, more than a dozen buds have formed, and Peter grasps her hand. Tears start up in his eyes. "Think, Selena, you wouldn't lose that perspective of yours. You'd have a youth that is without arrogance, ignorance, without the stupidities of the young!" He presses her hand with such earnestness that she feels her own eyes well up.

Peter mistakes her compassion for self-pity and hastens to offer greater reassurance, that their life would be a cornucopia of excitements, ever flowing outward, to travel to new adventures, bullfights, cars, endless renewals as their shuttle plane took them back and forth from those precipices of twenty-nine to forty-one.

And then her heart does go out to him, for she becomes sure of what lies behind all this zeal in Peter, his terror of what is beyond that precipice of forty-one for him—impotence.

"Peter," she says firmly. "I'd rather go for a more conventional eternal life. Like dying."

"Christianity!" he slaps his forehead, almost dislodging his wig.

"No, I'll come back as an infant and start over."

"Worse! You've fallen for all that ICH and DU stuff."

"Reincarnation," she says.

"You're crazy." Peter is beginning to lose his feeble hold on his emotions. "You're just a crazy old street freak—what was I thinking of?"

"What's crazier than *never* dying?" she asks.

"Coming back to this misery!" Peter cries crazily.

Then a momentary inspiration gives him the power of temptation. Of course, older women tend to go for dotty salvationism and cannot easily grasp matters of scientific research. But he can appeal to that irrational element as well. "Selena, this is an opportunity to go far beyond reincarnation. I hoped you would be ready for it. The woman who goes on this trip becomes *She*, the she of the eternal flame, at one with the Great Mother, with Kali and all the rest, a goddess, no longer on the Karmic wheel, to use the popular cliché. I offer you a leap beyond, but you're too busy following your nose. Have you no passion?"

Selena's resistance begins to waver. Eternal She? Selena's own

AMA man has warned her that unless she goes under the knife, she may die. Was she just a silly old woman seeking faith-healing (as she has done) to avoid the facts? Dying because she is too stubborn to go to the doctor? True, many silly old women go to doctors repeatedly and then die anyway. But her expectation was to go forward, to another life. This backing *up* and going forward again in the same body throughout eternity . . . mmm . . . Suddenly, Selena can see a larger element in it. She imagines herself and Peter, shuttling through the ages, flying back and forth between here and Mexico, having become an eternal demonstration of Selena's lesson to Luna, to Carrie, to whoever can observe it, that to strive for continuity is to imitate the continuousness of the eternal.

And so she considers herself with Peter, the countless plane trips throughout time, the bullfights in Tijuana, the what-all in Rio, the racing cars one after another. Eventually they might even travel down with only fly-packs on their backs. Then at Peter's words, "Have you no passion?" Selena sees herself as Gretchen to Peter's Faust, and their Mephisto in Mexico has a sting in his needlelike fire, and the smell of burning flesh penetrates their careless laughter; the dancing and the singing call for the reinforcement of liquor and of infidelities, for there must be met the unending hell of Peter's eternally erect penis!

"An old person," Selena says resolutely, wondering if given a nobler pursuit than an erection Peter might have persuaded her, "is very passionate." She is thinking of passion unimpeded by debased desires, free, flowing passion—grace.

"Absurd!" Peter cries. "Passion in the old is absurd!" But then Peter's invective becomes so heavy quotation marks could not hold up under the strain of it. He accuses all women over forty of insidious pretense—they can always spread their legs, but if they were a man, could they get it up? He calls old women names—smug old birds, zany weirds; he describes an aging vagina as a disaster area, a dried-out arroyo, and accuses old women, most regrettably, of "cunt rot"—speaking obliquely, of course, but still with enough aggression that he soon feels the guilty burden of rash words, feels agonized by his uncontrolled attack upon this particular old woman who never did him any harm. He shudders, his eyes fill with tears. He says he's cold, complains that it's gotten so it's always cold in the evenings even in June; California is becoming a miserable place to live even if one were young.

In short, Peter collapses and begs Selena to drive him away, down the hill, and by that time he is sobbing, and so Selena compassionately allows him to burrow his head in her breast, there on the bench in the rose garden, where tennis players whose balls are thonking on the nearby courts may imagine them to be old despairing lovers. Peter noses in, seeking that maternal flame in her despite himself, in her sagging but still warm flesh, where there is a scent of roses, and where, his lungs filling deeply with the scent, a hope is kindled in him, wistful, forlorn. *Could* he be reincarnated as slim, elegant and winning as he has been in this life? And Selena's wrinkled, knobby hand, simply by stroking his hairpiece tenderly without the least investigatory move so that he does not yet have to concede that he wears a wig, transmits to him the knowledge that a forlorn hope is a step up from a false one.

The delicate wings flutter over the images of Carrie and Harrison, of Selena and Peter, their bodies undulating with the shadows of Carrie's strawberry arbutus tree. Ladybugs, she thinks, so tiny, so intent upon their lives. There in that rock, *they* are as much as we! They fill an equal time and space. All the agonies of entrapments, remorse, ecstasy, disillusionment, loss—all the sequences of a thousand novels and screenplays were now as in the flutterings of two tiny aphid-eaters.

And here is Luna now, waiting at the studio door, still pouring out more words.

She has turned to Selena and asks, "Did you say something about chelating again, Selena?"

Selena is arranging her karate gi at the neckline and looks up innocently. "No. Not me."

Luna says, "I could have sworn it was you!"

Selena shrugs. "Philomen, maybe?"

"Oh, Selena," Luna cries, "what *do* spirit guides think they are doing?"

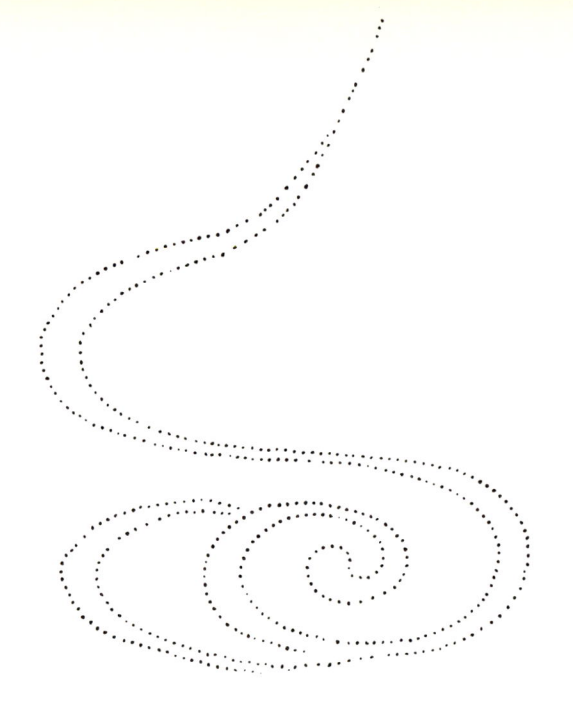

New Atlanteans

Luna's impertinent question comes when there is no time to answer it. In fact, such questions are not answered; they are dealt with in a more efficient manner. However, I am now going to return to the Claremont Hotel.

A meditation is in process on a balcony of the hotel, a summons I respond to out of a concern for Selena's involvement with DU, and also because I realize there is a fourth woman in our scheme. A triangle has its symbolism, as Luna has told us, but four—well, Luna may or may not tell us about the meaning of *four*.

Sometimes when a certain percentage of this city meditates—say, .02 percent at once—the activity of mending rips in the astral plane is enough to demand the attention of a thousand guides. Imagine the astral plane of a city as a large canopy above the smog; in an ordinary city it will be full of tattered, flapping shreds, like rent panels in a parachute beyond repair. Such a canopy over the cities of the San Francisco Bay, next to the last urban area of the United States to go under the smog cap, can be imaged as full of colored patches. Bright prints, candy stripes, and polka dots are favored by a city of celebrants, whose guardians repair as the people meditate. Whenever a meditator calls me, such a repair job takes place, metaphorically speaking.

The couple on the hotel balcony are Bubba Burr and a girl named Evi. Bubba sits tailor-fashion opposite her, but Evi's pelvic muscles are supple enough that she easily maintains a full lotus position. Their knees are almost touching, but their bodies actually touch at one point only; the tips of their forefingers meet opposite one another at the level of their shoulders. Their eyes are fixed, locked in place. The man's eyes are focused upon Evi's left eye, hers upon Bubba's right, so that they view one another on a diagonal.

They are naked except that Evi wears a silver ring inscribed with the letters DU woven together with letters spelling THOU. The same inscription is woven in silver on a necklace Bubba wears. The necklace moves with the even intake and outflow of his breath, to which he is trying, not too successfully, to pay attention.

Evi usually does not enjoy this DeFix at all, which Bubba has taught her and thousands like her. She prefers simpler meditations, or more active ones such as chaotic meditation with its snorting, screaming, pounding, writhing, dancing, flowing, its summons of the kundalini, in a chanting of the presumed now-known name of God (disclosed by Ali Pshaw), Hu, Hu, Hu, Hu (Hu-*Man*). Evi has required a dozen or more sessions of sexual hypnosis before waking up to the knowledge that her body—already a hive for drones, a lily pad for frogs, a field for blooming daisies, such an *object*, a pool for men to dive into and drown in lust—has had no need for release beyond nativity itself, but for making some coherent connection with her stintingly endowed mind.

Today Bubba feels irked that Evi has sunk into this DeFix with apparent ease, without even her usual little nervous cough. Being still and staring at his right eye usually arouses her fear, for ultimately he will disappear after first assuming feral, cross-eyed shapes like a bearded wolf or hyena or some mythic wonder. Evi is still so used to depending upon male admiration that her body usually will shudder as his own begins to disappear from her perception. No matter how deeply she draws on her breath or how slowly and evenly Bubba guides her in releasing it, the tremor would continue as she falls victim to her deepest insecurity, that fear of losing her allure. She might begin to clear her throat constantly or have a dry fit of coughing.

Bubba has always enjoyed that part of it with Evi, for it gives him a chance to work on himself. He has a residual brute in him, he knows, which her trembling torso appeals to. The loss of balance upon her coccyx, the bobbing of her breasts, the waver of her arms, the little gasps, the cough, the unspoken plea in each shudder—all bring into his awareness a favorite belonging of his adolescence, a rare and enviable collection of porno picture books, in which girls with boobs like Evi's were chained and beaten beside just such bedsteads as they have slept in the night before, a brass bedstead from the Claremont's palmier days.

Surprisingly wide, the range of a fixed eye, Bubba reflects, trying to consider his breathing instead. Not only can he take in the bedstead far to his right (though his eye is fixed upon Evi's left), but he can also take in part of the San Francisco skyline visible from the balcony, nesting in its bank of yellow smog, the pyramid tower of the Transamerica building visible just at the tip.

Other edges spring instantly into his visual memory, again yanking his attention away from his breathing. Luna doing Tai Chi beyond his eye, while his fingertips touched those of some earlier aspirant for his affection than Evi. Luna was in the Andes with him, received by Mamacita's order on his say-so, partly because Bubba's mind was on her apparent fiscal resources, not because she had evolved enough in Bubba's opinion to attain a Plus state. Luna, he reflects bitterly, incapable of seeing his potential as a Big Man on the Path, sloughing him aside because he is—yes, she said it scornfully—too ambitious! Could he help it if he still has work to do on his New York upbringing? What would Luna be if she, instead of being from an orphanage in Iowa, had had to fight her way through DeWitt Clinton High School?

Clearly Bubba is now in such an intensely retrograde state that we must back up with him, in the words of the *Sayso*, in order to advance, if the Psychic Reality wedding is to take place this day.

Humans often remark upon the elaborate, sometimes indecipherable pattern of their lives. We spirits have webs of even more amazing intricacy. It happens that one of my recent assignments, a delightful and adventurous one in which I helped obtain a section of the astral plane for humans, is closely linked to this present one. The chief occupant of that seat is none other than the glorious Peruvian child, Mamacita.

These sections of the astral plane we are bringing down for human use are all part of our general design of fostering the female principle. Therefore, to say they are being homesteaded is appropriate. Each one is in the care of one of the great all-time sages. Some are more successful than others, like all homesteads. One that is getting off to a somewhat slow start, for instance, is that one in India which is devoted to the teaching of susceptible statesmen and politicians in their sleep what they need to know about the female principle. Politicians are susceptible, as everybody knows, but astral persuasion is another thing. All over the world they learn our rote lessons while dreaming, but they are the most earthbound creatures on earth, and so we cannot boast of any conspicuous success in that sector. We have one of the most devoted sages who ever lived as leader there (His name is Legion), and as chief assistants Queen Elizabeth I and Gandhi. Some high and recently assassinated personages have come as apprentices, and so it is possible a late harvest from this sector may surprise us.

In Peru we have as teacher One whose name I may not even mention, working with the Little Mother. Astral fragments, once they are on the earth plane, are beset with earth problems, unfortunately. In Peru, practically the first persons to move in, frightening the native inhabitants, were psychologists.

Among them was Bubba Burr.

The visit I am tuned into now is Bubba's third, and he has brought twenty Americans with him, among them Luna, to receive instruction from the Sisterhood.

The central room of the retreat has wall-to-wall flooring composed of the *dojo*, the sacred mat of Oriental martial arts. It is an enormous room, large enough for twenty people to lie down with their limbs extended and still have circumference enough around them that they need never be anxious about touching one another by accident. Each individual enjoys its own space, even though at times pairs—or as these entities prefer to call them, dyads—may be formed. At the moment, they are alone upon the mat, twenty naked, free bodies, male and female, floating on a mat—a magic carpet, one might fancifully suggest, beside a high picture window which looks out on clouds and the Andes and the wondering native inhabitants. The latter, incidentally, often spend their days weaving llama images into ponchos which are worn in Berkeley, California.

In the work, the Sisters speak English, although Mamacita does not. However, she seldom speaks at all, scarcely more than a word at a time. The American disciples appreciate that the Sisters speak their own tongue to help them search for spaces beyond words. They have to master the complex terminology of an ancient system with modifications the Sisterhood has evolved in conference with Bubba Burr. For our purposes I shall simplify it, but there are a few terms I must define at the outset.

DeFix is applied to many techniques whereby the mind is freed, unfixed, from social conditioning, unconscious bias, and so on. This state of freedom is attained through many forms of meditation, one of which we have seen Bubba and Evi practicing on the Claremont balcony. Other means are used, such as encountering one's partner in a *Fix*, which may at times involve all the initiates and novices, or may be performed in dyadic privacy. *Fixes* can and frequently do lead to the PL, *Prodigious Leap*, but a PL may also be achieved in solitude. The only progress that may not be made alone is known as MT: *Multiplex Transmission*, a self-evident term. Despite the power of solitude, the teachings here show how knowledge serves evolutionary ends—that is, changes humankind for the better, through the controlled function of a Group. Mamacita's group works together daily, gathering and sharing psychic force. One method for this gathering is the *Murma*. A *Murma* is rather like a mantra, but it is on a tape loop, not in one's head; certain incantatory words are repeated over and over again. The *Murma*'s purpose is achieved when one is freed from

Meaning, achieving a state of power. *Meaning* is any rational, linear state.

Luna is about to witness her first *Fix*. A *Murma* has begun in the enormous room, and all twenty initiates are listening to it. One of the Sisters has started the tape loop, and four of them stand witness to the group, one at each corner of the *dojo* mat. The participants move about in response to the tape. They sit or lie down; sometimes they dance. The repeated words are given equal emphasis by the fact that the taped voice has spoken each word only once, and the tape repeats it again and again. "Mother marry mother marry mother marry mother..."

Luna lies in her space, somewhere between Bubba and Strong Elkhart. Bubba has told her that with this particular *Murma* she would probably run through an entire iconography of Motherhood before letting go of *Meaning*. And so she begins, first trying to visualize the mother she never knew, having been an orphan, then letting the image of Mamacita drift across her mind's eye, then entertaining the notion of being uplifted—married—by or to some unearthly mother.

Meaning does not release itself easily from Luna's head. She keeps hearing the actual tape. She suspects everyone else on the path has gotten free, because they soon begin to move, croon, dance and jiggle about.

She sees Bubba crawling past her on his hands and knees toward Elkhart, weaving his way through their companions. One or two of them are sobbing "Mama-mama-mama," in a rebirth-neuter-death sequence. Bubba has told Luna he now has easy access into and beyond such states as that. She watches as he gently prods Elkhart, with an eager whisper.

This surprises Luna. Bubba's attitude toward Elkhart is at this moment friendlier than it has been. Bubba has been working to overcome his resentment of Elkhart's coming to Mamacita's retreat, where he appeared without having been invited. For many days now Bubba has attacked this problem in private Fixes with Luna as witness. He has told her that the resentment goes back to their having come from the same Bronx neighborhood, except that Elkhart's grandfather left him railroad stock, freeing him to acquire an Ivy

League hauteur and Madison Avenue cool, while Bubba was destined to fight his way up through the New York streets and beat out the competition for scholarships at NYU. He has also shared with Luna the knowledge that Elkhart frequently has worked for the CIA. Nobody knows how many assignments he has had. He may even be on a CIA mission at this very time, Bubba has declared. Yet Luna could see that Bubba was drawn to the notion of covert activity, as if it were a vibrant jungle branch that might turn into a rapacious insect. His manner now is friendly; he touches Elkhart with something like a caress.

He whispers, "You are coming up into a Plus-plus. Just go with it. You need stay no longer among those in Minus states."

Elkhart groans, not focusing on Bubba, and mutters "Mother" in the voice of a three-year-old. If Bubba were not so excited, Luna imagines, or had a shred left of the suspicions he expressed before, he might have heard an insincerity in Elkhart's voice, a fake hollowness.

Bubba says urgently, "I see you up there—part of you anyway, Strong. Come on. The guides are waiting."

Elkhart frowns at Bubba crossly, gesturing him to go away. But something has happened to Bubba. He has been into Plus-plus, where the Path of New Beings says the spirit guides abide. He says, "Elk, your ear. Your ear is up there. I saw it."

He is still on his hands and knees in a crawl posture, but now comes halfway up so that he appears to be kneeling before Elkhart.

"Don't put me on, man," Elkhart says and closes his eyes.

"Listen," Bubba urges. "Come with me before your ear goes back down." He glances up over his shoulder, up where he has just left Elkhart's ear. He has also left himself there, in an out-of-the-body state Luna has heard a great deal about but never experienced.

Elkhart frowns crossly, giving Bubba a push that nearly knocks him off his knees. Bubba persists. "Your guide looks like this, kneeling, Elk. It's got gold wings and is a praying mantis. Mine—listen to this, Elk . . ."—he nudges Elkhart as if he believes the man shares his elation—"*mine* is . . ." He laughs almost helplessly. "You know they assume any shape they feel like. Mine at first was Moctezuma, now it's a"—more helpless laughter—"a kickball!"

"You're flipped out," Elkhart says.

"You, too, Elk, if you but knew. You're on your way, ear first."

"We're not supposed to talk during the *Murma*," Elkhart snarls. "You're blowing it."

Bubba whispers more urgently, "The ear, Elk, is the *first psychic receptor*!" He reaches out as if he would caress Elkhart's face.

Elkhart speaks loudly now. "Man, why don't you bug out!"

Bubba reels away, stunned, as if he cannot understand Elkhart's attitude. He seems torn between two states and gives an unpleasant glance at Piggy, Elkhart's wife, who is apparently in a rebirth state as a pig and is making wallowing movements and grunting and nosing the *dojo* mat near Elkhart. Bubba says vaguely in a neutral voice, "Hang back there then, with the pigs of your previous lives."

Bubba returns to his place on the mat and lies down. Luna sees that his face is immediately suffused with a blissful detached smile that she imagines indicates a Plus-plus state.

Elkhart is tugging at his ear lobe as if he wants to yank it down out of Plus-plus.

Luna would probably not have given their dialogue much thought, for she has seen many unusual exchanges since she arrived in Peru. She has been working on a primary DeFix called a DeJudge. Judging others is severely frowned upon at Mamacita's retreat, and is thought to be against all major spiritual advice of the ages.

In their joy at having a section of the astral plane, the Sisterhood has fallen into the human tendency to make too much of a good thing. Although ordinary humans can survive in these rare vortices, which are intended for their development, the Sisters have taken a risk in admitting so many novices. Spirit guides follow every human, and not all guides are benevolent, I regret to say. I can see that the Sisters are alert to certain rude presences, but not entirely in control. The DeJudge DeFix may be working against them here. In its narrowest application, there are dangers to the unwary mind in this DeFix.

Luna is confused, but not altogether unwary. She has been told to work on this DeFix by imagining herself as inseparable from the one she feels like judging, imagining herself in the same flesh. That makes it a nearly impossible DeFix for her when it comes to Strong Elkhart.

He stands up, now apparently ready for a complete Fix with Bubba, just as Luna is trying again to rise above the *Murma*. She is twisting her foot to the rhythm of the *Murma*, wondering if she can enter a rebirth state as a sea lion. She feels she is almost *there* when Elkhart speaks in a furious voice.

"Call me a *pig*, will you?" he is shouting. He has seized Bubba by the shoulders and stood him on his feet.

Bubba says, "I only wanted you to trip out with me."

The others on the mat, like a cloud of naked angels, form a circle about the two men, making room. They move into lounging postures to bear witness to the Fix. Everyone concentrates upon the DeJudge DeFix, knowing that in such confrontations neither can be wholly wrong. Their circle of flesh opens like an eye upon the *dojo*, so that all may *see*. The four sisters stand like four compass points, completing a perfect mandala around the storm center.

Bubba is foggy from being wrenched from his bright guide. Gently he inquires of Elkhart, "Can you *see* me?"

"I see a piece of shit," Elkhart says, his fists clenched. "I'd like to clean this place up, get the shit off the mat."

Now Bubba is roused at least to do verbal battle. "Don't talk to me like one of your ICH neophytes, Elkhart. You may get away with your crude put-down techniques in ICH. But save the shit for those clones you call latter-day Zen masters, those creeps who work for you for nothing, slaves, zombies—"

Elkhart raises his hand like a whip, but he too lashes with his tongue. "You know your cheap West Coast operation is no match for mine. Which came first, damn it, ICH or DU?"

Bubba's head nods up and down knowingly. "You thought you'd come down here to proselytize for ICH, take me over! Check us out for the CIA! Or maybe grab off the whole nunnery! Farfuckingout!" He advances threateningly. "What *do* you want here, Elkhart? And don't give me that crap about clarifying your spiritual soup! Murky metaphor!"

Luna recalls that when Elkhart arrived, bringing with him only his wife for a dyadic partner, he had gazed at Bubba, saying he had awakened, come *to* and wanted to clarify his spiritual soup. "My life is like split-pea soup, cloudy green, when I want it to be a clear broth—refreshing, clean."

"What I *want*," Elkhart cries, "is to bust your fuckin' head!"

Both men are highly trained in the defensive art of HoHo (which, as any Chinese waiter can tell you, means "superior, excellent, very good"), developed by a wise old man of Chinatown who in a flash vision saw the shortcomings of other martial and defensive arts and synthesized them all in one. As its weapon, rather than the ungainly tong and club of other methods, HoHo uses the more easily concealed ivory chopstick, whose advantage as a sudden projectile or as an object for insertion into the orifices of the body can be readily imagined—into a nostril, for example. When asked about the practical value of HoHo, inasmuch as its spiritual value goes unquestioned, the adept may suggest that bad vibrations stay away from the practitioner of HoHo, that aggressive, underdeveloped people turn and cross the street or slink into alleyways. Seldom is the chopstick resorted to.

Neither man can use the chopstick now, not having it concealed on their naked persons. But they assume the defensive stance. They make a few defensive passes of one another.

One of the four sisters who have supervised the *Murma* leaves the room. She goes for the Little Mother, who usually stands witness to such a Fix herself.

Luna, watching Elkhart closely, perceives a look of slyness as the sister leaves. He seems to decide not to risk losing to Bubba in Mamacita's presence, even though he outweighs him by about thirty pounds.

Dropping his HoHo stance, he runs up to Bubba and gives him a shot with the heel of his hand right under the nose. It is a stunning blow. Bubba sits on his behind, grabbing his face. But before Elkhart can come down on him, Bubba leaps up and grabs Elkhart in a primitive wrestling grip. They both fall to the floor.

The tape loop has been running: "Mother marry mother marry mother . . ." But suddenly it stops dead. The eyes of all in the circle turn in response to a presence. Mamacita has arrived.

She moves to the *dojo*, placing her tiny eleven-year-old body directly in the center, her flowing blue chiffon robes creating a glow around her slender frame. She holds her two hands palms together, in the gesture of a virgin madonna, and lowers her eyelids. This move to the center of the mat is in itself a minor miracle, for her physical body has interposed itself between those of Elkhart and Bubba while the two men were locked in their fierce embrace. Now from postures on either side of her, Elkhart clutching his own throat, Burr gripping a shame-covered face, they are totally separated.

The company waits word. Usually a word is as much as Mamacita utters. The word arrives, and she flowingly departs.

"*Por Dios*," she says.

The *Murma* recommences, and sobs are heard throughout the enormous room from those instantly endowed with MT, Multiplex Transmission.

"Mother marry mother marry mother marry mother . . ."

I mentioned before some rude presences. One becomes especially active as Mamacita departs. Purity has a way of activating unfavorable spirits.

Burr and Elkhart sit opposite one another. They gasp and weep. They grope for each other's hands, which they grip, gazing at one another. That unfavorable spirit, whom I can see but cannot recognize, takes over Elkhart, who completely fakes what follows.

It is a great frustration to me not to be able to make some direct attack, but I cannot attack a demon unless I can identify him, and in this case I am getting mixed identity signals. Moreover, I am under those orders to restrain my demon-expulsion capacities. And so the best I can do is to make Luna aware of Elkhart's act.

As she has been conspicuously unsuccessful at the DeJudge exercise, she can cooperate with me.

Elkhart gasps, "Once I killed a man. It was in the War."

Luna thinks: If this is real, I am a sea lion giving birth to a girl cub.

Bubba nods his head up and down in response to Elkhart's confession. He refrains from mentioning his own surely more elevated behavior as a draft protester in Berkeley, his prolonged life as a student which has kept him suitably removed from the great disaster arenas, the panoramas of which they have enacted here in small.

Bubba speaks in a quiet voice. "Strong," he says, swallowing. He grips Strong Elkhart's arm, his face showing an appreciation of multi-level nuances in the man's very name. "Just as *she* was leaving, I flashed on a cosmic truth." *She* apparently is Mamacita. "The new power of the earth can be realized only in using our female strength, Strong. That is why *she* has been given to us."

Luna, listening from the vantage point of a sea lion bearing a cub, hears Elkhart's reply. "I see what you mean."

"The authentic man of the future," Bubba goes on, relying on Luna's term in his eagerness to express his insights, "will not be in argument with the divine, which has been the male trip in the past. Always arguing."

Elkhart tunes in to this opportunistically. "Yes, no more argument. Response."

"Right!" Bubba cries. "Woman's natural responsiveness is what the world needs." He speaks under the spell of the seminar rhetoric that has sustained him since his Berkeley FSM days. "The male dialogue with the divine is at an end. It is time for the *female* quest to be fully articulated."

And Elkhart rises in the mode of oratory that has always stirred his followers: "Not the subservience of history, but the service. Yes, the dialogue is changing. Not a struggle *against* the divine, but cooperation *with* the divine."

Bubba says, "The female element will evolve the *true* dialectic—"

Elkhart interrupts: "Male tension being supplanted by female *attention*—"

"Yes, standing for resourcefulness in the exercise of divine will, in peacekeeping—"

"In ethical restraints—"

Their rhetoric is reaching competitive dimensions, but Elkhart checks himself now, sensing that what he has come there for is about to happen. He cries, "My God, Burr! With a thesis like this, you must see that a marriage of ICH and DU is inevitable!"

Bubba does not answer in words. He only gazes straight into Elkhart's eyes with a steadfastness that eventually causes Elkhart to blink and shake his head. He puts his hand over his heart to indicate a swelling there.

That evening Luna drops a casual remark that annoys Bubba so much he tells her she needs a Fix. "You didn't understand anything that was going on, Luna. You couldn't understand because you were in a Minus state. You were frozen in a block of ice."

"Not true. I was in a rebirth state," Luna declares.

"Impossible. You had an ice pick plunged into your heart. Your heart was gray, like the ice. I saw it."

"Bubba, that's ridiculous. I was watching the inception of human evolution."

"Sweetie, at best you were in a glacier. Believe me, Baby, I'm experienced at reading these things."

"I might have been in a glacier once. But I came out as a sea lion!"

"Wow, Luna. Just wow is all I can say."

"I was the beginning, Bubba, of mammalian development!"

"Jesus."

"I had a female cub!"

"Luna, stop putting me on!"

"But I mean it, Bubba. I was seeing how women have evolved throughout time, and how subservience is going to be usurped by the male principle." She laughs. "For Lord's sake, Bubba. You didn't believe him! You *know* that he was faking!"

Bubba shakes his head. "Claire de Lune, you'll never get anywhere if you keep laughing at the process."

"But I'm not laughing, Bubba. I'm just giving full articulation to my female quest!"

"Bitch!"

"I'm just at *attention*, yielding, responding, serving..."

Bubba begins a private Fix in order to remove her negative vibration from his psychic field.

Bubba never has to complain that Evi might laugh at the process. It gives her that link she needs between mind and body, in its vocabulary.

Rising from her meditation on the balcony, she says to Bubba, "I felt a jolt to the etheric that time, Bubba. The *real* me. Like, I didn't quake today. I think my chakras are open and balanced for the first time since Atlantis."

Bubba is putting on his tie, a wide paisley, predominantly pink, which he is feeling doubts about. Should he be wearing this Pierre Cardin suit, purchased in Elkhart's company, or the garb of Mamacita's country? Or should he have worn American buckskins? The range of costume available is now beyond consideration, but he regrets Elkhart's influence on his wardrobe.

Evi impinges upon his thoughts again. "Don't you think, Bubba, that I'm getting close to reprogramming my Fourth Center? After all, that's what's been hanging me up ever since Atlantis."

Bubba pats her on the arm, which is still covered with chillbumps from the bay breeze. "Don't strain, Evi," he says, "you'll make it yet."

"Just into Plus, that's all I want. I don't ask a Plus-plus, that's too much. My Consciousness-Focusing is not aimed that high! I was so conceited in Atlantis, you know. That was the problem." She gazes into the mirror, at her long blond hair, her wide-set blue eyes. "I was just an empty vain thing, trying to play off one man against another, both of my warriors. No wonder they killed each other when they learned how unfaithful I was. Do you know, Bubba, I used to *lie* to one of them whenever I was with the other. I hadn't learned the DeFix that makes it so simple for me to make it with both you and Elk. I have to make up for all that bloodshed, Sarinha Bock says, maybe in this lifetime." Sarinha Bock is the medium who has instructed Evi about her past incarnations, Atlantis in particular. Evi often meditates on what she did after her lovers met their fate: she took the rope belts off her lovers, tied the ropes together and hanged herself. Sarinha's caution that suicide costs from six to eight incarnations preys upon Evi and has aroused in her the modest ambition that she may find a way in this life to be of enough service to compensate for those past misdeeds. Evi sighs, giving her habitual little choked cough, a hangover from that former life, or death perhaps. "I blew it in Atlantis," she says.

The telephone rings as she is pulling on her blue velour robe. "That must be Mamacita!" Bubba cries. "Don't tell Elkhart she's here. Promise?"

Evi is puzzled by that, and when Bubba finishes receiving confirmation that the Little Mother has arrived from Peru and is in the lobby, she asks, "Why don't you want him to know?" Evi, as we shall see, has an inquisitive turn of mind.

"Baby, I want to make a small point, that's all. Mamacita has come because *I* invited her, not ICH. That is, not Elk."

Evi looks at him, enjoying the warmth of her soft robe. "Bubba, what difference does it make?"

"None," he says briskly. "The minor victories that occur among men are of no importance." He checks his tie one last time. "So why not enjoy them?"

"It's against the basic tenets of DU, Bubba," Evi says. "But I promise anyway."

"Baby, you're telling *me* about basic tenets? The most basic tenet is that there are no tenets." He gives his mirror one last glimpse of his hair and his bushy beard and slips out the door to greet the Little Mother.

As soon as Bubba leaves, Evi reaches for the telephone and asks for a number. "Elk," she says, "Bubba's gone out for a while. Are you free to Fix me up?" She giggles.

I leave Evi for now to her past misdeeds. I am uneasy about going, though. For no sooner do I consider the Yin of Evi's limitations than the Yang of her potential swells before me. Well, all in good time, as a *Sayso* says it.

Karmic Creation

Carrie goes to the sink in a corner of her studio and washes her hands. She takes a bar of Ivory soap from a carton underneath the sink. Soap is the humble material she uses to make models of her sculpture. Selena, dressed in a karate gi, assumes the "chop" posture Carrie wants to carve.

Outside the studio window, the gardener, Ginseng, is talking to Luna about a new planting he has done. Ginseng once figured in Luna's private life, and she still appreciates his charms. Isn't he a tall Chicano, a distinction on two counts, and doesn't he murmur seductively in Spanish, half joking, half smoldering? Except for the chaos of his mind, he might be her lover yet. However, she came to see his chaos as a travesty of her own dualism, her need to be both skeptic and believer at the same time.

"I'm going as Ginseng now," he is saying to her, expecting her to understand, in that Luna is also a self-designate. Ten years ago at a Haight-Ashbury street dance, she discarded the ugly name assigned by her orphanage. "It started the day the helicopters began," he says.

"Helicopters?"

"You know how they come over now all the time. So I changed my crop."

"No," she says. "What helicopters, Goliath?"

"Ginseng. After the root. You see, I switched."

Luna shakes her head, lost in his incoherency. "Tell me what you're telling me, Goliath."

"That, just *that*. How could you miss the helicopters? Every day, they're looking, searching. The police—" Ginseng is also a part-time tour guide on Alcatraz Island, a prison predating police helicopters, now a tourist attraction. Ginseng's work there has made him more conscious than ever of police activity.

"I don't get it, Goliath. Not yet," Luna says.

"Okay, Lun-ita Lovely, my name is Ginseng. They came zooming down over this backyard scanning me. They have telescopes, you know. And it was ten feet tall. I had more than five plants too."

At last Luna realizes that in a burst of unparalleled paranoia, responding to police helicopters that were probably in search of some criminal they could take seriously, he has destroyed his marijuana crop. Saying he has done with chromosomal damage, he has replaced it with ginseng root and changed his name. He has also planted the root on Alcatraz, between lectures to visitors on the criminality of prisons, upon the entrapments of the human psyche, upon the infringements of freedom at every turn.

"And so, I am Ginseng the Gardener now. It has changed my life." He has noticed that Luna has her video equipment in the studio, and draws a parallel. "If you want to change yours with video, good luck. It beats the fascist guru trip!"

Ginseng has urged Luna not to go down to the Andes because of what he calls the "fascist guru trip," and when she questioned him as to what he meant, he could only say he was "working it out." Now he brings from his pocket a copy of a flyer about the Psychic Reality wedding, which Strong Elkhart has issued with photographs of himself, Tsinghai Yana, Mamacita and several other luminaries. "It's coming together in my head now, Luna. He wants to corner the gurus.

The way I see it is this—the guy gets a few dozen gurus in his pocket. They all agree on one thing all the folks who follow them got to believe. Then the folks got to do something for the sake of that *one* thing, make a sacrifice. It'll be for God this time, not the state, you cut off your balls, or something . . ."

"Oh, Goliath!"

"Ginseng." He turns away. "Never mind, I'm just a philosopher with a chaotic, paranoid mind."

Inside, Luna puts on the tape of Carrie's reading with Jim Smith for Selena to hear, and begins to gather up her equipment, uncoupling and looping cables. She sighs her annoyance with Jim's analysis of Carrie, occasionally giving little exclamations of exasperation. He tells Carrie to allow her "heart chakra to release itself, to yield its constriction, so that the flow, the pranahaorgonotic flow might go up through the heart, through the crown chakra, and out." He urges her to give up the fears "that keep her contracts with men neutral, that indicate she has given up on commitments." Luna dismisses such terms as "neutral" and "fears" as unsuitable for Carrie.

Carrie, however, realizes such words make her feel so defensive there may be some truth in them, even though "given up" is not the most flattering term for her poised detachment. She does not feel resigned, defeated, bleak.

Jim says, "I am receiving a symbol out of a Leonardo sketchbook. It's one that demonstrates the pattern of water flowing into a pool. The water looks like curls of a woman's hair, swirling into a circle, toward a center hollow. You know the one I mean, of course. To me, this is a symbol of the marriage of art and technology. I see this symbol often nowadays. It appears with people who are coming into an awareness of how great the world need for change is, who are at a time of immense personal change. In you, I sense a cellular change, almost alchemical."

Luna switches off the machine in disgust. "He told me to guard against a detached configuration too. But prescribed for me random sex. Starting with *him*!"

Then Luna appears to change the subject abruptly. "I've decided to move away from the commune."

The Spare Change Commune, as it was originally called—now known to the four women who stuck with it in an economic venture of Tantric posters as the Tantric Arts Commune—has been her home for two years. "I have evolved beyond the group style," Luna says.

"Whatever that means," Carrie comments, chipping at her bar of soap.

"Well, it doesn't mean a reversion to the ideal of rugged individualism, which has no future, despite its glorious past in America." She can just now only decide what the move means to her pragmatically. It means a change in diet; she will no longer eat "brown food," which the sister devoted to cooking has imposed upon them—brown rice, brown breads and vegetables browned by soy sauce. She will also start putting her dividends into a personal bank account.

Luna is encumbered with a bulky income, source of many problems and pleasures, the fortuitous settlement of her one marital experiment with an electrical designer who, although the inventor of a fixture used in beer billboards all over the country, was otherwise inaccessible, except that Luna had the fortune to discover him *in flagrante delicto* with a gay veterinarian who had come to spay their cats. Luna's decision may be a death blow to the economy of the Tantric Arts Commune, although she says, "The poster business is self-supporting now anyway. I'll probably move back into my house in the hills." She has leased the house these past two years to a psychiatric couple whose fashionable body therapy bears their own name, Bahf or Bahfing. "I'll have my money, my house, and so I'll probably have a baby."

The two older women exchange a glance of alarm.

"Are you pregnant yet?" asks Carrie.

"Oh, no, I only had the IUD removed yesterday," she says. "I'm considering Jim Smith."

"I thought so," says Selena.

"He said something critical might happen to me today."

"Getting pregnant—that's critical," Selena says.

"He repeated it. 'Be careful *today*,' he said."

"So, having taken out your IUD, you figure the most careful thing you can do is start a family with Jim."

"Oh, well, I wouldn't live with him," she says dismissively. "But on my way here, I saw a girl riding in her Volvo with a baby in a sling seat and Pampers on the rear ledge, and I thought, it's a whole scene you go through and I'm already twenty-nine."

"A sling seat and Pampers!" cries Selena. "But you haven't been chelated yet!"

"I can do that afterward. Just think, a little Karmic creation waiting for me to give it material form. My next meaningful work." As always, Luna is half satirical.

"But if you won't live with him, how about waiting for the authentic man?" Carrie suggests.

"Carrie, if I put four of the best men I know together I might get one whole person. Men are in even worse shape than women—you know that!" She is packing up her cassette in her spangled bag. "Even Jim said there's no such thing as an authentic man. But a psychic! Genetically what could be better!" She urges them to consider his strong body, uncontaminated by habits, cigarettes, liquor, dope. She reflects that it is even the right day of her cycle, and more, the ideal month. Conceived in June, the child would be a Pisces, naturally psychic. "I can see it now, doing psychic readings from its crib! I'm going to try it!" she concludes.

"You fruitcake! Motherhood isn't just something you try," Carrie says.

"Some mothers get to thinking of it as a life sentence," says Selena.

"Well, so is *life*!" Luna has them there.

But Selena is not at all ready to let her go, for she is under my instructions. "Stay a few minutes," Selena says, "I have a story to tell you."

Luna groans, knowing Selena's stories always get to her in some way, if not when they are told, then later. The story relates to Luna's insolent question about what spirit guides think they are doing. No self-respecting guide would give a direct answer to such a question. I will say in this report, however, that we guides believe that we are needed. We think people are in such bad shape that they need all the help they can get.

Selena is my channel to Luna at the moment, and Luna plops in a chair, knowing she must listen; no matter how she may disregard a lesson, she will hear it.

Carrie takes up a fresh bar of soap, unwraps it and gazes at the white rectangle as if she doesn't recognize it. That means she is already dealing with another onset of layering. Carrie can receive messages from a vessel as complex as a radio telescope or as simple as a crystal ball or, as in this case, a piece of soap.

Selena begins her story. We shall look into both story and soap in whatever order we can find.

Selena's story:
"Three elderly mothers decided to take a pilgrimage to Peru to visit the Little Mother, hoping for help with their problems.

"The first said: 'My son, who is a forty-year-old hippie, expects me to send him money every few weeks in Nepal. He says it costs more to live in Berkeley, so if I send money there he'll cost me less. If he comes home, I'll have to support him and his stream of girl friends. I've already paid for three abortions and five bails, all of which he has jumped.'

"The second said: 'My daughter makes it worse for me. She has forgotten all I did for her when she was growing up. She and her husband decided to take a trip around the world, but it didn't occur to them to recall that I'd never been out of Alameda County. They left me at home with the grandchildren. As a result, I broke my hip, and my enormous hospital bills have to come out of my own income, and they think I'm just a clumsy old fool.'

"The third mother spoke up at even greater length. 'My mother-in-law came to live with me, and she is ninety-five and helplessly senile. I have to lift her in and out of the bathtub. My husband became a helpless drunk shortly after she came. One night, driving home with some woman he picked up in a bar, as he usually did, carrying God-knows-what germ with which he intended to infect me, he got smashed again for the last time—head on. It took cutting torches to get his body out of the wreck, and his insurance wouldn't cover—drunk driver. And then, being dead, he is now unable to help me get his mother in and out of the tub, and so the strain has made me tear my bladder and have to have major surgery, and even so my bladder still leaks. That is because my bladder has always been weak, ever since I bore my first child. On that night, my husband went out, and I had to have the child all by myself, and the water burst, and I have had a weak bladder ever since. And whose fault *is* this motherhood, anyway? It's *his* fault that I had those children and his fault that my mother-in-law is wrecking what's left of my life, and there is no one who cares anyway and I'll be left alone and thrust penniless in an old-age home without even Social Security because *he* would never let me get out on my own and work . . .' "

As Selena tells the story, Carrie is looking at the Ivory soap. At Selena's word "motherhood," she finds herself dropping farther away from her studio, yet somehow closer to her friends, who appear in mingling images.

We can inspect them as she did before we hear the end of Selena's parable. Incidentally, I have remarked about enjoying Carrie's layers, but haven't mentioned that at times I direct them. They too are part of my assignment in consciousness. And as long as I am present while Carrie "nicks out," she is not in any danger.

The resentment of the old women seems to be her own, yet where does she fix it? On her daughters? No, yet *who?* she asks herself. Her former husband, for leaving her, then dying? Hasn't she moved beyond that?

The rectangle of soap turns into a piece of paper held in Carrie's hands. She has seized it from the hands of a young man. He mutters, "I can't go through with it." Who *is* he? How young their faces look —can they be twenty-five? How cramped his face there in the soap bar, now showing above the paper, which has turned out to be a marriage license. Carrie's own face is wistful, unformed, a face with no sculptural interest, she notes, framed in a conventional haircut. She wants to marry him! And he, blond, gray-eyed, frightened. Such a pouty mouth! Sweat pours off his face with amazing abundance. Then even more liquid—he bursts into tears! Horrible! Absurd! Carrie crumples the paper, for which he has just paid a fee. She tears it—at first it won't tear, so strong a paper a marriage license is printed on!

But then it falls into tiny pieces. It looks as if those hands, unflawed, tender, could never accomplish anything, except for the hint of ferocity with which they are moving. They release the bits of paper, extend themselves like a model's hands. She might be posing for a soap ad. The paper flutters beneath them. And now Carrie has burst into tears! She and the young man cry together. It has just occurred to him that Carrie may want a child. It is too much for him. He already has two children. He is not ready for more. He was not ready for those, ran away as soon as he saw the years-long stretch of nurture ahead. A life sentence, indeed, the rest of his youth! How could he have imagined such a criminal act as marriage again! He tells her the sentence, the cell of the American home, a stretch with more children, years of alimony and child support, a life sentence with no time off for good behavior. He would prefer solitary! Carrie has begun to throw something—what is it? Glassware. Where has it come from? She is methodically shattering an entire set of Tiffany crystal goblets against the wall of the soap bar. The young man gathers up pieces of broken crystal and clenches them into his fist until capillaries break and blood trickles down his arm, spilling like a travesty of the rite he cannot bring himself to pass through, weeping still—what a *baby*!

The soap bar becomes another rectangle, a soft fiber, a Kleenex tissue. Yes, it is being used by someone who is with Selena Crum, the tissue flattened out on her belly. Selena is undergoing psychic surgery, not to be confused with the brain amputation known as psychosurgery.

Selena's operation has been arranged under the auspices of DU, and is taking place there in Berkeley. Other psychic surgeries are more elaborate: some of those arranged by ICH, for instance, call for jet charters to Peru, where an Indian discovered by Elkhart removes without anesthesia or knife troubled, swollen or shrunken organs, tumors, warts, etc., and holds them up for all to see and marvel over. Selena's surgeon, however, removes nothing but the negative energy in what he calls the Other Body, allowing for the free flow of health to reestablish itself. The blind have seen light, the halt have walked, the deaf have heard the drop of a pin.

Needless to say, the philosophical differences in the two approaches are another source of friction between the two groups, DU and ICH.

A DU neophyte discovered their surgeon in Oleg's Coffee House on Shattuck Avenue. The neophyte, a young Chinese student who calls himself Flo Blue, was grappling with a headache caused by a Minus state. The annoying throb was heightened by a garrulous Irish voice at the next table. Flo Blue immediately saw the situation as an opportunity to work on a DU DeFix. In order to attack his headache he must enter into another irritant with his entire being, thereby shifting his energy configuration. And so Flo Blue quickly engaged himself in conversation with this noisy Irishman, listening for a few moments to coarse jokes that ran throughout a bar-style narrative, until Flo Blue became aware of an acute difference between what he was hearing and what he was seeing. What he *saw* was an aging man with a severely ascetic and finely wrinkled face, a man of quiet and simple dignity. Flo Blue knew somehow that his companion was the victim of a double, possibly multiple personality.

Consulting others at his table who seemed to know the man well, Flo Blue quickly confirmed his opinion. The man was none other than Hubert Fred Halley—an Irishman, true, but not the Black Irish brawling vulgarian his body was playing host to that evening; no, Halley was a priest and healer. Halley's friends who were sitting in a circle around a table at Oleg's explained to Flo Blue. The man often went into "states." And so Flo, remembering another DU technique, asked Halley if he would let him exorcise the noisy rogue, so that he, Flo, might talk to the priest aspect of Halley. Halley said, "Oh, I can take care of the rotter meself," and clenching his small fist, he took a swing that landed himself a solid pop on his well-chiseled jaw. He swayed and nearly fell from his chair. But then he put his arm around Flo Blue. He stood up and led Flo out of the coffeehouse, speaking in a calm, responsible voice, shed of its cracks and crankinesses. With an awesome precision, he directed his forefinger and thumb to the spot on Flo Blue's forehead that had been throbbing with pain from his Minus state, and then asked, "Better now, isn't it?"

Halley's noisy rogue is actually an obnoxious spirit I am acquainted with on this side of time, one who has died of drink a hundred times. For some reason, Halley, tolerant soul, enjoys playing host to this creature. Halley is of a high enough order to exorcise this demon for good. He seems to enjoy these visits occasionally, though, perhaps the better to radiate what knowledge he possesses in his higher human state. This is a manifestation of how people resist living at their peak capacity.

Hubert Fred Halley's fame has spread quickly throughout the ailing city. Under the authority and cloak of DU, he is at last able to practice with minimal risk of prosecution, for he now serves technically as a nurse's aide to one of the many licensed physicians of DU who are actually always standing by during his operations, eager to learn healing. Selena has booked weeks in advance, and Halley has two M.D.'s in attendance.

Hubert Fred's patients adore him, for his movements are quick and graceful, his touch light, his tongue sweet. He is small of foot and limb and his eyes are grave, watchful, piercing. "Hubert Fred Halley has X-ray vision," one of the M.D.s explains. For Halley looks into the body, not just *at* it. He does not poke and probe as an M.D. might. He comes right up to the spot that hurts and looks inside as if he is peering through a microscope. It is not necessary for the flesh to be exposed. Halley can see straight through clothing. He even prefers to add another layer, a Kleenex. He places a tissue over the site of the ailment, flattens it into a rectangle, then looks through the tissue, as if it were an X-ray plate, into the body.

"We are out of tissues," he tells Selena. "The last person I operated on was a weeper. I've never seen anything like it."

"Did you hurt the patient?" Selena asks, having assumed knife-free surgery was pain-free as well.

"Oh, no," Halley hastens to reassure. "Tears of joy, pure joy. Next time I'll have to treat her ducts."

"Well, I came prepared," Selena says, taking out a purse-size packet of Kleenex. Halley, delighted, unfolds one and lifts it up to his face, blowing his nose.

"Slight sinus from the smog," he says. Then he takes another, asking Selena where her difficulty lies.

Selena tells him what happened to her some mornings before. According to her kitchen clock, for fifteen minutes she had undergone a complete loss of physical capacity, stumbled to a table to keep from falling, sat down and began to breathe deeply. Deep breathing seemed most likely to sustain her contact with the light through the kitchen window as kitchen-window rather than cosmic light, and to sustain the sounds of birds in the patio as bird song rather than universal vibration, to maintain in the pause between breaths the fine silvery thread she could see weaving her into the familiar narrational events. In this manner, she waited for some return of focus, for a vertiginous weakness to leave her limbs, either that or for her breathing to stop altogether, to end her stay in this body. "I was so unattracted to that light and vibration," she tells Halley, "that I knew it wasn't time for me to get into it." She tells him that she went to her old internist about it, who cut short her account by saying, "A near faint," and prescribed X-rays, after which he recommended exploratory surgery.

Halley does not inquire what the X-rays revealed. He thoughtfully waves a Kleenex, murmuring, "Don't let them cut," and then asks Selena to lie upon the Japanese mat raised about a foot off the floor of his study. He spreads the Kleenex upon her flat belly. Down to tissue level goes Halley's face, his body bent over, his one eye squinting, the other piercing its way through the tissue, until he has satisfied himself. Then he shifts eyes, and peers into the other side, an eye for each ovary. Then he eyes Selena's uterus.

"Buy some chaparral tea," he whispers. "You won't like the taste of it, but drink it anyway." One of the licensed surgeons, who are acting as nurse's aides, chuckles humorously.

Halley drops the first tissue into a basket and asks Selena to sit up. He then trips around to Selena's back and places a fresh tissue in the flat of her back, bends over and turns his head so that his eye is no less than an inch away from this tissue. He looks and looks. Minutes pass. Then: "I shall be going inside the Other Body."

Halley straightens, asks Selena to lie upon her back again and spreads another tissue over the wool dress covering her solar plexus, her third chakra. With his middle finger thrust forward like a knife, he probes into the center of the tissue, and—the finger disappears. Selena glances down to see the finger vanishing into the tissue, and the licensed surgeons draw their breath. "I am always amazed at this juncture," one says. "It never ceases to cause me awe too," the other M.D. declares. "Breathe deeply," he tells Selena, "and relax." Each of them takes one of Selena's hands.

Selena breathes as instructed. "Do you feel something opening inside?" asks one of the surgeons.

Selena cannot deny that something *has* seemed to penetrate the wall of her belly, has stirred inside her uterine wall. Halley's index and fourth and fifth fingers now writhe on the outside of the Kleenex, then his entire hand seems to disappear.

Suddenly the M.D.s gasp, and Selena, breathing, sees Halley spring back, away from her living body, and her Other Body as well, she imagines, and his entire hand is outside. The tissue clings, rumpled, to Selena's dress.

"Ah!" say all present, looking at the tissue significantly. Halley's severe expression is broken by a radiant smile. "That's an excellent sign. Whenever the tissue stays put, the operation has been a success. I don't know why, but such has proved to be the case."

Selena touches the paper clinging to her dress. "Static electricity?" she asks.

Halley nods. "Yes. But with other wool clothing it has come right off when I moved my hand, to the disappointment and subsequent demise of the patient. I cannot explain it."

Selena sits up. "Besides," she says, "what is more mysterious than electricity?"

Hubert Fred Halley looks at her face, draws his eye closer to it. Halley sees straight through her skull to her brain cells, looks into them, perceives her highly evolved state and takes her into his arms.

He asks, "What sort of man do you like, Selena?"

She looks closely at him too, perceives the fineness of his skin, the character wrinkles, the gray, gallant eyes. She says, "Oh . . . small, elegant, gifted."

"Would you be annoyed if he started to tell lewd stories in an Irish brogue?"

"Damned right," she says wryly.

Halley sighs. "No matter. You are a beauty."

Selena blows him a a farewell kiss, which he ruefully catches in another Kleenex. "We'll meet again in another life," Selena says.

The rectangle of Ivory soap is also a bed, Luna's bed, Carrie believes. She is with Ginseng (then Goliath). First they are at a lecture, where he is gazing at her unhappily, for he is losing her there. A professor of shamanism at UC-Berkeley is speaking that evening at the Berkeley Psychic College.

Before the lecture they watch a dozen students of psychic science give an aura cleanse. The students are wired, each wearing microphones like necklace pendants to record impressions of the volunteer they are cleansing. The volunteer is weeping from insight—more tears! They mingle momentarily with those of Carrie and her lover holding the Tiffany glass, with Selena's Kleenex.

After the cleanse, everyone listens to the distinguished professor, Daniel Hitzig, who tells what he knows of the Huichol Indians. Luna is lured by his white-templed sagacity, seduced by the depths of his esoterica, and by his obvious interest in her own blond loveliness, as he talks of the Huichol quest for peyote cactus deep in the deserts of central Mexico. The audience is awe-struck when he tells how, under the guidance of their benevolent shaman, the Huichol shoot the peyote as if it were deer; Luna feels stabbed herself and then dazzled by visions as he tells how the Indian eats the peyote in a ritual meal as if it were deer meat. His eyes glitter like stars shooting into her own with incredible speed. But the most blinding persuasion in his glance comes as he speaks of a discovery he says he made himself. He offers it as information that will transform his academic circle, offering it first to these psychics because, as he says, they have surrounded themselves with the white light of trust. He reveals that the deer itself is not shot with an arrow but captured alive with clever nooses and only then killed. And it is the manner of the killing that causes Luna's breath to catch and strangle, for Hitzig says the shaman places his mouth upon the deer's own and collapses the creature's lungs by sucking its last breath. Luna's own lungs undergo a desperate constriction, and she imagines her very last breath passing into this extraordinary adventurer old enough to be her grandfather. As Hitzig takes a deep breath, acknowledging the admiration of all the psychic students, Luna's soul enters into him, she feels, in the same way the deer's enters the shaman.

Needless to say, by the end of the lecture, Luna is ready for the professor to take her anywhere he will—for hasn't he gone with the Indians who call their pilgrimage an occasion to "find their life," and can he not therefore help her to find her own?

Hitzig shows an inclination to take Luna on no higher adventure than home to the Tantric Arts Commune and to bed. After weeks of this fairly familiar pilgrimage, Luna learns that Hitzig is expert not only in the matter of benign shamans, but is more intensely schooled in the arts of black magic. But then, Luna has fallen helplessly under his spell.

Evil emerges in a final episode. He makes an effigy doll of a rival anthropologist, a younger man who is about to publish a paper that would reveal how the trapped deer is killed. That would have scooped Hitzig, and so the younger man falls victim to the academic occupational hazard of jealousy, falls into a trap Hitzig designs for him. He becomes the apparent victim of a teenage drag race on Alcatraz Avenue at two A.M. one Sunday morning when he is run down and killed. However, later that day Luna finds an effigy image of the young man, smashed by a bound volume of the *American Anthropologist*. Later, Hitzig performs a ritual in which he exonerates himself of guilt-by-effigy in the death. Luna, pregnant by then, imagines she must have an abortion or possibly suffer some fate similar to Hitzig's rival. For she remembers in terrifying retrospect other craziness from this aged lover. Like most Don Juans, Hitzig has a mother hang-up. Luna has thought little of it, in that all the other men she knows do too, but now she remembers his baby talk, his curious little-boy looks, which she has discounted on account of his age.

After the abortion, she takes refuge in the simple comfort of Ginseng (then Goliath). They are at the Tantric Arts Commune, lying on Luna's bed, surrounded by houseplants. Perhaps twenty plants hang in baskets and ceramic bowls above their heads, trailing down in a circle about their bodies. Through this screen of maidenhair, asparagus and Boston ferns, through creeping ivies, English and Swedish, through several varieties of wandering Jew and hanging cacti (non-hallucinogenic), Luna accepts the comfort of Goliath.

She gazes at the posters beyond the tangle of plants, the Tantric Arts posters she and the other women of the commune are producing and selling at a great rate and with which she has lined the walls of her room. Eventually she will roll them all up and give them to Goliath when she sends him on his way. But for now she is appreciative of him, of the simple, good-humored devoutness in him that is free of the unearthly complexities she has found in her older lover Hitzig.

Goliath removes her hand, which she is pressing against her belly where there is a pain, and gently puts his lips there. He has been considering her personal plight against the structure of politics as he sees it. Luna recognizes in him a nostalgia he must have grown up hearing of in the thirties; she imagines Mexican workers in southern California, where Goliath has come from. He has just begun to work for the Forest Service on Alcatraz Island. He tells her about former prisoners (*more* sentences! Carrie thinks). He relates all society's outrages to Luna's predicament. Goliath's Mexican accent deepens so that she seems to hear his father's voice, talking of injustice, and in Goliath's touch, she is comforted by the round hands and lap of his indulging mama.

She says, "The doctor did the abortion on the day my period was due. He thinks that allows for less interruption of the organic flow." Goliath winces at these words, having been brought up to know abortion as evil. Her mind is still in the clinic, where Muzak played "I Left My Heart in San Francisco" throughout the operation. Luna begins to shake, to tremble. Would she *never* find her life? She burrows her head onto Goliath's shoulder.

Goliath, offering what he can, inadvertently reminds her again of her shaman. He says, "You're really in a black hole." She gazes out the window, seeking through the lacing of ferns a glimpse of the stars. The anthropologist has told Luna about black holes.

She now passes on what she knows to Goliath, telling him that a black hole is postulated as a collapsed sun, which has increased in density so much that it is charted as a black spot, but actually it is a dense energy area; that although through a telescope it may look to be about five miles in diameter, a spoonful of it weighs thousands of tons. "Imagine, Goliath, if you could get hold of a spoonful of it, you couldn't lift it. And it's not just a black hole, it's a *suck*. The gravity is so dense that light cannot escape; instead, it pulls everything into itself. It is ever-growing, yet ever-compacting."

Goliath gazes out at the night sky, where dense billows occasionally yield a view of glinting stars. "You mean, it could take in all the light there is?"

"Space, too," Luna declares. "Space is curving down into it, everything plunging into the black hole. So—conceivably everything in the universe could get inside, and be swallowed up."

Hitzig has discussed this philosophical inscrutable with Luna and elaborated a further possibility, which she imposes upon Goliath's capacities, that the energy entering a black hole might empty out into a different time scheme.

Goliath is holding onto his head with both hands, as if to hold his mind together, for Luna goes on to speak about the Greek God Chaos (whom she has also heard about from her anthropologist), Chaos who devoured his children one by one till none were left and till Zeus came along and forced him to stop, and moreover, Luna is linking the increase of light and curved space within a black hole to Creskendo, cosmic origin, having to do with an increase of the *moon*, and he, Goliath, is bothered by all this to a terrible extent, and all he can consider is that Luna has once told him that *he* has a chaotic mind, which now begins to swarm and fragment, and he realizes that she is right. Clutching hold of a single coherency he has read in the San Francisco *Chronicle* he picked up in the Buttercup Coffeehouse, he says, "But, Luna, they have found a second black hole. How does that fit in? Two universes? Two Christs?"

Luna widens her gray eyes playfully. "Consider the possibility that there are two of everything."

Goliath claps his forehead, taking relief in humor. "They try to swallow one another up. They become *It*; *It* becomes more and more compact. It becomes the *One*.

"Until—bang!"

"Total rebirth!"

And Luna, until he says rebirth, is laughing too, but that word reminds her of the embryo she has just given up. The psychiatrist renting her house in the hills, Ernie Bahf, is humorously working on something he calls a placebo fetus, to pacify his wife's yearning for a child; he wants a mechanism to fill the hole, that hungry hole inside a woman, tugging, sucking at life itself, which says, impregnate me, I crave gestation.

I might mention here that these black holes have been charted by scientists under our close supervision. I myself have not taken part in these ventures, and they may well be on levels of understanding that are beyond my range. But many of my friends have guided these scientists in their explorations into this particular form of concavity, and it, too, is a part of this general assignment of expansion of the female principle. It's no laughing matter, though on all levels, from Goliath on up, we may hear laughter. Our mission is of high seriousness, even among those of us who do not thoroughly understand it. It is the same here as with earthly knowledge; the direct question-and-answer mode seldom yields much. We can know only what we are able to know.

Luna *must* laugh to keep from crying. But it doesn't always work. Inside her body now as she laughs, she feels a rip, a tear from the same tugging Ernie Bahf's wife feels, a pain from her recently evacuated uterus. And the smallness and yet intolerable size of her own universe and her own inability to function joyfully in it, her cravings for its attachments, her need for someone to hang onto, and the unlikelihood of that being a solution to the human problem for anyone—all these thoughts bring Luna to a well of tears. She begins to cry, holding onto her head now, holding the pieces of her own fragmented perceptions inside it, trying to hold something together.

Goliath, touched, tender, takes and holds her body, kisses her tears, knowing they are helpless to help each other, finding that knowledge of no earthly use. Yet he kisses her throat and her breasts, and lays his hands gently upon her belly until the throbbing there is soothed.

These rectangles, Luna's bed, Selena's Kleenex, Carrie's marriage license, all come together in the soap bar, as Carrie, with a sob, gives up her early lover because she might want to bear a child, as Luna turns to weep for the child cut out of her body, and as Selena senses at the root of being, at the solar plexus, something missing in the divine flow, the way an engine misses, Harrison might say, beyond the help of any earthly healing. Carrie looks up from the soap to hear Luna ask, "So, what did the Little Mother recommend the old women do to relieve their miseries?"

Selena smiles. "You know, the Little Mother scarcely ever talks. They were outside in the clear mountain air. One of the women complained about the altitude and how dizzy she felt. The Little Mother put a rock in her hand at that. Then, two of the Sisters, taking that as a signal, applied the treatment. The Little Mother directed them by telepathy. Each pilgrim received a basket and was told to hang onto it no matter what. For every grievance they had expressed they received a rock, each weighing about a pound. The Sisters named each rock: 'hippie son,' 'bail,' 'hospital bill,' 'mother-in-law,' and so on. Naturally, the mother whose troubles outweighed the others had the heaviest basket. Then the Little Mother spoke her *Sayso*: 'Go to Town.' The nearest town was ten kilometers on foot. The old women objected—what, walk all that way with such heavy loads? They had palpitations, high blood pressure, weak bladders; it would kill them. But the Little Mother didn't answer; she just gave them her blissful smile and, entering a Plus state, left them to figure it out for themselves. 'Go to Town.'"

Luna looks at Selena, waiting. She realizes she usually wants an explanation at the end of Selena's stories, and that explanations are not forthcoming. "Did anybody get there?" she asks, knowing she has probably missed the point.

Carrie laughs and says, "Well, I wonder if one of them at least had sense enough to let go of the stones!"

And at that phrase, "let go," Carrie hears a clatter, as of the sound of falling rocks, in the driveway, which Ginseng goes to inquire into. She realizes that Harrison is arriving now, with a load of equipment, as he has in her earlier visions.

As Harrison comes through the gate, Selena goes out to him buoyantly, pleased and uplifted by his spirited arrival.

Carrie turns to Luna. "Why didn't I realize it before? I'm *psychic!*"

Luna smiles, gathering up. "One of Selena's other stories, I think, had the point that the most apparent things are sometimes hardest to see."

"Where are you going, Luna?" Carrie asks, for Luna is at the door and looks determined.

"It'll be a long time before *I'm* a whining old woman!" Luna says.

"But . . ." Carrie is about to say, "But that's not the point," when she stops, considering how each of them must have a differently developed apparatus for receiving levels of meaning. Later she will realize *she* is the one who has benefited most from Selena's story, when she lets go of her *own* impediments. Such are the unpredictabilities of our lessons. For now, Carrie tries one last appeal to Luna, suggesting Jim might not want to be a father, even with no strings.

But Luna is imagining being with him in the hills, strolling among the daffodils.

Useless to remark that daffodils have died out since April or that Jim might feel used. "Among the poppies then," Luna declares.

"Poppies have been gone since May!" But Luna is leaving, is at the gate with her tape recorder in her spangled Pakistani bag, and is only momentarily being overtaken by Ginseng. "Take some ginseng root," he cries, bringing forth a plastic bag in which he has placed the root. He tucks it into her bag, and she rewards him with a peck on the cheek. "Thanks, Goliath." He winces but doesn't correct her again. He calls after her, "Come out to Alcatraz soon, Lunita. I'll show you what a real-life prison is. I'll give you some of the root from the island. That's what you need, Luna, roots, roots!"

But she is off, hustling toward her destiny, heedful only of the signals that tingle and spark, that flash sunlight through her tender flesh. That too, of course, is destiny. Oh Luna, youth! If they had stopped you, I would regret it.

For we care! Some people think we guides watch only distantly, with our cold advice of self-denial. But would we linger around the earth if we didn't care for those who have trouble following our advice? We are not like self-seeking Greeks looking down from Olympus and occasionally interfering. No, we are only ex-people, as I have explained. The human quest is ours. We care.

". . . on the edge of the second coming of Atlantis."

"Would she never find her life?"

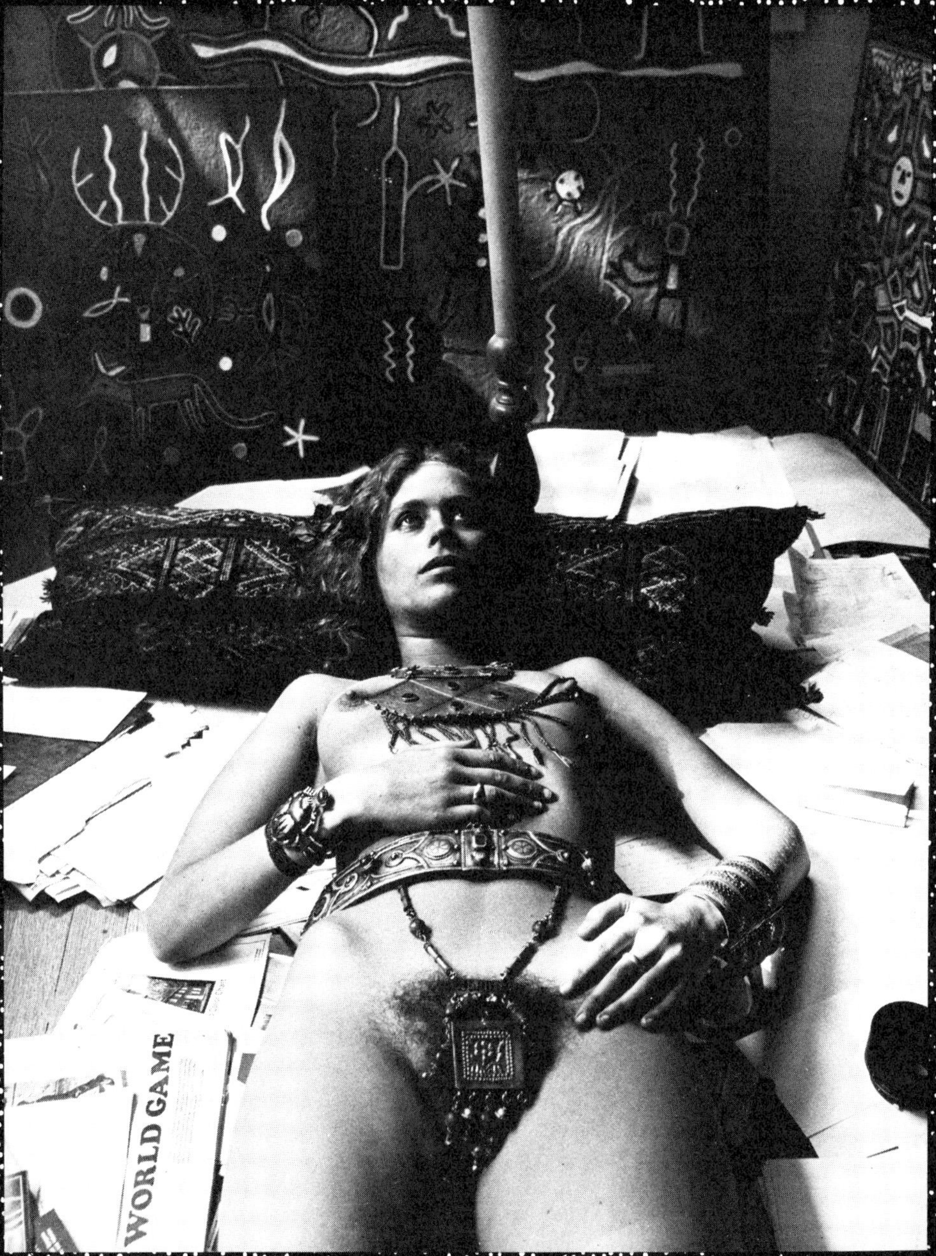
WORLD GAME

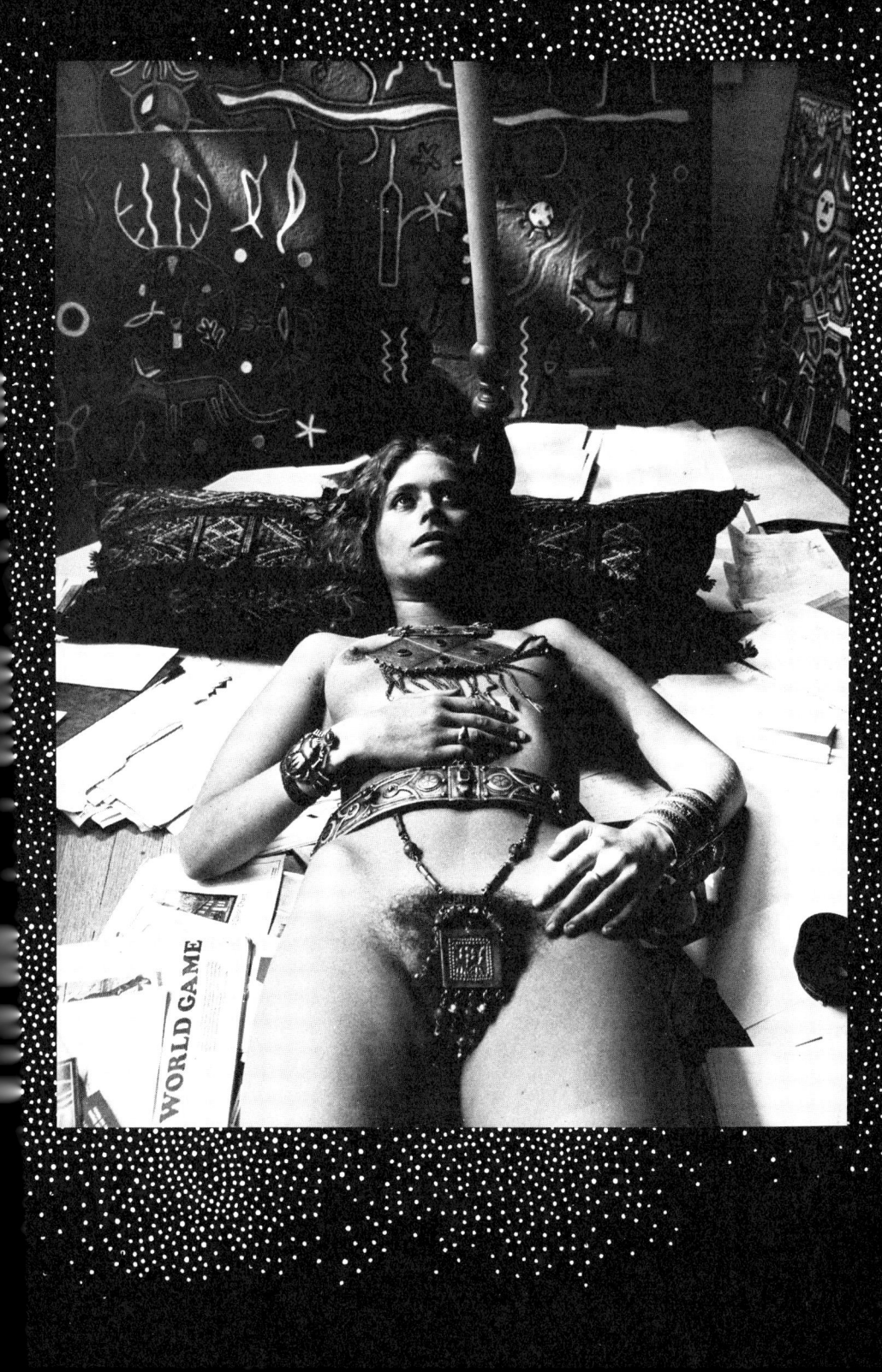

"... above the human sequential state."

"Where else would there be no need of a leash law?"

"...scene of early-morning Tai Chi devotions."

Lessons in Leaping

Despite Bubba's skill at teaching the DeFix, Elkhart sets up a stronger fluttering in Evi that she does not quite understand. Has he gone further than Bubba, she wonders, and if so, where? And if not, does her attraction to him spring from some hidden blot in herself harking back to those dismal days in Atlantis? Is she fated to play one man against the other through this life too, when she really wants to find her Soul Mate? She knows not everybody succeeds in doing that on the Earth Plane, but she hopes she is not destined, as some are, to meet her Soul Mate only on a Soul Plane.

She is wondering about these things as she runs a bath. In Elkhart she recognizes all the classic appeals—height, darkness, handsomeness, plus a mystery ingredient. For one thing, he talks to her intellectually in a way nobody else ever has. He tells her infinitely more details about the workings of Knowledge than Bubba does. He is steeped, as far as Evi can see, in Lore. Yet, she doubts he is her Soul Mate. Probably not. She has the uneasy thought that she may have to wait to find her Soul Mate after the holocaust.

The tub, a high Victorian vessel on clawed feet, is so long that Evi cannot lie down in it without wetting her hair. She sinks into the water, putting her feet up beside the fixtures, the faucet spouting between them. Elkhart likes her with wet hair. He likes her altogether wet.

She reaches for a bottle of bubbles and pours it on her breasts, then strokes them until she is buried in suds.

"Cunt," says Elkhart as he comes into the bathroom. (Paradoxically, Bubba, who seldom speaks to her intellectually, calls Evi a "sexual genius"). Elkhart undresses and slides into the tub with Evi, displacing a large amount of water, some of which runs on to the well-tiled floor.

Evi sighs, letting her head roll back in lather. "I love making it under water," she says.

"That's because it is the female element," Elkhart declares, sloshing against her hips, grinning at the vacuum the water creates between their bellies. He looks at her hands, which have become crinkled. He is having trouble finding his way inside. "How long have you been in this element? You're shriveled." Evi giggles. "No matter," Elkhart says with a curse and a ruthless thrust. "I can make out." The vacuum between them sucks loudly with each rotation of the water.

He begins a chant, calling the name of a water goddess with every push: "Lorelei, Lorelei, Sirena, Sirena, Circe, Circe . . ." Evi thinks it begins to sound like one of Mamacita's Murmas. "Venus, Venus, Ganga, Ganga, Yamuna, Yamuna . . ." How has he ever learned them all? In his research on the female principle, she wonders. He accelerates his chant with no regard, as usual, for Evi's own pace, but she is too entranced by his chant to care: "Shakti, Shakti, Padma, Padma, Rusalka, Rusalka, Esther Williams, Esther Williams, baby, oh baby *doll!*"

What usually constitutes the more intellectual nature of Evi's relationship with Elkhart is that he, still weighed by lawsuits and lawyers' formulations, will discourse at length on the nature of ICH, its greater complexity than DU, its pyramid shape, which arose when the rod of power was given him by Tsinghai Yana. That was an occasion when the monk was indulging in the favorite pastime of his order, the imbibing of a native Tibetan plum wine. Ever since then, Elkhart has been engaged in the elaboration of his pyramid, which was given a much more definite shape and relationship to the known world under a secret sorcery he learned in the Andes. He has not yet told anyone of his instruction, but he yearns to.

He has set Evi down before the mirror and is combing out her damp hair, enjoying an indulgence a person inclines toward after intimacy, so that when Evi asks her question he wants to open up to her, to enjoy her trust. But that has been forbidden.

"The differences between ICH and DU—I guess I still don't get it, Strong," she says. "It's like the way I get mixed up on the lama and the man who discovered the name of God."

"The lama," Elkhart says, "is Tsinghai."

"I dig his name," says Evi.

"And the esoterica expert is Pshaw, with a P. He's the one who will talk. He's spilled ancient secrets, especially to Bubba, who went to Mecca with him once. But you don't need to be discouraged, Evi. Sometimes even Bubba doesn't understand the difference. He doesn't yet see that all bearers of knowledge must enter the pyramid of ICH, the better to penetrate supra-space."

"But, Strong, don't we get into supra-space using DeFixes?"

"Now I see where you're mixed up. From a DU DeFix you come back. DU in that sense is just farting around. Thousands of DU-bys are doing Astravel and don't understand why. It's unbalanced."

"Bubba says ICH's unbalanced," says Evi innocently. "He says sometimes he thinks you really believe in the pyramid."

Elkhart lets her feel his stunned amazement. Then he says, "Evi dear, I see now that you need a lesson in PL."

Evi winces, having forgotten what PL stands for, and also because Elkhart, fixated upon her hair part, has tugged at her tangles. She takes the comb away from him. "And PL is what?" she asks for a reminder.

"Prodigious Leap," he explains patiently. "Let's start at the beginning, Evi."

She straightens herself on the dresser bench, spreading her behind Zen-fashion like a cushion, to make herself comfortable. This is preparation for another DeFix; she straightens her spine over her plump cushion, pulls her shoulders down and gazes into the mirror as Elkhart goes on.

"Pay attention to the fact that the earth's resources are exhausted. Pay attention to the rest the earth needs—from the ravaging hordes that inhabit it. And then you will begin to see the purpose of the pyramid."

Elkhart gazes out the balcony, and in the bright haze he sees hanging there just at the base of the astral canopy his own conception. In the mundane reality he knows it to be the Transamerica Building, which an architect recently told him was designed as an ironic comment on the power structure of corporations who rented space inside it. Taunting cynic. One of the most elemental lessons of ICH is that the pyramid is a device designed to blend the geomagnetic current of earth with solar energy!

Elkhart's eyes narrow, for many souls are entering the pyramid of his mind, and he is counting. "No matter what the courts may say eventually," he muses, "my pyramid is not to be destroyed. People will continue to throng into it, with the purchase of their passage to eternity. The pyramid cannot be done away with by a courthouse; not even the Supreme Court can touch it because as far as it's concerned it is *invisible*."

"So that's why Bubba says he can't see it," Evi says.

"Mmm. Bubba's been out here on the West Coast so long he's lost touch with true power. That's a danger in this post-hippie love-in of his."

He sits next to her on the dresser bench, gazing intently into the glass. "Evi, I have a vision of a world restored to its primeval wonder, its natural splendor. All the human restlessness and misery we inflict upon ourselves, all our driving self-destructiveness has a purpose. Even those who are scornful of Knowledge—scientists, scholars, even politicians—now recognize that the human race is going to blow itself off the face of the earth. ICH offers those souls who have joined the pyramid a place to go. We are on the edge of the second coming of Atlantis."

Evi looks at his intent gaze, notices as he flicks a glance at the balcony when he mentions the pyramid, wonders anew at the notion of the Prodigious Leap he has in mind. "I still don't see, Elk. It seems so vague. How do I get *in* the pyramid? I mean, once I've bought my thousand-dollar ticket and have gotten others to join, how do I get *inside?*"

Elkhart chooses an indirect answer and says, "Think of it, once the holocaust comes, all of us who have recognized the relative insignificance of the physical body in relation to other aspects of the entity, all move at once to another life form. And the earth has a chance to be restored."

Evi opens the neck of her blue velour robe, loosening it to her waist, looking at her silky skin; she runs her fingers over the rosy tips of her breasts. Such phrases as "aspects of the entity" might dazzle, but the idea of somehow side-stepping her yummy (if insignificant) body wasn't very warming. She says, "So the Leap is right out of this world?"

Secretly she tells herself she doesn't buy it. "Try putting it another way," Elkhart says. "Right *into* the invisible world."

"Ah," Evi says with a little cough, the legacy of her fate during the first Atlantis.

Elkhart says, "Now you begin to *see*. There is no visible way. Try Fixing that!" He strolls out to the balcony to resume his soul count.

Evi is left to her dry little cough. Thoughtfully, she goes back into the bathroom, stoppers the tub and runs more water, in preparation for another of her favorite DeFixes. When the tub is half full, she removes the stopper and perches on the rim of the tub with her feet in the very cold water. She stares into the small whirlpool created by the drain—a slow drain. The Victorian plumbing of the hotel provides the ideal movement for this DeFix. The water whirls gently into a small, slow eddy, where she lets her being glide.

I see that I must back up now to those other lessons in leaping Elkhart has had. I have a reluctance about it, because it will mean approaching his demon, and my instructions will be a restraint. I believe my report would be incomplete without this unpleasantness, to retrace his sorcerer's apprenticeship that he has been slyly alluding to in his talk with Evi. You can imagine how grateful I am for my ease of transport. If I had to use earthly means of getting around, I would be hard put to accomplish my many tasks. As it is, my colleagues and I are understaffed. Fortunately, we have no clock and need no sleep. All our time is Overtime.

And so back to Peru.

There is one disadvantage to having heaven on earth. These astral planes we have brought down for human use are especially vulnerable to unfavorable spirits. That is why people should be careful that only the most high be given access. And even they are subject to residual Karmic weaknesses such as pride, greed and gullibility. Americans have an infectious conviction that the more people there are doing a thing, the better it becomes. The Peruvian Sisterhood has been taken in by this odd conceit.

Otherwise, Elkhart would never have been admitted.

After he has been in Peru for a few weeks, shortly after his Fix with Bubba Burr, Mamacita sends him upon a Solitary Task. All novices go upon these journeys into the desert alone to work on their individual Murma for sixteen hours a day. Commonly they return having made an individual PL. What is uncommon about Elkhart's PL is that he makes it under false instruction. Usually a seeker on a Solitary Task would find the native hallucinogens, peyote and mescaline affiliates, and would undergo a solitary trial of deciding whether to relieve the isolation and loneliness by ingesting them. This is an expected part of the Leap process, for drugs are strictly forbidden by Mamacita, who would prefer not to have a novice attain at all rather than attain through such jolting, crude means, of whose side effects she has no certain knowledge. Individual attainment is not Mamacita's concern, but evolution; despite a widely circulated theory that mind-affecting drugs were created to improve human genetics, she prefers her ascetic approach.

Scarcely anyone studying under Mamacita is more zealous about evolutionary process than Elkhart, but he is so obsessive that it is like a magnetic force for underworld fanatics. One such fanatic has led him by a painful path to a mind-bending root. We shall call it Knuckle Root, although its name shall be disclosed at the proper time in a book by Ali Pshaw.

On the first day out, Elkhart undresses, and in his urban ignorance sits in the sun, placing his bare behind on what appears to be a slight elevation. It turns out to be a nest of scorpions, and he receives several stings. So intense is his agony that concentration upon his Murma becomes impossible. To increase his distress, a vulture begins to circle above his new place of meditation. At that, he seeks refuge in a spot of shade under a Joshua tree cactus, whose arms hover over him as if threatening to embrace or throttle him, and no sooner is he settled than the ground beside him makes a short tearing sound, like zipper teeth ripping. Looking at the earth opening, he gets his first glimpse of Knuckle Root, a twisted yellow tuber like a yellow yam.

Sensing a miracle, and suspecting Mamacita is behind it, he tears out the root and eats it, enjoying the soft yamlike texture. Instantly, the pain from his stings stops. But he has fallen into grave error.

Knuckle Root has uncanny effects. It opens a huge appetite in Elkhart (who is supposed to be fasting), and he tries to eat all he can find. Each bite creates the desire for more. He begins to see himself at a feast in the court of Louis XIV, as a gustatory stream flows in and out of his vision. At length he falls into a glutted stupor, his private Murma forgotten. At this moment, he is easy prey to any evil spirit.

I mentioned during the Fix with Bubba that I was aware of a malevolent presence but was getting mixed identity signals. Now the picture clarifies somewhat, but I am not entirely convinced of what I see myself.

Lying in his Knuckle Root stupor, Elkhart sees through glazed eyes a naked form, neither man nor deer, a short, heavy-footed creature, hooved, with a majestic head set with five-point antlers and cool, commanding eyes. Trying to sit up, Elkhart realizes that a power has surrounded him. The spirit has created a force field around Elkhart to immobilize him.

"Call me Bielbog," he tells Elkhart. "I have grasped the future and know how to make it work." And with this sentence, Elkhart's instruction begins.

I look closely at this demon, who is incapable of seeing me. He can sense my presence, however, if I am not careful. I do not believe that this is Bielbog, who is quite dangerous and with whom I have previously tangled. It strikes me that Bielbog may be the victim of name theft, a silly game imps are fond of playing. But who have we here, and how serious is the game?

Elkhart is soon persuaded, by shrewd and twisted flattery, that he can do a vast and necessary service to the world. We know of Elkhart's pyramid scheme of psychic development. It is this concept through which the demon works, first complimenting Elkhart upon his genius in conceiving it. "I picked you as my human counterpart because of your pyramid. But you can succeed with it only if I am your unhuman counterpart." He convinces Elkhart that the pyramid will vaporize in the outer atmosphere without the grounding, the underpinnings of earthly reality, that he, Bielbog, can provide for it.

Having always vaguely sensed something amiss in his master scheme, and weakened by cellular alterations caused by Knuckle Root, Elkhart submits totally.

On the second day, the two meet beside the Knuckle Root source, as appointed.

Suddenly a black shadow comes out from behind a bush and pulls itself over Bielbog's antlers like a sack.

Elkhart, alarmed, reaches out to try to remove the shadow. But Bielbog lets out a shriek. His voice is so piercing that Elkhart draws back, immediately afraid.

Bielbog's voice, which has in it a petulance I think I recognize, sounds from under the black cloud. "You must learn to live in a world of omens, you fool. When a force like this comes, let me handle it."

There is another zipping sound, and the antlers break through the shadow, dispersing it. The deer-demon asks, "You did not understand the significance of the scorpions and the vulture your first day here, did you?"

Elkhart shakes his head ignorantly. He takes out a notebook into which he begins to put all this teacher has to say. He thinks some day he may put it into a book. "The scorpion and the vulture," Bielbog slowly articulates, "enabled me to introduce you to Knuckle Root, didn't they?"

Elkhart looks at him in amazement, seeing the unity of these signs.

Yes, if he hadn't moved, he would never have sat upon the Knuckle Root. He writes in his notebook.

"And what of this shadow?" Elkhart asks.

His teacher laughs, watching him scribble in his book. "When you are ready, you will know," he says.

Elkhart nods; his fatal flaw, that he wants to trust someone, is in operation. If ever teacher and disciple were matched in weakness, it is in this pairing. For the demon, too, wants to trust his disciple. This enables me to find out the identity he has stolen, for he has gone beyond mere name theft. Later in the day, after Elkhart has eaten a pound of Knuckle Root, Bielbog approaches him closely and whispers his real name. However, I hear it and realize I have been obtuse. Of course, all that prancing and stamping on the ground is not Bielbog's way and should have betrayed the source—Rumpelstiltskin!

Many people believe that when he stamped himself through the floor and out of the life of a certain princess he was tormenting that he stamped himself out of existence. But it is now more widely known that demons do not die, and all these years Rumpelstiltskin has been seeking an opportunity to disguise his identity and do something really big.

I have a long-standing relationship with this imp. My most recent adventure with him was to impede his dream of glory; it was I who kept him out of Germany in the thirties. Whether Rumpelstiltskin could have done much in that highly competitive situation we can only speculate. However, by now he has gotten together quite a large scheme. His assuming the identity of someone so much higher in the Pantheon than he could prove a nuisance.

When he hears the name, Elkhart laughs in great amusement. "That's very funny!" Bielbog joins in, laughing too. They slap one another on the back and roll upon the desert sand.

But Bielbog sobers suddenly. "You must never say my real name. Forget you have heard it! If you ever mention it, especially in spite—" Such spirits are ignorantly superstitious. He shivers, almost as if he senses the nearness of a benevolent spirit. I draw back, for it would never do for him to guess *my* identity.

On the third day, his teacher laughs scornfully when Elkhart begins to write in his notebook. "Automatic writing," he says contemptuously.

But by that evening, Bielbog is supplying Elkhart with automatic drawings, too. They are elaborate plans, which emerge to perfection on a very small scale in his notebook. Without ruler, compass or measure of any kind, these plans are marvelously complete. Elkhart can easily have them reproduced in larger portfolio size for engineers to read. Even I am impressed with their thoroughness.

But their content! Well, it makes me regretful of the restraints I am under once again! If I could simply zap Bielbog here and now, without having to teach some living female how to handle this, much energy would be saved.

Elkhart's head reels as information flows from his hand onto the pages. He has no control over the drawings. Sometimes Bielbog's voice sinks to a murmur, yet the drawings come out in the notebook with great clarity.

Elkhart becomes more convinced that their co-creation operates upon parallel planes, Bielbog's work being of the material world, yet Elkhart necessary to implement it; while Elkhart's pyramid is of the spirit world and cannot take off without Bielbog's practical scheme. In his delirium, Elkhart feels singled out, Chosen, almost divine.

On the fourth day, Bielbog explains that in order to execute the plans, Elkhart will need many Recruitment Officers, more than he now has working within his pyramid structure. Thousands of them would come to him, Bielbog promises. "I am choosing them now. For every Recruitment Officer assigned to round up volunteers for service, there will be a corresponding guide." The guides would be chosen from the best stock of goblins, imps, afrits, and djins, from the three-headed associates of Balan, from others with cloven hoofs, horny brows, spiky tails and fiery eyes, all of whom Bielbog in his new-found maturity would lead in the proper action at the proper time in the proper place with the proper people.

Even to Elkhart, it sounds a trifle grandiose, but he sleeps on it. The next day, the fifth, he rises troubled and very anxious.

When Bielbog appears, Elkhart consults his notes. "I don't see how we can recruit them—the female finalist volunteers, the FFV," he says.

Bielbog speaks with perceptible disappointment. "You still understand very little," he says sourly. He has waited for centuries for this opportunity, believing in the ancient dictum that teacher and student find each other when the time is right. Somehow he feels he deserves a brighter pupil, despite Elkhart's ingenious scheme.

"Women aren't so cooperative as they once were," Elkhart says.

Bielbog does not address himself immediately to this point. He says, "Do you know how stupid you are?"

Elkhart only stares in a mild daze, more anxious than ever but willing to attribute it to his breakfast of Knuckle Root.

Bielbog shakes his head, then laughs with the same affection he has shown before. "You don't even know that you cannot tape what I say."

Elkhart's anxiety deepens. He stammers but no words come.

"I know you have hidden that tiny recorder inside your jacket. There is nothing you can hide from me. But you are so stupid you don't even realize that nothing I say will go onto tape."

"I've been having writer's cramp," Elkhart complains.

Bielbog, still laughing, asks, "Tell me, are we equals, you and I?"

Now if Bielbog has experienced some disappointment, so too has Elkhart. He considers his Ivy League education, his life on Madison Avenue—indeed, even his long-term secret work for the CIA—and wonders in the light of his well-groomed past if he ought not have been given a higher tutor than a minor underworld thief, whose real name does occasionally slip out in a Rump or Rumpel . . . But Elkhart has not betrayed these feelings in any way that he is aware of, and so he says, "Yes, you are every bit as good as I am!"

Bielbog laughs wickedly then. "You fool! Picking up my crumbs like a magpie! You have not yet learned the first command, total submission to the teacher!" This unexpected outburst silences Elkhart, stuns him. He remembers the first command from Mamacita (to whom he has always paid overt submission), and to hear it from Bielbog reinforces his belief that Mamacita herself has directed him to this other teacher. He feels humbled and confused. He has been given a unique opportunity to redeem the earth through the help of this guide, and he has proved ungrateful. He withdraws the tape recorder from his pocket and smashes it against a rock, breaking the tape so as never to be able to test Bielbog's assertion that he is untapable. "I *am* stupid," he says. "I might as well be working on a Ph.D. dissertation. Please help me." His tears fall down onto the cold sand.

"That is more like it," says his teacher in a conciliatory tone. He draws in the sand with his cloven hoof. "Now you must follow my directions to the letter." He tells Elkhart that the next day he must return to Mamacita and that soon thereafter he must go back, to California this time, to continue his work. He instructs Elkhart to speak to no one of their plans, to none of his assistants, nor to Mamacita, until he is contacted again. "I shall visit you in the West. I am not merely a desert lord, you know, but can function in cities, and have always liked San Francisco as a stamping ground." He paws the desert. "The Recruitment Officers will present themselves when they are ready. Be patient. Be alert. My surrogates are instructing them in their sleep. They will also be speaking to the FFV in their sleep."

Elkhart smiles in understanding. "So you have answered one question after all. We get control of the volunteers in bed!"

Bielbog's mouth curls with crafty humor. "Isn't that where we've always done it!" His laugh becomes a roar. "The female capacity for self-sacrifice is inexhaustible, you'll see."

On the last day he receives parting instructions. These concern Knuckle Root. Bielbog describes how Elkhart will start a business for ethnic freaks, although he will never sell his stock until further instructions. It will be apparently harmless trade beads from the Peruvian desert. Actually the beads will be made of compressed Knuckle Root. "They will be called hare-hare beads," Bielbog says, "and will be ingested by every volunteer, at the proper time."

Elkhart murmurs an ecstatic delight in this cover. "*Hare* means deer. From the necklace that Shiva wears," he says wonderingly.

Bielbog nods approval. It is of some value that his disciple is addicted to Lore, as Evi has observed. "Whoever enters an R.I.P. unit will already be a user of the Root," he says. "Herding becomes a simple organizational matter. Like herding chattel."

He enjoys a deep, malevolent laugh. His hoof marks the ground. Elkhart shivers, beset by shadows.

"You have further questions?" his teacher asks archly, as if impatient now to be gone.

Elkhart can scarcely look at him. The sun has gone behind the Joshua tree where these meetings have been held. Thunder shakes the air. Elkhart finds himself muttering a question which surprises and alarms him. "Are you the devil?" It has the resonances of a medieval mentality to his ears; is not the question a man like himself asks. It makes him afraid.

His teacher laughs again and phrases his answer as a riddle: "Is it of any use if I say that I am?"

Elkhart does not know what to say to that and can only shake his head dumbly. The teacher laughs again. "You still do not understand the difference between us. You must learn it once and for all. Say it to yourself over and over that you *can* be named. Say it and remember, Elkhart: '*He* is a spirit! While I—I am a turd, a clod, a pile of manure! A human!' Repeat it like a Murma, Elkhart, and you will slowly understand our work and will revere it. But you cannot expect to be my equal!"

His self-assurance, his implications about naming disturb me greatly. He seems to have forgotten his humbler identity altogether and to have his mind set for an even bigger game than Bielbog's. I do not like the feeling in the air at all.

His laughter sounds again, a deep bass roll that resounds over the high, clouded mountain. He scrapes his hoof upon the ground, then stamps his way out of Elkhart's presence; their lessons in the Andes are complete.

After his retreat, Elkhart awaits a sign from Mamacita, believing that she has sent him on the Task in order that he might encounter Bielbog. But when none is forthcoming, he remembers to make his plans to take leave of the Andes, amassing in secret a huge shipment of Knuckle Root disguised as trade beads.

Although the other students perceive no change in him, being deeply involved in their own work, Piggy, his wife and dyadic partner, becomes a difficulty to him.

Elkhart has never trusted Piggy, despite his desire to trust. She has always dwelled upon error and unpleasantness. He believes it is Piggy's fault that nasty rumors about his sexual preferences have been spread about. She knows him, knows his sly muscular contractions about the eyes and mouth; she hears his voice speaking its own will in the dark when he sleeps, spilling secrets. Within a few days, she is begging him to go back to the States to his old shrink. Finally, after a few futile Fixes in private, she asks the group to let them Fix openly.

She catches him unawares, or he would never have consented. She catches him during one of the tape loops: "Under standing under standing under standing under . . ."

The group obligingly makes a space for them, but it is not to Piggy's advantage. There she stands in the center of the *dojo* mat, feeling that she is standing under the world's weight. She can only scream: "Strong, you've gone crazy! You're insane!"

Strong Elkhart finds an inspiration that wins the day for him. He asks, "Have you been reading my notebook?"

All craziness is supposed to go into one's notebook. Anything is okay there. He doesn't imagine Piggy *has* read it or seen the drawings so exquisitely made, so clearly the work of a master craftsman, so obviously beyond his talents. But reading a notebook is taboo—not, of course, on moral grounds. Read Minds, not Words, is the word. Elkhart has so clouded his mind for the others that he is unreadable.

Piggy cannot bear his outrageous accusation. She never intentionally spies. She begins to babble even more incoherently.

Hardly anybody has thought much of Piggy. A skinny woman past her attractive years, lacking self-confidence; it is a bad match, people think, since Elkhart has always had such success with other women. Few are sorry when, her head bobbing, her mouth drooling at the corners, she says that she is leaving.

However, Elkhart is not content merely to have her go. He realizes she knows too much. He insists on taking her himself, a gesture scarcely anyone can fault him for and one which gives him an opportunity to smuggle out his shipment of Knuckle Root. The next day, he arranges to have Piggy committed to a private hospital in Tucson. There she resides to this day, claiming in a sad monotone that her husband wants to kill most of the women in the world, that he has spoken of his plan in his sleep, that this extermination may happen any day now. She speaks often in Spanish in the hope that at least the Mexican cleaning women will hear her and take precautionary measures to hide out. (Perhaps in Amsterdam, she tells them plaintively.) She is constantly given tranquilizers, and in private interviews with her psychiatrist receives the compassionate treatment reserved for hopeless, paying paranoids. The official opinion is that the spiritual exercises she undertook were too much for her.

Among the women at Mamacita's, Luna alone has liked Piggy, for as we have seen she has a respect for women of greater experience than her own, and as we shall soon see dramatically, she has a way of finding virtue where others cannot.

When Elkhart returns to gather the rest of the available Root, Luna is still suspicious of him, and it is he who is the cause of her break with Bubba Burr. Bubba, seeing that Elkhart has lost his dyadic partner and deeply compelled by his recently aroused feelings of brotherhood, offers Luna the opportunity to replace Piggy in Elkhart's dyad.

"I won't," Luna says disappointingly.

"Just for one night," Bubba says.

"Nuts," says Luna.

Bubba engages her in a short Fix. She has to understand that in certain respects she *is* in a cube of ice, a square. The task of the Fix he imposes on her is to enter a circle. They are to meditate upon these two forms, he upon the circle, until a fusion occurs and square and circle overlap. When that happens in their psyches, according to Bubba, a triangle will be formed with two base angles of fifty-one degrees. This, incidentally, is a Fix created by Elkhart, for the triangle, so conceived of male and female principles, creates a pyramid.

Afterward, Bubba says, "If *I* have no objection, how can *you*?"

"How can I what?"

"Not go fuck Elkhart, Baby."

Luna sighs wearily. "If you have no objection, Bubba, I am going back to Berkeley."

Bubba cries, "But I do object. You haven't completed Multiplex Transmission yet!"

"No, and I'm still in my block of ice, to tell the truth."

Bubba sighs, gazing at her distantly across the levels of evolution. He sees that she will not give up such antediluvian morality as the notion of "loyalty within a pair bond," Luna's rationalization for that most degrading of hang-ups, jealousy. He sees that she lacks the female responsiveness he needs to reinforce his intended announcement to the world of the emergence of the female principle. She is not for him, at this important moment in his career, for he has decided to buy into the vast empire of the Intergalactic Cosmic Hookup.

Suddenly, as the last of the bathwater disappears down the whirlpool, Evi lets out a terrified scream. She stands up in the tub on feet numb with cold. She is shaking out her hands loosely, staring wildly, crying, "I'm not there! I'm not there!" Through the workings of her DeFix, her image has gone down the drain.

Her shrieks bring Elkhart from the balcony, and when he appears she finds herself again. She falls upon him weakly and cries, "I'm growing, Elk, I know it. One day soon I'll be able to disappear and not get freaked. I have so much to overcome." Tears trickle down onto the lapel of his Cardin suit.

He guides her out to the balcony where he can peer over her trembling shoulder at his pyramid again, which he has only momentarily stopped considering. He tells Evi to look at it, suggesting she imagine that the Transamerica building is the ICH pyramid, going up into the sky.

Her sobbing subsides, and quieted, she only half hears his words. His voice lulls her; she listens to the resonances in his chest. He is saying, "Think of those who are bringing their fiscal strength to it. How fortuitous it was that I hit upon the pyramid recruitment system, a metaphysical insight, an intuition that won me the support of my Other Teacher . . ." Here he catches himself. This is as close as he has come to betraying his teacher to anyone. Evi's eyes are closing restfully.

His mind constricts, throbs, undergoes a sudden, explosive expansion as that shriek of steel sounds in it again, and as something goes down the long metal chute inside his head, and as he hears the grinding, splintering scream of a whirling blade.

So vivid is the force of Elkhart's vision that he cannot help speaking of it. He tells himself that Evi is stupefied and cannot understand, but another part of him tries to make it as clear for her as possible. He speaks of the natural parallel between money and metaphysics, of the integral salvationist aspect of material power; more than metaphor, money was *means* whereby souls might enter the structure in which everyone worth saving would be rocketed home to the new planet, their spirits in the safety of the metamoney pyramid, while bodies were at work in the Earth Restoration Project.

"It is given," Elkhart says, assuming the language of prophecy and squinting at the base of his pyramid, "that when the great takeoff occurs, some souls with balances outstanding may fall off and crash into the rocket flames." But on the whole, everything would be conducted in an orderly fashion, no elbowing, shouldering, nudging, gouging, not even among those who failed to recognize the pyramid's strength. It is true, in every society there have been rebels who preferred to writhe in their self-styled Dantean agonies. He could imagine some recalcitrant, undisciplined hoods, on so vast a globe as this, might get hold of a small arsenal and attempt to undermine the great adventure. Arabs might make trouble, or the French. Resistance forces might join those who had fallen off the pyramid for one reason or another—he did not expect 100 percent success, for history was against that. But he could not conceive of failure. All resisters would eventually be consigned to the Hog.

Evi's eyes open with a renewal of the panic she has suffered at the tub, and she asks, "Elk, what is the Hog?"

He laughs, hugging her close. "One day I shall show you the blueprints. I keep them with me always. The sample model, the experimental Hog, is now being built. I inspected the chassis last week in Idaho. It is being readied for a trial run."

"But, Elk, what is it for?" Evi is now trying to disguise her sense of dread as she searches her memory cells for some gossip she heard about Elkhart's wife and her pitiful accusations against her husband. What had they been? Evi says, "It sounds like everybody who doesn't make it into the pyramid gets fed to the hogs. Sort of like a Roman circus." Her voice quavers despite her effort to appear normal. Her cough scratches at her throat.

He looks down at her with some surprise, gives her shoulder a shake. Suddenly he seizes her with both hands in a fiercely cold grip. His hands feel like clamps to her; his voice is a hiss. "The earth is dying. Everybody says so. It has got to be restored. And by those who have consumed it. My own personal guide has conceived a relief for the situation. He is a great spirit who can turn straw into gold. He is now going to turn the wretched straw persons who have wrecked this earthly paradise into the means for making another. This is an alchemical process!"

Evi is holding her body perfectly still, trying to think of how to proceed with a DeFix that will enable her to get free of him. He gives no indication he is even aware of how tightly he is holding her and speaks in broken sentences, murmuring about Recruitment Officers, the Hog's power and versatility, its readiness for an experimental trial run. Evi remembers now that she has an appointment that afternoon for an aura rinse, and the notion of keeping it becomes precious to her.

Elkhart looks down, suddenly tilts her chin up. "You!" he mutters, his eyes glazed. "I may be called upon to make a sacrifice. Like all the saints—" He releases her so quickly that she loses her balance. He reaches into his pocket. "Evi, I have a gift for you." He brings out a very delicately made necklace of macramé and what appear to be finely cut shell beads of yellow. "These beads are made of Knuckle Root."

Evi gulps, finding the necklace immensely attractive. She takes it from him, but her throat constricts, like an alarm.

"Keep it with you always like a rosary," he says. "Take one of the beads now. It will get you closer to that Leap that you must make." He puts it around her neck, raises the center portion to her lips. "Eat a bead, Evi. Eat one now."

Evi looks at the necklace with a horrible fascination. Some instinct makes her decide to put him off. "Not now, Strong. I—you—" Her mind stalls. Then an inspiration comes to her. She doesn't recognize it, but I whisper it to her. "Mamacita has arrived!" She yields to a violent fit of coughing.

"Who? Mamacita?" he asks dazedly. He seems to try to remember her, his mind having been focused so strongly upon his Other Teacher. "Mamacita! Why didn't you tell me?"

"I—I forgot." She groans inwardly, remembering her promise to Bubba and how she used to tell lies in Atlantis. How will she ever sort it all out?

But without realizing it, Evi has been enabled through this encounter to make a spurt of growth, like a plant given a shot of nitrogen in its roots. She may not yet be able to take a Prodigious Leap, but a new assurance possesses her. She realizes that Elkhart is not her Soul Mate, whoever he may be. She knows that she must not take Knuckle Root for reasons obscure to her, and she also knows that she must try to find out more about the Hog. No sooner does that occur to her than she realizes why she has broken her word to Bubba. She must have the way clear to go and search Elkhart's room. There are times when danger enlarges the mind as much as suffering does.

Elkhart straightens, breathes deeply, and that aspect of his entity which has so frightened Evi recedes. He chucks her under the chin, giving her a large-toothed smile. "We'll try the Knuckle Root next time, cunt. You'll make that PL yet, you'll see."

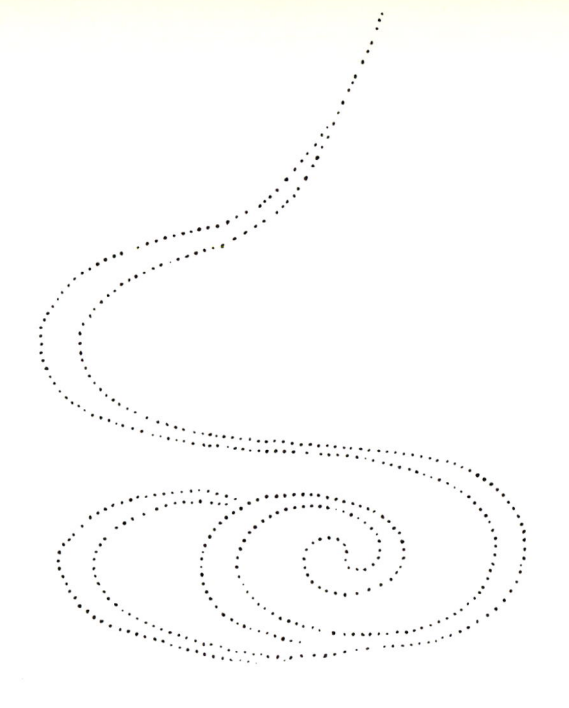

The Corner of the Eye

Now about Harrison . . . here is a man intent upon another path, the highway system. Those who ride the concrete web that covers the globe, the highway users, are his target for salvation at the moment. Unlike some salvationists, Harrison believes the earth is worth saving, although human perversity and wastefulness bother him to a terrible extent. At times he imagines he might be more pleasantly occupied in trying to save those varieties of falcons, tigers and whales now growing extinct.

He is bringing equipment into Carrie's garden. Ginseng is backing in, supporting one end of a distilling tower about five feet high. Harrison is about to place it on top of a cluster of carefully bonsai-ed cotoneaster bushes, when Ginseng sees where he is heading and skillfully side-steps the mishap. After all, the bushes are Ginseng's own workmanship. They land with the machinery disturbing nothing more than a bed of baby's-breath, although Carrie's calico cat, which had been resting there, is obliged to run for her life.

Carrie watches uneasily from the studio. "Now for those retorts," says Harrison, heading back out to his truck. They bring two retorts and make another trip, this time bearing an automobile engine on a dolly. Harrison and Ginseng roll the dolly straight toward the French doors of Carrie's studio, where Selena is sitting for her in a yoga posture of the Plow.

"Carrie," Selena says without shifting her position, one she can maintain comfortably for half an hour and which is very good for her varicose veins, "you see what they are about to do?"

Carrie's "Hummm" of recognition is from seeing much more. She has offered to let Harrison unload here because Selena has told her he has an early-afternoon appointment in San Francisco, where his equipment would be unsafe in the truck. But she is seeing now in his glance at her an attraction that he is not even conscious of, a wanting in him to reach that moment in Carrie's earlier vision where he can make free with her space, time, affections, food. But all this is unknown at this juncture, which Harrison may now see only dimly as a first step (and not a step from which there is no easy turning back) in an only faintly familiar ritual.

At the studio door, while Carrie is interpreting that look of his, he is saying, "I won't disturb you with this. I just want to stick her in the corner for the night," and so Carrie opens the door, clears some canvases out of a corner, and looks on while he and Ginseng lower the engine to the floor.

He pats it. "Sixty to the gallon," he tells Ginseng, who caresses the engine, saying, "Man, I gotta see this."

Harrison is planning the next day to put the engine into Selena's car, a 1937 Packard, which is now in the shop being worked on today by two young women who run an Auto-Healing Center and who have refurnished it with everything except an engine, including an eight-track stereo.

But for now Harrison leads Ginseng back outside to the portable distillery and closes the door behind him. They are seen bending over Harrison's machinery. Only an occasional phrase ("tested for hydrocarbons," "five hundred thousand miles," "retort head through this tube") penetrates the French doors.

The following exchange occurs inside the studio:
Selena: "Aren't you curious?"
"Are you?"
"Well, of course. It's interesting."
"You think so. Well, come on . . ."

And then they are all outside, around the still and its retort and its retort head, while Harrison attaches a tube from the head to the condenser. Harrison is not secretive about his invention, only at the subtlest depth. "You see," he says, gazing at Carrie, unaware that she simply blanks out over anything scientific, a trait which may cause him difficulty, "of all the demons set loose upon the world, I have one of them cornered." Here he is using imagery he knows will appeal to Selena's interest in the invisible. "I have created a combustion inhibitor which successfully exorcises the demon, you might say. And so my pollution solution"—and here Harrison may be making a rhyming appeal to the childlike quality Ginseng has betrayed to him—"is a simple additive, something called a vanadium catalyst. The catalyst is bonded to a hydrocarbon molecule, which can be mixed with gasoline and remain suspended uniformly in the gasoline, so that when the gas is burned in the engine, it will catalyze the combustion. The emissions of the engine will fall easily within the limits of the federal standards for emission contaminants."

"Federal standards?" asks Ginseng, who has not understood much more than Carrie but who has decided opinions about federal standards. "Are they low enough for contaminants? We know how low they are on morals."

"When I say 'fall easily,' I mean fall to *zero!*"

"Harrison, how does the additive get into the gasoline?" Selena asks.

"Ah, that's what I'm working on now, partly. The plan is that it goes in at the refinery. It is to be sold in carloads to gasoline companies and added to storage tanks."

"But they already got low and no lead gas," says Ginseng, bewildered.

Harrison explains the difference, that it is in his "hydrocarbon molecular bond," and he points to his retort head, the tube of which is leading to the condenser, which he says is a "fractional tower, in ordinary refining a kind of separator of the various elements of petroleum," but which he is using now as a means of projecting the layers for his molecular—

At the words "fractional" and "layers," Carrie is lost to them. Her calico cat brushes up against her, and she picks up the animal and gazes at the tower as it becomes an immense layer cake. The tower is the scene of three layers of activity, where she, Selena and Luna are entrapped with other fellow creatures.

On one layer Carrie's former husband, Roger, is seeing her as a *thing*, a complete disaster area, an ugly mess. He gazes at the unsightly geography of Carrie through the mirror of her dressing table. Beside the mirror is an old print called "All Is Vanity," which depicts a woman at her dressing table but which may also be seen as a picture of a skull, for the bottles on the dressing table are also grinning teeth and the mirror is the shape of a skull, the woman's head its nose. The print offering these simultaneous images may have been Carrie's first layering experience, in fact. To Roger, it is one of many items of rubbish in Carrie's life. Roger is disgusted by it, by the general untidiness of Carrie's housekeeping, by the double life she tries to lead as mother/housewife and painter. Roger wants her to stop painting and fixes on the piles of paints and canvases as a huge disturbance, is revolted by the heaps of clay she leaves about the house for their two small children, as if her own messy studio outside were not enough. A small reenactment of Carrie's marriage is taking place there in the distillery, on one level of it, as Roger thrashes about in the hatefulness he finds, not only in her work but in her child-rearing methods, and he faces only her reflection, unable to meet her eye to eye. For in her eye, Roger might find a reflection of what Carrie is re-seeing inside her hand mirror, a scene she has witnessed only that afternoon, a meeting between Roger and Marianne, a woman who has enabled Roger to alter so dramatically his image of Carrie that she has become inept and incompetent as a mother, unworthy to be his wife. Marianne, Marianne. Strolling past the hill behind their very house in the North Berkeley Hills, down to Rose Walk. He could not have foreseen that Carrie would be so maddeningly forgetful as to miss her dental appointment. Soft-eyed, entrancingly wealthy Marianne, with Roger sauntering beside her. Roger sauntering! Cool, professorial Roger, who stands above Carrie's dressing-table mirror, posturing his disapproval, his disgust, while as Marianne's lover he saunters. "You give the children absolutely no sense of order," he complains as Carrie's mascara creates little stains on her cheeks. Here she is twenty-nine, and like Luna, who wears no make-up at all, Carrie follows the fashion of her own time and paints her lashes. "You sit there crying, feeling sorry for yourself, when you might be doing something worthwhile. The girls are not learning anything a woman needs to know. Amy might learn to cook if you had the slightest interest in it yourself. Emily has a talent for clothes you've done nothing to help her with." The mascara stains widen into rivulets, flash floods. Carrie tries to imagine her dog-eared cookbooks on Marianne's kitchen shelf but sees instead crisp new volumes, a black maid from West Berkeley in a white apron, Marianne ringing a service bell and Roger gormandizing, toasting her blond loveliness, while he now berates Carrie: "There is no routine in your life!" But hasn't she seen the routine of their lives flung into the winds of a summer afternoon on Rose Walk, during the hour of Roger's own Wednesday lab, where students wait in vain with their routine projects, where an entire university system is obliged gently to inquire of itself, what has happened to our systematic Roger this afternoon? Marianne, Marianne, a name as fateful as the sea, invoking her own imagery, and here Carrie listens to the surf just below the office of a psychiatrist Roger has decided they must visit to make their break-up orderly. The psychiatrist explains that what Roger is seeking in Marianne is "the archetypal image of youthful purity and beauty which often beckons a man after either seven or fourteen years of marriage." "The cycles," he declares, "tend to go in sevens." Marianne, Marianne, sounding against the rocky cliff, more certain than stone, strong enough a name to bring a man to his knees, or to empower him with new strength. Roger's body has become firmer, straighter, more toned than it has ever been in the years of his marriage to Carrie. Can his rounded shoulders have lifted, his slouchy belly have disappeared? Why shouldn't Roger, then, say to the psychiatrist, "If these cycles make a man feel like this, I'll take as many as I can get."

Carrie smiles at this layer of the distillery. Roger has taken all he could get: a Mercedes 220 SL, a swimming pool built for their distraction, a totally new wardrobe—a year and a day with Marianne. Then she left him to sail to Greece with an archeologist. And here Carrie runs the risk *I* often encounter, of falling into a seeming tributary of consciousness. For now she is drifting into Marianne, sounding in the surf of her mind: Marianne trying to be Roger's vision of purity but at length offering her archeologist a perfect collection of Balinese statuettes, offering a man always something he cannot resist, especially when she accompanies it with his own image of purity; Marianne, trying to make a pure, selfless gesture and losing herself in it. Here Carrie calls herself back to Roger, the tiny speck of their life together passing, reeling across the years, the falling of a leaf like that one drifting down now from her strawberry arbutus tree onto Harrison's portable distillery. Occasionally Roger—sober, systematic, round-shouldered Roger—has come and gone thoughtfully through their lives, visiting his daughters (neither of whom has become in the least concerned about their incapacities in the domestic arts), talking to Carrie, the old pervasive obliquity of their tie the same, indirect, as through a looking glass.

"It works both ways," Harrison is saying, "that is, the vapors separate at varying rates—" He is pointing to the layers of his condenser there in Carrie's garden as Selena and Ginseng try to follow his explanation.

And like vapors, ghosts or steamy figures move inside the layers before Carrie's gaze. Roger has died of a heart attack at forty-five, now a ghost himself.

On a separate layer, there is Luna, looking like a lovely ghost, moving in a vapor: she talks to Emil Jewels. "In my struggle to stop being a sex object, I've made objects of men," she says. Emil Jewels, who has come to Calistoga Hot Springs to conduct a workshop he calls "The New Woman: Down from Goddess or Up from Guttersnipe," strokes his long gray beard and gazes out from a face so skilled at being a projection screen itself that his patients, whom he prefers to call disciples or spiritual friends, can see him variously as a toad, God, Reich, Beethoven, Gloria Steinem—whatever suits their inner need. That Luna's entire commune, the Daughters of the Tantra, are taking the workshop is no challenge to him, and he will, given occasion and cooperation on their part, take them all on for sexual therapy afterward, or in the steam baths in what he likes to call Interviews. Under the popular spell of the East, he prefers to give Interviews rather than Therapy.

The Calistoga Hot Springs, open to the moon and stars at night, is a bit run-down, having seen its height as a spa before World War II, but with the organizational energies of Selena Crum, who remembered the place in its heyday, and the mind power of Emil Jewels drawing people there, he expects it to become the world's leading growth center—a term which in more informal moments he says sounds like a tumor.

Within the steam from the hot spring and the vapor in Harrison's condenser, Luna gropes in the fog, conducting her eternal search. "Who *is* the Authentic Man?" Emil Jewels wants to know. Luna articulates slowly, in a logy voice: "He is intelligent, spiritual, dashing, accomplished, charming, kind." She is floating in the vapor of this layer with a dim lantern held up to faces of easily rejected men, one after another doomed to sink into a mist of inauthenticity. "He must have an authentic calling, excel at it, be physically strong, in command of the material world, able to survive in the wilderness, and yet delight in urban variety and have no fear of the city's competition." Luna is clearly, at the time she is speaking, a hopeless case. Sunk at the bottom of a well. "He must, moreover," she echoes hollowly, "understand the nature of reality's illusion."

Emil Jewels rubs his hand over his balding dome and inquires, "What do you lack that you need so much from a man?"

And the other three Daughters of the Tantra wait for her answer, knowing its application to themselves as well, yet not moving to defend her—Lotus, Daisy, Dandelion, all three hope their failure at communal living is somehow Luna's fault; let *her* be the scapegoat because she wants more than all of them put together. Daisy would settle for a man who would take her to an organic farm forever; Dandelion knows her moto cross-mad marvel is no match for her in the upper story; and Lotus, who has been seeing a man on the West

Coast *Wall Street Journal,* is more confused than all of them. But Luna has the money that the others lack, has taken care of them all for months, has mothered them, has given them hideous cause for resentment. Let *her* sweat it—what *do* you lack, Luna Newcome?

And Luna pauses, her face seeming indeed to break into a sweat, out of which pours the resentment of the Daughters of the Tantra. She vaporizes inside the layer of Harrison's condenser and rematerializes in her effort to take some definite form, to gather herself together, feeling as fractioned as the parts of raw petroleum (what *is* Harrison saying, Carrie wonders—"paraffin oil, diesel, machine, gas oils, asphalt, tar . . ."). Luna holds up her lantern now, to the faces of the Daughters of the Tantra. And their faces change into those children with whom she lived as a child, in an orphanage in Iowa—Opal, Ruby, Pearl, those sisters all bearing the names of jewels instead of flowers, blond, innocent, evil. They are spread on the grass before the orphan home, like a cask of neglected ornaments, all of them waiting for a neighboring child to go home. It is dusk, almost dinner time, and often they have heard a voice calling that little girl, who enjoys playing hide-and-seek with them at the orphanage, a voice calling her home. She is someone's darling, and the voice often sings across at this lonely hour before dark: "Eleanor. Elean–*or*," an upward inflection on the last note, as if she is something more priceless than they, the very *ore* of life that they may be only set into, like artificial gemstones, easily knocked out of, lost. Come home, Elean-*ore* and be kissed before dinner, come home to be hugged, touched, delighted in. The four orphan girls despise Eleanor in secret, and yet they play with her often, for she exercises over them the fascination of the normal, the everyday. Eleanor is IT more often than she is a hider. She has looked for orphans under every bush, behind every L in the intriguing orphanage, admiring their agility, enjoying their sisterhood (for she is an only child with two parents, when the four of them together can't count one). Eleanor vicariously lives in the pleasure of their large household full of many voices, not just the tones of soft parental harmony. Yes, Eleanor learns from the orphans, perceiving only their joy; their difference is beautiful to her. She plays IT with a light heart. The orphans turn the ordinary little girl into a seeker.

How they loathe her! But Opal, the oldest, is the one who finds the subtle means of letting Eleanor suspect their feelings, to discover alone after she has left them that she is not one of them after all, not wanted. After the last orphan has run "Home Free," Opal turns and says, "Eleanor, your mother's calling you." The other three, Luna as well, in no way betray the lie but merely watch Eleanor's face as she wonderingly says, "Oh, I didn't hear," and Opal says again, "Your mother's calling you for dinner." And Luna, remembering that summer dusk, is chilled by the memory of Opal's voice, its veiled cruelty —and didn't Opal die two years ago of leukemia, at twenty-nine? In the vapor of memory, of frustration, Luna wavers before Emil Jewels' question: *"What do you lack?"* She wonders, if his name were different, would she have remembered the three girls in the orphanage? She looks at him, at his volatile image, as it changes into an old woman, the hair of his beard hanging at his shoulders—a wise old woman, giving, nourishing, sacrificing, a *mother*. And the Daughters of the Tantra, looking at Luna, sharing her disappointment in their hope of creating a better living style, fragile moon flowers, Lotus, Daisy, Dandy, none capable of mothering herself, although none with the record of an orphanage as a foundation for incompetence.

Carrie watches Luna wavering, fading. The three Daughters of the Tantra become momentarily the three witches of *Macbeth*. I step in hastily, unable to resist expelling *them* from Carrie's vision, but then they become Selena's three whining mothers, only to be replaced, finally, with the three who are the source of my report: Carrie herself, Luna, and Selena. She thinks: Yes, Motherhood is a mess! Weak, undermined, *absent*, to the extent that no one has confidence in *any* relationship any more. How else could she account for her dismay that Luna, even while withdrawing her displaced mothering from the Daughters of the Tantra, was taking on with such apparent lightness the dreary burden of solitary parenthood? Yet Roger wasn't right— disinterest in housekeeping doesn't make a woman unfit for nurture! Of *that* at least she is sure, despite Roger's appearance there in Harrison's machinery.

Carrie strokes the legs of her calico cat, looks down at the legs surrounding the portable distillery; Selena's legs standing in an assembly line among other machinery during World War II—what *is* this machinery doing in her garden? This inscrutable machinery! What has this to *do* with her life of art, dedication, self-denial? She remembers, then, Jim Smith's notion of Leonardo's drawing of water falling into a pool, swirling into curls like a woman's hair. She shakes her head—anything can mean *any*thing, she tells herself. Perhaps it means she ought to take a trip abroad, go to Italy, enjoy the Via Veneto . . .

Harrison has finished his sentence about the molecular bond, and Selena is asking: "Have they approved your marketing scheme, Harrison?"

Harrison, Carrie thinks, looks tired. The city tires him, despite an unusual reserve of energy. He comes there only when he must, when his inventions must be discussed, demonstrated, contracted for or dismissed by one of the industrialists he sells them to. He would never live up to Luna's Authentic Man standard, "delight in urban variety." Cities offer terrifying options to Harrison.

He slaps the retort on the head. "They say it's too eccentric. But they want this additive. You see, with this they can *maintain* and won't have to redesign." Harrison's plan calls for aerial video on national hook-up of the entire country showing the smog dispersal as it happens. He imagines the world tuned in all day. He says, "Every ecological move so far has been so stingy, so imperceptible, nobody believes any of it's worthwhile."

Selena says, "But isn't that like asking everybody in the world to pray at the same time?"

"Or pee?" says Ginseng.

Harrison shrugs. "That's what *they* say. I thought I could count on friends to say something more advanced."

Ginseng, happy to be considered a friend of clearly the most advanced inventor since Edison, decides to make a statement. "But that sounds to me like you may be playing into the hands of the International Oil Cartel. That is, getting every car on the road on the same day—even with your additive—well, isn't it going to do something maybe to the law of supply and demand?"

Ginseng, fogged by explanation, handicapped with a sloganized education, is nevertheless close to hitting on those depths of his invention Harrison does not wish to disclose. Harrison smiles and makes no reply.

His evasion of this question is lost in the distraction of Selena's departure. Her foot lifts the kickstand of her bicycle and she speaks to Carrie, having noticed the intensity of her layering experience. "Where were you this time?"

Carrie doesn't know what to say. In the past, she wonders? Yet she doesn't think so, despite the simple sequential import of what she has been seeing.

She asks, "Is Philomen around today? And maybe trying to get through to me?"

Selena gives a humorous shrug and pushes off. "Well, until this evening. By then you'll be having an out-of-the-body, Carrie!"

But Carrie doesn't feel satisfied with a good-humored attitude. She feels that I am trying to draw her toward something she hasn't seen before. My reading of her mind bothers even me. She thinks she is getting glimpses out of the corner of her eye of some unknown quantity, elusive and fearsome, which has nothing to do with her layers or nicks in time.

Perhaps in my effort to get on with this assignment, I have overloaded her. For whatever her sidelong vision shows, *I* know nothing about it.

Flying in the Icy Wind

Now all three women are scattered all over Berkeley, but thanks to my power of transport, we shall not lose them. On my way back to the Claremont, I drift past a billboard advertising cigarettes. A blond young man has a brush attached to the end of a pole and is wiping out a letter on the sign. One moment, it reads MEET THE TURK; in the next, MEET THE TURD. In a flash he tucks his pole and brush into a VW bus and flees the scene. Such sign "improvements" are a favorite diversion of Berkeleyites.

I am on my way to our fourth woman, for it wouldn't do to forget her. Evi, the fundamental one, perhaps the easiest of our women to understand, in that she has a way to go beyond fundamentals.

However, it will not do to cut her down. Evi is essential as long as I receive her signals, which come in strongly just now. She is about to commit a service besides. She doesn't know it, but does the orange tree know its merit, or the broom?

Standing before the mirror, she reaches with a nervous gesture for a cologne bottle and with trembling fingers applies some scent to her body. She starts to remove her robe, then changes her mind on an impulse she doesn't quite understand. "Piggy," she murmurs. "Piggy." She knows (as do all of ICH and DU) that Piggy Elkhart has been committed in Arizona, and she wonders again about Piggy's bizarre accusations. Her agitated body is trying to capture a thought; a question has focused in Evi's mind: "How can I get into Elkhart's room to look for those blueprints of the Hog?"

A DU *Sayso* comes to her rescue (thanks to me): "Many questions contain their own answer."

And so, no longer hesitating for an answer, Evi puts a white light of protection around herself with a brief Fix and leaves the room, wearing only her blue velour robe. She goes to the elevator, meditating on the question, and sure enough the elevator arrives, bringing her reply.

It happens that Rupert Oaks is trying out for a summer job as elevator boy. Rupert is a patrol leader in Scout Troop Number 7, the oldest troop in Berkeley, which meets on Tuesday evenings in St. Clement Church across the street from the Claremont. The boy is at that moment deep in a revenge fantasy aimed at his mother, whose current lover has only that morning told him that all Scouts are fruits. And now he is about to find some practical reinforcement for his revenge fantasy.

He has gotten no further than covering himself with pomegranate juice and standing over them in the dark of night, when Evi lifts his fantasy to another, richer dimension. "Hell-o," she says, entering the elevator, smiling as his startled gaze jumps from the opening of her velour robe, where her breasts clearly show, to her bare feet. Noticing that he is alone in the elevator, she asks his name. He stammers, "Rup–pert Oaks." Evi manipulates his neck gently. "Rupert, it's so lucky nobody's in the elevator," she says, "because I might be embarrassed. You see, I've lost my key. But you can take a minute off, can't you, to let me in?" And she gives him the number of Elkhart's room.

Now Evi is not one to chisel out on an implicit deal, even though the Scout is too inexperienced to realize that a deal has been implied. As Evi slips into the room, she runs her hand down his cheeks and tells him to come on in.

Rupert yammers incoherently. The elevator is buzzing. He gestures toward it, rocked by confusion. He's a large boy with large feet, which he tends to stumble over as he backs up toward the elevator. Evi clasps her hands in relief. She's eager to get on with her errand. But still she doesn't cheat. "Well, then, how about later on? This evening. The Jacuzzi whirlpool," she says. "About nine o'clock? I love to go down there in the dark."

Reeling into the elevator, Rupert nods, punches the door shut and punches himself dazedly down to answer the buzz of his patrons. This evening, nine o'clock, his dazzled mind records. Wait till his mother's fruity lover hears about this! How would he hint it to him? How, without letting his mother suspect that the hazards of a summer hotel experience might be an overload for his young life? He mulls it over and finally decides to keep his own counsel, to savor what comes and be silent, to forget about Mom for once in his life.

And meanwhile Evi, rummaging quickly, even deftly, through the dresser drawers, finds a briefcase filled with blueprints which contain a design so clear that even she grasps its sinister and outlandish intent. She tucks the case under her arm and takes the stairway back to her own room.

There she catches sight of her face in the mirror—and does not recognize herself. Who is that frightened dummy? she asks herself. She sits before the mirror in dismay. She is thinking of how she must immediately appeal to Selena, who seems to her the very personification of wisdom, one who can offer protection, authority, shelter, relief, nourishment, advice. And the face that stares back from the mirror is not her own but that of a terrified animal out of her memory, a ewe.

She came upon the ewe months ago when she was on horseback. The trail crossed a field where sheep were grazing, and disappeared into a slope that would take her into the hills. At the foot of the slope stood the ewe, immobilized. She was watching a German shepherd that had suddenly gone berserk and was heading toward her with bared teeth. At the sound of the dog, Evi's horse bolted up the hill, itself sensing a dreadful danger. The ewe's eyes were perfectly blank but not expressionless. They were completely without color; like a Greek statue the whole head was, the hair in tight ash ringlets, the eyes like carved marble, the whites the color of the creature's wool. As her horse took her up to safety past the ewe, Evi saw in its stance a slight swaying, as if it had measured the chances of flight and given up the impulse. Evi could hear the utterance the ewe made as the dog tore into her, a wrenching cry. But it is that frozen gaze of fear Evi looks at now, the ewe's transfixed eyes staring at the certainty of its own extinction. Earlier, looking at the tiny whirlpool the water made as the drain sucked it downward, she had been afraid. Now she knows that surely she will die.

Help! she cries without a sound, without moving her bright lips full of life. Selena, my God, help!

And she touches that strange yellow necklace Elkhart has given her, seized with a wracking fit of dry coughing.

Luna and Jim Smith are now exercising a tug upon me, partly because whenever they are together there is a mild explosion like a sparkler on the astral plane, my signal. I am obliged to shoot over to them at the Berkeley Marina.

Luna is remarking about the campiness of the houseboat where Jim is staying, knowing it is not his own taste to live in a boat at all, especially one done up like the inside of a piece of pop art, and probably designed with the notion that one would feel, reclining on the oblong mattress spread with an enormous crewel embroidery eye, blue with a purple iris, like part of someone else's fantasy. The houseboat is Jim's on loan, the possession of a psychiatrist who has taken leave both of absence and of his senses. Jim—boat-sitting for the psychiatrist until he can find his own place, having just been licensed to practice family therapy and not quite settled into the Berkeley scene –has begun to consider more inland sites, where a psychic therapist would not be quite so commonplace, and where he might indulge that taste Luna has observed in him for a simpler life style. He refers Luna to a book on the coffee table, a dog-eared paperback atlas in which he has been perusing the vastly unfamiliar regions between the East and West Coasts. "I'm thinking of cutting out," he says, as he brings in from the galley some sandwiches of salami, liverwurst and cheese and a pot of coffee.

It is now that Luna begins to guide him skillfully, she hopes, to her purpose in coming there, to the satisfying, indeed fulfilling, conclusion of her psychic reading, which Jim had been unable to complete before because his "sexual energy got in the way." Luna plans to take hold of that energy and use it to make her way into the beginnings of motherhood that very afternoon—if necessary, on that embroidered eye.

The salami sandwiches are the first impediment. Apparently they must be eaten before Jim can begin anything. Offering her the tray he takes a sandwich himself, urging her to "eat, eat." This has a decidedly maternal sound to it, reinforcing Luna in her intent, and so she takes a bite, wondering how she may remind him that if his sexuality has stood in the way of her reading there is an easy way to remove the obstacle. She decides to put it to him straight and begins to undo the fastenings of her Bedouin dress.

But Jim shakes his head, eating his sandwich calmly. "Lock it back up, Luna," he says. He is evidently very hungry and has undergone a change in attitude.

Luna offers her most seductive glance and asks, "Isn't it easier to see the aura of a person who is undressed?"

He shakes his head again, chewing. He has certainly regathered his resistance, and to judge by his appetite as he reaches now for a cheese and liverwurst sandwich, intends to strengthen it further, even in the face of Luna's obviously lowered resistance. Jim has in fact mobilized a regiment. He says: "You've been hiding behind your apparent sexuality for years."

Luna sighs and leans back on the big embroidery eye. "Go on," she says. "I guess your flow is not impeded any more. What else do you see?"

His regiment attacks with a series of devastating statements. Yet as he talks, that sense of his maternalness is strengthened in Luna's mind. Not only has he offered her nourishment, but as he goes on berating her, his limbs seem to Luna to grow rounder, and that athletic firmness is replaced by softer lines, an aspect of concernful gentleness. He might have been in the kitchen helplessly wringing his apron all these years, watching Luna from afar as she thrashed about in the wreckage of her youth. He tells her that her head has ruled her heart but without success; that the Work-and-Woman trip is just thrusting her body further away from her head; that in fact her head is like a giant dirigible, full of highly incendiary air, dangerous. "I see it up in the sky," he says, closing his eyes, "carrying below it a kind of strongbox with a combination lock."

Luna reclines on the eye now. If she can't take her clothes off, she will at least take it lying down, this insight of his, this unhappy imagery, thinking that at any moment she may explode, helium mixed with a scattering of brain cells all over the houseboat.

"The lunar moth," Jim goes on relentlessly, "is a symbol of the soul. Is that why you changed your name? To put your soul out where it was available, if in name only?"

"I'm available."

Jim continues with his sandwich. "What was your real name anyway?" he asks. The name, secreted away in her mental strongbox, hovers there heavily, leaden. She remembers the names of the other jewels in the orphanage, Opal, Pearl, Ruby—why couldn't she have been given a name like theirs, Emerald or Sapphire? Would that have made a difference? Whoever had named her anyway, a name from another age! The name springs out of the strongbox: "Bertha," she says.

Jim does not laugh but of course, being psychic, cannot repress the image of a tank that instantly replaces the strongbox, imposing itself over the slim waist of Luna, along with the dirigible that has covered her cascading blond hair.

He doesn't mention it; instead he muses. "Mmm . . . Bertha! *That* would have been more suitable. The German goddess. Like Artemis, who wore the crescent moon and whose followers wore antlers. She killed the stag of the golden antlers and bronzen hooves."

Jim cannot know how affecting this imagery is, how it pierces like an arrow, reminding her of past fatalities—with the demonologist Hitzig, for instance, who also knew about deer—of her lost embryo (an unborn creature wearing golden antlers!), and evoking as it does forests now buried under highways, trees taller than skyscrapers, silent woodland magic, arcane rites, sudden unavertible disasters. She sees the stag lying dead in the snow, its heart rent mercilessly, spurting warm, red blood against white down. Crystal tears start in the corners of her huge gray eyes. (The reader interested in psychic coincidence may want to know that at this very moment Carrie is bearing witness to a meeting between a man and a marvelous deerlike being, which because of the limitations of my medium I cannot bring you simultaneously.)

Still lying flat upon the absurd coverlet, her arms straight at her sides, staring at the ceiling, Luna herself looks like a sacrifice whose heart might be cut out and offered to the deity. She asks in a small voice, "Do you see any connection between this—mmm—dangerous headful of hot air and the strongbox?"

Jim smiles gently. "Now I'm receiving something more like a balloon at the top, not a dirigible, with a basket below it." She turns to look at him with hope lending a faint curl to her mouth. "But there's a blank at the heart chakra," he says, hastily calling his regiment, which has begun to scatter, sounding a bugle (his own imagery is once again beginning to intrude, he notices uneasily). "The balloon is there, holding inside its basket—ah, yes, I had thought it contained something softer—sponges for instance—but the safe is still there."

And at that Luna's tears come down, splashing on her clear skin. Her mouth, soft without the kind of defenses Jim might expect to see there, trembles. But she answers, "A rope is better than a sponge. You can tie things together with a rope."

Luna is thinking now of her notion of tying things together for herself, to bring out of her immobilized (locked-up!) body someone she can feel attached to, can feel she must nurture in the one unbreakable bond, that of mother and child. She is thinking that her life, messed up with waste, affluence, indolence, and lately desperation, cannot possibly pull together (even with balloon ropes) enough stability to make another creature comfortable, easy, pleasant, when her own being is creaking under the weight of odd necessities, tensions. She remembers Carrie's alarm at her decision, Selena's caution at her inexperience. And now she is sorry and decides to tell Jim that she has tried to lure him into a stupid plan without even telling him, for she sees herself completely unable to deal with motherhood or any other aspect of her life.

But Jim meanwhile has begun to lose control of his regiment;

routed by Luna's sorrow, his defense is scattering. One of the rebels, heedless of his commander, kneels and fires a fatal shot, a question which now issues from Jim's lips, disarming him hopelessly against Luna's power. He asks her what her mother was like. "I am an orphan," Luna says flatly, "and knew neither of my parents."

Flat as her voice may be, the shimmer of crystal still lingers in her eyes, enhancing her beauty without endowing the words with any self-pity whatsoever. Jim is done for. An orphan—a female orphan, since infancy trying to compose from scraps and pieces, like all of us, some sense, some fabric that will have not only a hang-togetherness to it but style, vitality, interest, some substance that is worth gazing upon, watching, taking part in. An *orphan*! Jim considers himself: from a huge family, he is the youngest, most precious son of adoring, clangorous older brothers, sisters, aunts, mothers and fathers—seemingly he had several. Surely this is why Luna's appeal to him seems so fundamentally unavoidable, so—yes, he seizes upon the word—so Karmic. He needs to fulfill something through her, something in his own life, and she through him will understand better what it is that she wants to create—oh, he is suddenly seized, all right, taken, whirled about on the Karmic wheel, bitten by its spiked hub, run down and over and taken up again, flung into a spoke as if it is a cabin of a Ferris wheel accelerating toward the speed of light. Luna —destiny. Luna, light, soul, ecstacy!

He touches her now, unable to resist any longer the unfastening of the Bedouin dress, empowered to thrust aside the unfavorable imagery of balloons, of strongboxes, of baskets, of creaking ropes. And as the dress billows over her head, the balloon takes on its natural expression as a flowing thing, floating, held by nothing, free. And Luna's entire lovely body is floating with it, also held by nothing (unless we may count the bracelet of hippie beads one of the Tantric Arts sisters wove onto her arm), held only by Jim's own hastily undressed body, not so motherly now, restored in Luna's eye and to her touch to its firm, athletic lines, to its full virility.

And Jim, drawn still more to the image into which he has flung them both—the cabin of a Ferris wheel, accelerating faster—yields to that part of him that craves soothing by recollection of the flesh. And he is down with her on the eye, moving with the rhythm of the rocking of the houseboat. Although he has been hard on her, his body, captivated by speed and light, rejoices in that fleshly notion such captives as they share, that things *are* reconcilable, can be gotten together somehow, by that compulsion of the body which does make human things happen. And one of the ironies of my tale is that it is he, the man who is embracing her, who sees all this, who in his emotional urgency gives Luna a glimmer of it, but only a glimmer, for she is still back at the juncture where he has raised a question in her about her capacities to nurture, where her self-doubt is aroused, where there is a huge caution against the intent which has brought her there and which, at that very moment, is being fulfilled, as the invisible world inside her cervix undergoes its dilative, tiny, transforming, convulsive drama.

"I tricked you," Luna whispers to Jim, who is breathing deeply into her hair, spent, her words partly another trick, she realizes, a maneuver to get him to shift his weight off her chest so that she can breathe.

"I know," he says, but neither of them quite understands the other, as is usual.

But because he says he knows, Luna decides not to tell him of her guilty scheme just then, to wait, to consider.

Another observable fact about how humans react to sexual expression is that they sometimes get in touch with insecurities and instabilities they were unaware of, and even those they have already talked about previously may appear in a new light, sharper, more focused. And so later, after they have dressed again and Jim has poured coffee, which he has kept on a warming plate, and they are all smiles and gentle touches, Jim, who is noticeably less complicated than Luna, if more of a seer, picks up the paperback atlas from the table and begins to speak of his own unsureness, of wanting to live in a more stable place, a less fluid town, where there is a quieter, less disturbed pace. He opens the map to point to another part of the country he has been thinking of, not yet imagining in any way that he might want to ask Luna to go there with him, or thinking of a particular future, but exposing, possibly to himself for the first time, his own fear of being a psychic minnow in this teeming reservoir of Berkeley. He points to a place called Thermopolis, Idaho, a town he says that must have thermal springs, but tiny (it is only a dot on the map), unaffected. And as he talks, there falls from the atlas an old photograph. Remember, the atlas itself has seen use, and this picture, which Jim offers Luna with some amusement, is almost fifteen years old, faded but readable.

"That's Selena Crum!" Luna says in astonishment.

Jim has only meant to share with her the amusing pose, in which he and Selena are sitting in the lap of a Mayan god, a Chac Mol, in the garden at Chichen Itza, a piece of statuary with a hole in the belly thought to be a large incense burner. Luna, looking closer, realizes that Jim cannot be over seventeen in the picture, a fact he confirms, and Selena—easily fifteen years younger than now! As he speaks of that trip, taken so long ago, into Yucatan with that "fabulous woman," as he calls Selena, who, as he put it, finished bringing him up then, something springs open in Luna, like a dark, unexplored box *inside* that strongbox Jim has seen. She feels she must get in there and look at it, for the opening has caused a sudden rising of emotion (can it be anger, rage, resentment?), and Luna feels some other part of herself hanging on in midair to ropes that are groaning in a quickening wind which threatens to turn into a gale.

She rises, gathers her things, prepares to leave, only to be stopped by Jim, who urges her to sit down, to let him look at her to try to understand. Surely it cannot be jealousy, he recognizes that at once, but something deeper, something he has missed before, and there again he glimpses the ropes in the middle of her body, right where her heart ought to be. And Luna bursts out with an expression of disappointment she herself does not understand. "Do *I* have to be your mother too?" She has certainly been no one's mother yet, nor had a mother herself, and has only just realized her possible unfitness to mother an infant, let alone a grown man; while Jim, convinced beyond a doubt that he no longer is in need of bringing up, wondering how to deal with this outburst of aggression, sees a word suddenly between those ropes, right there where Luna's heart ought to be: *Calamity.*

And he takes her hand, speaking patiently, almost like a mother again. "Luna, give it up. Give up the idea that all men are calamities that happen in the lives of good women."

But Luna, recalling that she has seen into Hitzig's underlying childishness, into Goliath's, surely into her husband's, and into that of every man she has ever known, is hurled about with emotion. She darts for the door. "You were wrong about the combination lock," she cries dramatically. "My strongbox has a key! A masculine symbol!" And she flings herself out the door and slams into her car, starting it up with a roar. Her mind is raging: What can *that* mean? That I'm not a woman at all? That I can never mother anyone?

She puts her car, an Opel, in gear, but not so quickly that she misses what he calls out after her. She realizes he too has fallen prey to anger as he shouts through the marina gate, "It was safe to say *something* would happen to you today. You've always got to star in some big production!" And she is trembling at that, with insights into his other accusations, honeyed over with desire. How has she let him get away with the insults he has stuck on her, balloons, dirigibles, ropes, strongboxes, all disguised accusations of heartlessness, of frigidity, of being unable to form an attachment—when again he has proved to her, like everyone else, that ultimately the only relationship a man ever wants is with *Mother*, someone to take care of him, to feed him (and here she remembers the salami and liverwurst sandwiches), or with a twist, to become a mother himself! Mother Jim! The idiocy of it, she exclaims to herself, to think that this is what lies at the bottom of sexual cravings. And to think she has wanted a child, who would grow up to engage in the same feeble groping all its life for the mother breast, who would probably be a boy, to search forever for the lunatic mother who had never given him enough, or a girl, to fall into the vast array of grinning traps (not the least of which is her present resentment) whose teeth have bitten out her heart, leaving a gnawing emptiness where ropes creak in an icy blast.

She realizes that she is speeding, has exceeded the limit on the road past the marina's Watergate Apartments. Her body is shaking. She glimpses Alcatraz Island out in the bay, looking like a giant dinosaur egg. Then suddenly a bright red egg of light splashes into her rearview mirror. A police car draws up behind her. She pulls to the curb, close by that deserted beach known as the Emeryville Mudflats, which contains an enigmatic collection of enormous driftwood statuary. She presses her hands to her mouth, wanting to scream. The policeman has stopped behind the car to take her plate number, giving her a moment to collect an appearance of calm.

"I was a little upset," she says, handing him her license.

He looks through the window at her wryly. He's a young man under a pressure he dislikes to write up a moving violation every day. The department, he feels, frustrated by unsolved cases of burglary, rape and assault, overcompensates in the avid pursuit of traffic violators. He writes the ticket and returns the license. "Mad driving is as bad as drunk driving," he says. "Why don't you get out and settle down for a while?"

Acting on that inauspicious advice, Luna gets out of the car and heads over to the beach. She has heard the driftwood creations here will soon be bulldozed to make room for another set of Watergate-style apartments. The impromptu museum appears deserted, as it usually does from the freeway, from which she has only glimpsed it before in passing.

She casts a sidelong glance over her left shoulder, and there stands a man with a high Afro hair style, dressed in lift boots, checked flare pants, and a crisp leather jacket. He might have just stepped out of Solomon Grundy's bar and separated himself from a cheerful, fashionably dressed crowd of blacks Luna has seen getting into their car outside the bar. But despite the snappy stylishness of his dress, his foot slithers and his mouth, as he slips a cigarette into it, is puffed like the throat of a snake about to strike. He says, "Damn pig! He give you a ticket?"

The boots draw closer. Luna finds herself momentarily rooted, aware without recourse to psychic power of his intentions. She lifts her hand defensively, and he grabs it at her eye level. She notices his ring, set with heavy chrome knobs, four or five of them, topped with red enamel. It fills an entire knuckle and looks like a gorgeous weapon.

He grins, showing yellowed teeth. He holds the ring out for her so that she can see it better. "Like it? That red stuff's pig meat."

As he has let her hand go, Luna bolts. But he has blocked the way to her car, and she must turn toward the beach. In a moment she is standing on the totally deserted beach, surrounded by the tall statues made of driftwood, tin cans, styrofoam and other waste thrown up by the churning stomach of the bay.

Moon Garden

Harrison has asked Carrie a leading question: "Why is Selena such a *subject* to you?"

Having found herself alone with him (Ginseng has disappeared shortly after Selena), she has offered him lunch there in the garden before his appointment in the city. She is placing the contents of the luncheon tray on the wrought-iron table with its glass top and has motioned him into one of the wrought-iron chairs. Harrison notices that she has made a cold avocado soup. He does not like cold soup. The sandwiches are of cheese and alfalfa sprouts. Can she be a *vegetarian*? An alfalfa-sprout salvationist? The table is below a gigantic avocado tree that does not yield, the avocados in their soup having been trucked up from Mexico. The tree shades their faces, but Carrie is uncomfortable.

In fact, she is embarrassed. She feels turned inside out, completely vulnerable and conspicuous. At the same time, she knows that is all in her mind, as one of the symptoms causing her embarrassment. Menopause! The end of moon change!

It has happened suddenly, just as menstruation did, she recalls. She feels like an adolescent, too. She remembers her daughters just a few years ago and wishes they were here to laugh with her as she laughed with them over the discomforts of their growth. It isn't considered growth at the end of the cycle, she thinks, but a kind of decay. And yet she feels like an adolescent, giddy as a girl.

How often in those years of lying alone Carrie has been annoyed by the uselessness of her cyclic bloodletting. Yet as it wanes now, coming in unexpected clots, sometimes seeping onto her skirts, as it did with her daughters, and stopping its flow as suddenly, she feels regret. Life is undeniably waning, but it isn't decay. Surrender maybe. The end of her long marriage to the moon, perhaps not as painful as the end of her human marriage but more poignant somehow, in its way surely more personal.

We have noticed that human visitations to the moon have not altered its force on earthly life. Some tribespeople like the Maoris think the moon is the permanent husband, true husband to all women, its slender scythe cutting in a ritual deeper than a husband's. Carrie does not imagine herself more understanding of the world than a Maori tribe informed by long service to nature. The moon as male and female has taken her and used her for many more years than she needed it, yet her life's movement is tied to the moon, turns toward it, making a few last spasmodic gestures as she is released of its demands.

She has not yet answered Harrison's question, being aware that he does not like the lunch. What a difficult person he seemed to be! Contradictory, as full of jerks and starts as she feels herself to be during this period of change. She finds she cannot eat the lunch herself. She is disturbed now by an odor in the garden, so pronounced and repugnant to her she feels she has to apologize for it. But no sooner does she suffer the apology than she blushes, her face coloring in blotches, for she realizes that it is not from some fertilizer Ginseng has been using but is the pungent smell of an animal marking its territory. She glances at her cat, spayed two years before, usually a fastidious cat. How can it be? Harrison, to confound her further, shakes his head. He denies smelling anything and shrugs indifferently.

. . .

Carrie can scarcely breathe. She takes a sip from the glass of iced tea beside her place. Can she imagine it? Can she herself be the source of the odor? It flows across her nostrils like an effluvium, fetid, pervasive, a much stronger smell than cats in the garden have ever made, goatish, unfamiliar, the smell of rut.

And as suddenly as it has filled the air, it goes, and a sweet breeze bearing the scent of her rose blossoms allows her to breathe again.

Harrison is inquiring about the sound of water from the other side of her studio. Out of his sight there is a pool, where we hear a faint but constant sound of splashing water, a soothing plop with a lingering vibration. Ginseng's experiment in Oriental gardening, she tells Harrison. The water falls in isolated drops into a clear pool that drains over sea-worn rocks and is moss-encircled. Street noises from beyond the garden wall interfere with the continuity of the sound, but in moments of quiet the drops fall in calm resonation.

"I'm thinking about your question," she says. She realizes that what Harrison wants to know is whether she shares Selena's fascination with the occult. "Selena is a subject I don't tire of, it's true. She moves. There's nothing static about her, no way to freeze her in time and space. A challenge."

Harrison says, "It's all fantasy, you know."

Carrie looks at him until he has to glance up at her, then says, "Go on."

Her brevity disconcerts him, tempting him to be equally brief and scornful. As a matter of fact, he wishes Selena Crum had never introduced him to Carrie, because it is like being handed some inconsiderable reality, like having an orphan baby in a blanket dumped in his arms by a crazed woman babbling with a broken accent.

"Well—" Harrison begins by looking at her eyes, which are so clear and direct he has to shift his gaze to her hands, where the wear of her work is evident, her fingernails as stained as his own. He thinks: She's an artist, she ought to understand. He says, "The sculpture—it shows me you must think about the primary problem—what in hell we're doing here." Carrie only nods, waiting, which makes Harrison all the more aware of his own uneasiness. "Simply to accept a system like this crazy DU," he says, "it's nonsense. Why is one theory any better than another? Why not forty-seven chakras instead of five or six; what if Buddhas float on clouds alongside of ascending Christs; what if there are Tibetan monsters stabbing Greek gods?"

I'd hate to tell him, but that *is* the way it is. Totally chaotic, everything ever conceived. Harrison's education might lead him to think the Greek gods, with their foundation for Western culture, are the most interesting and audacious, but he doesn't know what is happening. He doesn't *have* to know—many people don't. And many more couldn't tolerate the really weird mix of Scandinavian, Tibetan, Hindu, Chinese, Christian, Aztec and Egyptian lords, not to mention their various prophets and sages, recently roused from their slumbers and all communicating frequently with some earthbound person. No wonder groups like DU proliferate. Humans have a need to try to bring order out of chaos. Harrison knows this, but he says, "Why close off any possibility?"

"But you've just done that," Carrie points out calmly. "You said DU is nonsense."

"It's making some absolute assertions," he asserts. "That's even potentially dangerous, aside from its stupidity. It leads to such engaging heroics as the Crusades, for example, or the dunking and burning in Salem, not to mention more recent forms of spiritual fascism."

Carrie thinks of Harrison's own experience in the outer world, where his inventive devices deal with social manifestations of chaos. She says, "I imagine you must worry about the value of what you're doing sometimes, about whether you're right or not. Or whether what one person can do in a practical way is of any use."

This evaluation annoys Harrison immensely. It is accurate as far as it goes, but it strikes him as a complete evasion of what he's been saying. It's true, his mode is oblique. He hasn't just come out with the fact that he thinks Carrie, with her visions and spells, her obsessional working of one figure over and over, is in need of medical, probably psychiatric, attention.

"I used to think I was crazy too," she says maddeningly. Recovered now from that olfactory trance, she reaches for her sandwich, taking some of the alfalfa sprouts in her hands. She places them between her teeth with her fingers, making Harrison more aware of her creatureliness, her unavoidable bond with the kingdom of those who feed themselves with their paws, who conjoin, reproduce, digest their sprouts, defecate and die, untroubled by the dreadful human problem of cosmic awareness. He does not want to hear her tell him she *used to* think she was insane but rather than she *is now*, and that she is going to have herself committed that very day and taken out of his range of concern.

She says, "After all, it's peculiar to have people who are dead or who you don't even know wander in and out of your garden and realize nobody else can see them." Here she gives a light laugh. "It's crazy!"

Carrie's calico cat is stalking something and leaps up on top of the retort head, where she glares at a thrush in the arbutus tree. She springs up onto one of the branches of the tree, leaving the machinery unbalanced. Harrison says nothing, thinking that Carrie hasn't noticed. He plans to return as soon as he possibly can from the city and retrieve his material (and his *life*! he thinks a bit presumptuously) before that animal can destroy everything.

"We can put it in the studio before you go," Carrie says.

He blurts out, "I don't like having my mind read."

Carrie laughs. "Oh, were you thinking the same thing?"

"Thinking what?"

"What I was thinking. I can't read minds, you know. At least I don't think I can."

Harrison bites hugely on his sandwich. "You've done it twice."

She waits a moment. "Maybe we should tell each other what we were thinking. It couldn't have been the same thing after all."

Harrison doesn't answer, is wondering that this small woman has made him aware of how cranky he has become. Like Carrie a few moments before, he has a passing difficulty in breathing. He feels a physical cramp in his belly, not from eating the infant alfalfa but from being cramped in his psyche, invaded. He realizes a fear that she has it in her power to take over; after all, she was a woman, wasn't she? Everyone knew that women call the shots even if men do fire them. Why else has he stayed away from women for so long, if not to avoid the insanity of human aggressions? He has his scientific projects. He can rely upon them, but life has proved, since his Catholic childhood, a perilous process, a shoot-or-be-shot situation, and Harrison, as he has said, has no yearning for absolutes. He likes the element of doubt science demands, which has filled the gap faith left in him, a faith he had buried along with his wife, who died in childbirth. He seldom thinks of her, never if he can help it, yet there she is now, lying in that glittering hospital where his child had tried to come to life, dying of childbirth *fever*, an obsolete disorder of the womb which had somehow gone undiagnosed. Surely one of the last women in modern society, he imagined, to die in childbirth. He had been done with women since then; his unresolved pain could riot in his dreams, startle him awake and stalk him on insomnia walks through the Valley of the Moon, but daytime would come, and he could go back to work.

Carrie is interrupting these reflections (Can she have read them again? he wonders with a start). She says, "Many of the things I see don't happen, are as impossible as dreams. Some are distorted memories. I used to feel disturbed by it. But lately I feel strengthened. It's because I have changed. It's a tiny move, to believe, but it changes everything. If you can believe life is a divine trust—well, that sounds pretentious—"

"Go on."

"Trust sounds too solid, like a bank. What I feel is just the opposite, a lightness." She gestures again, as if trying to create a stack of layers of lightness with her hands. "What an enigma! Words are the best thing we have for giving information, but they're useless in giving —in receiving—" She stops again, shaking her head.

"Giving what?" he insists.

"I want to use another word like trust, but it's even more difficult."

"Grace," Harrison says harshly, finishing it for her, reading *her* mind, dredging up one of the loaded words of his childhood.

Carrie, who cannot read minds, reaches out and touches his sleeve. Her voice is carefree, almost caressing. "Why, Harrison, you didn't tell me *you* were a mind-reader!"

Then she is suddenly aware of her earlier embarrassment, and now it invades the lightness she has expressed. She feels awkward again, adolescent, and she recognizes what it is. She wants to be touched, held—if not by this man, then by another. How awkward, she thinks, for these feelings to be aroused, visibly surfacing, spilling out all over the garden. She wants to burst into tears of frustration, as she has inside her soap bar earlier. The embarrassment of continuing all these years to want to be touched, embraced!

I send her word that she is engaged in a useless struggle, which she seems to hear, for in the next few moments she grows calmer.

A helicopter has begun to circle overhead, at first only as troublesome as a fly. But then it has closed in, making a hovering circle only two hundred feet above the garden. This is the police helicopter, the kind that brought on Ginseng's paranoic fit in which he destroyed his marijuana plants. It is a familiar noise because of the frequent criminal activity on College Avenue nearby. Carrie explains it to Harrison.

He has read of the bank robberies, the burglaries, the anarchy in the streets here. He glances again at his machinery—will it still be here when he returns? Should he take it somewhere else for safekeeping? Where was there a place in these crime-infested cities?

If Harrison is seeing himself as cranky today, you should not be misled into thinking him a simple crank. Think of him rather as the survivor of some other age, the age of inventors, say, since that is what he is, one in whom the ethic of the Western frontier still asserts itself. A farmer's son, he has a practical sense of the basis of that ethic: society valued an individual because his body was *needed*, if only as an earth mover, a tiller of ground. He sees the humanistic ideals people built around that as obsolete now, undermined by insane urban development, which has brought on the anarchy signaled by the helicopter overhead. Strong Elkhart, Bubba Burr and other city spiritual leaders teach exercises for "sensitizing" the body; a drive into the city is enough to sensitize Harrison—his senses set off signals of fury at the stench and decay. What could a single human life be worth in a world that already looks and smells like kitchen middens, heaps of stinking waste not quite rotten enough to be turned to any earthly good? The helicopter, its blades making futile thrashing gestures against chaos, grates on him, and now he can smell that odor

Carrie has spoken of. He feels a disorder in the atmosphere even more intense than usual. Suffocated, he begins to speak aggressively.

"Selena's hope club, DU," he says, "it's just so much wishful thinking, group hypnosis. They've lived in cities so long they can't see themselves as part of nature. They glance away from their role in this strange world, in which all creatures devote themselves to tearing one another into shreds—biting, gnawing, gnashing, grinding—and they say they are devoted to human evolution! Every animal alive comes equipped with something they can destroy other living matter with; everything born looks for something else that has been born to gobble it down, consume it, digest it, and then turn away, only to be eaten itself." Here Harrison takes another large bite of his sandwich of baby alfalfa, while Carrie stares in alarm. He seems so upset! "We see this pattern in all life," he says, "and among men we are coming to understand that war is probably not a curable condition. Can the fiendish way in which we destroy one another be less natural than the ruthless earthquake that buries alive whole towns, or the tidal wave that washes over a quarter of a million people like so many shrimp? And what of the *shrimp?*" he goes on. "Consider how the sea destroys its own life every year. Do those in Selena's group who imagine human life is evolving ever think of their own relationship to the pine tree that scatters thousands of seeds from its cone in an effort to create a forest, only to have perhaps one small seedling rise to light in a decade, perhaps none. People are no more special than the thousands of infant ants eaten by the anteater, while one or two escape; than the turtles born of a nest of fifty eggs who rush to the sea, hurrying to the armored mouth of gulls, and possibly one among them able to mature in the ocean depths. We can only observe the same thing over and over; decay creates the fertilizer which enables birth, and there follows the multiple spreading of seed, from pine trees to humans, which leads only to more death, more decay, renewed fecundity. We live on a planet of creation and destruction so impenetrable that we can't understand it. Grace is a word for the past, and the inventions these psychics imagine for the future—the new Atlanteans and so on—are childish daydreaming."

Carrie is gazing off now toward the garden pool, which is out of

Harrison's sight. He has been speaking above the whir of the helicopter, has had to raise his voice almost to a shout, and now falls into a gloomy silence.

Suddenly Carrie's calico cat springs forward and leaps upon the finch it has been stalking, as if to confirm all that Harrison has said. Harrison assumes that this is why Carrie rises from the table with a strangled gasp. The cat grips the finch, tearing at its neck, spilling blood on the ground-cover of baby's-breath under the strawberry arbutus tree. Even Harrison finds the cat's appetite reduces his own.

But Carrie is not looking at her cat. She moves from the table toward the Oriental pool at the other side of the garden. Unknown to Harrison, she has not even seen the cat's luncheon feast. She gives a cry that Harrison cannot hear over the helicopter. An overwhelming scent of musk penetrates her nostrils, and Carrie sways before an outrageous sight.

Usually she has believed the things she has seen. They are familiar to her, although they are sometimes like dreams, as she has told Harrison. But she has never before seen a creature like the one who is standing there beside her pool. The sound of the helicopter ends abruptly. She is surrounded by silence, and her vision spins, tunnels. The garden seems to curve upward, to make a circle, and at the center of it stands the figure of a human-deer.

Someone else is with this being, who has staggered against a lawn chair, as startled as Carrie, a man she has heard of but never seen before, Strong Elkhart.

Carrié is to witness a scene between these two, Elkhart and his teacher, newly arrived to bestow further knowledge upon his favored pupil. How she is enabled to witness it is something for parapsychologists to ponder, or poets. I am neither, only a spirit guide, and can offer no explanation. But the two are there before her at her pool, just exactly as they are also at the Claremont Hotel pool as far as Elkhart is concerned.

Approaching a chair at the pool, Elkhart has suddenly felt weak. He has heard the roar of the helicopter making its searching circle overhead. As it has in Carrie's garden, the machine seems to circle above the hotel, just above *him*, and although Elkhart is inclined to favor helicopters (for reasons yet to come), the sense of being stalked by some unknown hunter raises the hair all along his spine. And then he, like Carrie, smells the heavy odor of musk.

The Bielbog who stands beside the sunlit water is somehow much larger than before—his antlers many-tined and golden, his hide very white, but his feet no longer cloven. He has become more a deer and somehow more human, more dominating. He is smiling and very dangerous.

Elkhart is frightened. His desert mentor has been changed from a capricious, malefic horned imp, toward whom he felt some superiority, into a presence that shimmers with magnificence, so awesome in aspect that Elkhart nearly collapses as the support goes out of his legs. He falls into a chair, swallows dryness and aspirates, "My God, what are you?"

The creature makes no reply but looks about both garden and hotel, looks wherever those bottomless brown eyes may see.

I recall the misgivings I felt in the desert about the transformations of Elkhart's teacher. I realize that I myself am as afraid as Elkhart of what may happen now, that I share Carrie's surge of apprehension as she draws closer to look at the terrified man in the chair, at the lofty being, at its downy white chest, its impenetrable gaze. In all my work at the expelling of imps and demons, I have seen nothing like this. I might have worked an exorcism upon the Bielbog Elkhart knew in the desert, but I have no power now over what he has become. I listen fearfully for his answer to Elkhart's question.

The being speaks. The voice, coming from some deeps I have never penetrated, has yet a gentle sound to it, a strange tenderness and at the same time a lofty condescension. An indescribable fascination is contained in its sound, and its utterances are careful and slow as it never spoke in the mountain desert. Gone is the impatient tenor, the petulance. The lofty resonance that blends with that tender strain is like a necessary counterpoint in a fugue. But this being is beyond my descriptive words; even its own words intensify its mystery. The vibrant voice rises in a chant, spellbinding, sustaining an inhuman wrath.

"You asked me to name myself before, Elkhart, and I gave you

Bielbog. And you wanted to know if I am the devil! Now again you wish to limit me by insisting that I have an identity. You see, identities are temporal and transient; I am not. If you had lived in Paleolithic times, I would have appeared to you in a deep, secret part of a cave, and for the occasion you would have worn a headdress of horns yourself and carried a box of ocher and treasured relics. You would have painted the walls with pictures of animals and of me. With fire and dancing you would have evoked me. Our tête-à-tête, horns to horns, would have been about death—yours and the animals you might kill, a conversation simple and satisfying to me about death and rebirth.

"If you had lived millennia later in the age of open sunlight and free-standing sculpture, templed mountaintops and round theaters, I might have appeared to you as a white goddess rising from the water and gone with you to a cliff where you would chant in sonorous Greek. I would reveal myself as the creatrix, the eternal mother, the deliverer, the watchful eye, and you would swoon in ecstasy and love for me, as you now faint with fear. You might even grow wise enough to know that in every Isis there is a Hathor, in every life a death. I would leave you suddenly, for I never reveal too much at one time of an eternal pattern. You would be overwhelmed with wonder. You would seek me everywhere. You would find me in the logarithmic spiral of the conch shell, in the power and relentless motion of the whirlpool. You would see me reflected in the spindrift gaze of the sea lion. Twisting, whirling, eddying, reeling, my motion might be found everywhere."

The voice pauses, and in that momentary silence all of us are more conscious of our terror. Elkhart has thrust his knuckles into his mouth, chewing them as if they have been magically transformed into Knuckle Root, whose power if he were to remember it now might seem trivial. Carrie has had to sit down on the grass, her fingers up to her lips, and is again having trouble breathing. She is very sensitive to the smell of rut. Her own body is throbbing; the flow of blood she has suspected before seeps from her uterus. Her face feels like melting wax. And I—I tell myself I am only a vessel, a channel, and try to let my own fear out into empty space as the being speaks again.

"And in this forgetful age, you still evoke me. If you ignore the water, I come on the wind. Your weapons, which have always reflected me, as in the spiraling flight of the arrow, are subtler now but just as strong a call. I fly in your bullets, in their gyroscopic spin to their victims. Even the very atoms and their particles in orbit now are spinning out my deadly work. Spinning, spiraling, whirling, I can still make humans reel. And reeling, you try to gain your balance with definings, rules for religionists! Absurd! I am *never* what you think to find. You came looking with your love of eternity. And now that you have forgotten the first rule, obedience, your plans are as irrelevant as dust. My gift is what you may receive instead. My gift to those who love me!"

In a weak voice, Elkhart says, "I only wanted to know the truth."

The majestic foot stamps, no longer the petulant stamp of an imp who has stolen a name; the sustained rage of that being is poised for release. The voice sounds again. "What in hell is truth? Have you the delusion I have given it to *you*? I will tell you this. Each age earns the god that it desires and deserves. I have come again in your murderous century, the horned one, the *cernunnos* beloved of barbarians. Someone here conjured me today, who spoke of the absolute, someone who understands what pleases me most—birth, death, regeneration. I gave you an invention, Elkhart, nothing more. Can you imagine I would give the truth away to a mortal? No, the truth is not my gift."

Carrie falls down onto the grass and speaks in an anguished whisper. "Oh, please—" Elkhart has broken into a sweat and lies groaning on the chair. The antlers turn on that lofty head; the ears twitch as if Carrie's whisper has reached them. "Let us live!" she cries.

It seems to her that the two beings telescope, become very distant from her and are slowly surrounded not by her sunlit garden but by the night sky, or rather that she is looking into a sidereal view, has fallen into a slow moment between two nights. "What *is* your gift?" Elkhart pleads. A sickle moon intervenes between Carrie and the distant pair, gleams on the antlers, then comes between Carrie and the two figures, draws closer to her, penetrates her body. She feels saturated with fluid. Her heart spins, flutters. She falls into a faint.

Harrison, who has been watching her, has also been distracted by the calico cat, whose cutting teeth have made quick work of the little garden finch. The bird has been processed through the side of the cat's mouth, with shearing teeth that have crunched the delicate bones, so that very quickly nothing is left but fragments of wings as clues to a tasty meal.

When Carrie begins to speak, Harrison runs to her side. He is very alarmed by her whispering plea. What is she saying? "Let us live . . ." Let *who* live?

The cat springs up onto the tree again, by way of his distillery, upsetting it. He scarcely notices. His earlier misgivings about his material have vanished in the light of Carrie's apparently endangered state, and so too has his critical attitude of her.

He must save her, he thinks confusedly. What does she mean—let us live? Her voice, an anguished whisper from her will to life. Has *he* brought on this strange attack from which she seems to be suffering? Has the death of the bird affected her so strongly?

Harrison has a terrible conscience, the consequence of his upbringing, his asceticism. He has presented her, he realizes, with an unbalanced picture of the world, in speaking of all its death, of its habit of recovering itself at the expense of life. He has overlooked the sun! He gazes down at her; her face appears to have sunspots as she lies there in the bright daylight. The irony of his proud summation strikes him now, creating a steady pounding in his head. He sees the Oriental pool, and each of its sunlit drops of water seems to strike blows at his forehead; he seems to hear the resonances of a song sung in Greek floating in the sunny air—it is the shriek of a siren on the other side of the garden wall. The sun, which also enables fertilizer to do its changing work, now strikes him with reassurance, stirring his roots to life. He rubs his head, which has banged against more of his own rhetoric: Carrie lying on the grass is no longer an infant in a blanket; she is the surviving sapling grown up to the sun from the thousand spores of the solitary parent tree; she is the full-grown queen of her mother's ant hill; she is the giant turtle who has made a hundred trips to lay her eggs upon the beach and left them there heedless of whether one will grow to her own size. *She* has grown, fortuitous or especially chosen —what did it matter? She was a being with days of grace, yes, left in which to thrive in that survival, in the sun.

All of this flashes in his mind on the length of a sunray, and he touches her cheek with its spots of red about the eyes. She is hot, burning. Her eyelids flutter open. Her hand goes out to cover the stain on her skirt, but Harrison scarcely notices. "Let me help you!" he cries, lifting her from the place where she has fallen.

A loudspeaker now comes from the helicopter overhead, a police voice sounding from the vortex into which Carrie's vision has whirled. "They went into Mystic Street . . . behind the Blood Bank . . ."

Carrie says, "They've robbed the Bank of America again."

She looks at Harrison and realizes a change in his attitude as he presses her hand, carefully settling her in the chair beside her table. She sees that gloominess has been displaced by a panic not unlike her own. Yet she also knows he has seen nothing she has just witnessed.

Yet Harrison's own words have summoned that resplendent being—hadn't the creature said so? Harrison had been the one to speak of the absolute. It was Harrison who had evoked death, rebirth, and the ruthless way in which it comes about. Harrison, the unbeliever, has called up that being of majesty and mysteriousness.

Risen from her fall and looking at him, Carrie thinks of an old word which she hasn't heard since she sang it in a ballad as a schoolgirl, yet the word, *plighted*, resonates through her. Their pledge is unspoken, not yet recognized. Their plight, there in that garden surrounded by the siren calls of a collapsing society, fearsome and lovely, comes like a gift out of the vortex, late to their lives.

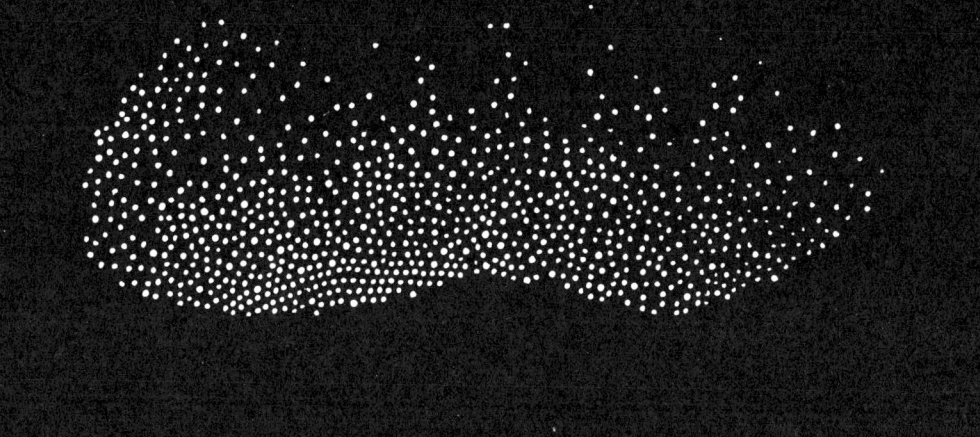

"*I am* never *what you think to find.*"

"Which came first, dammit, ICH or DU?"

"Could he *be the Authentic Man?"*

"Cities offered terrifying options to Harrison."

". . . other aspects of the entity."

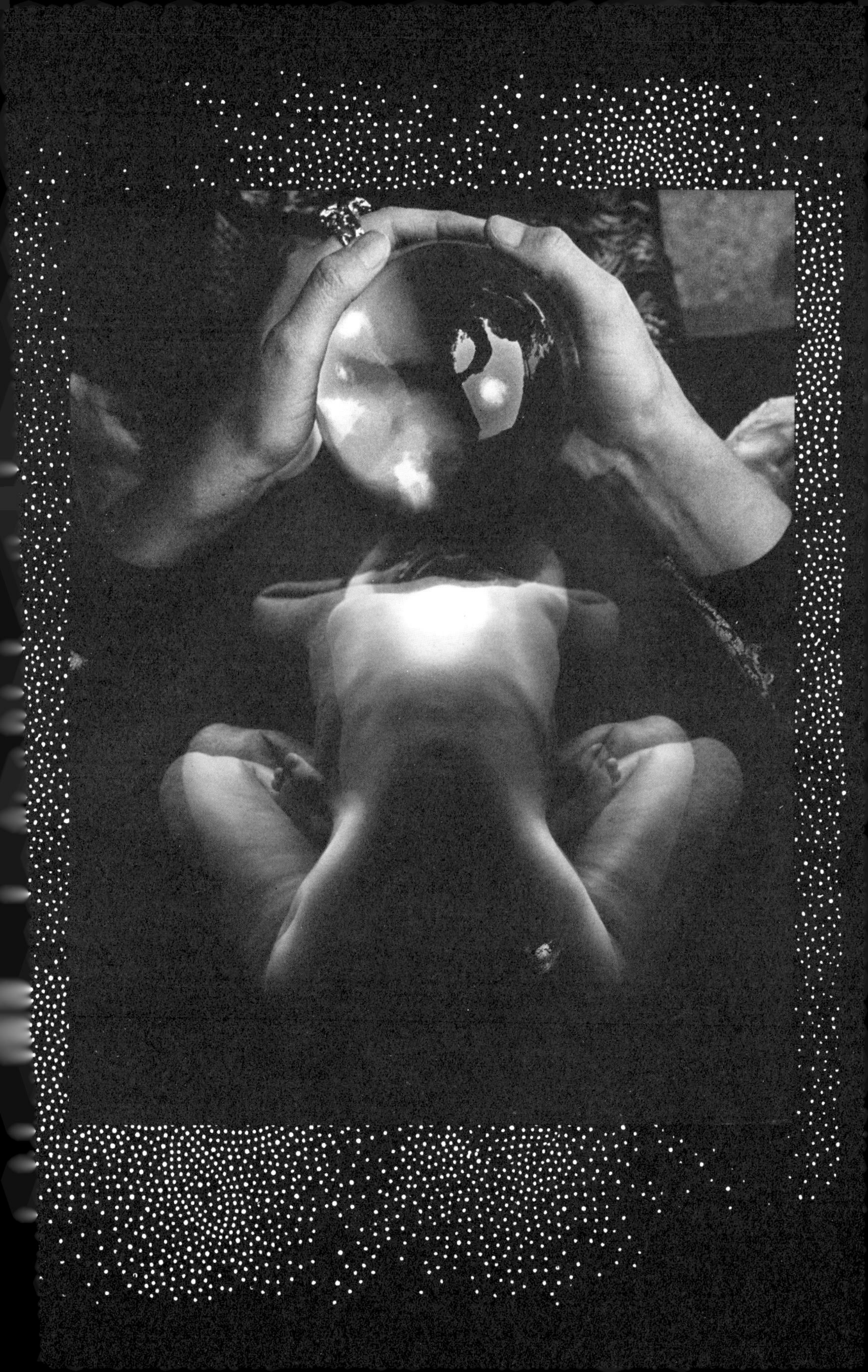

Reap the Whirlpool

Selena is lunching alone at her apartment across from the Ho Chi Minh Park, site of early-morning Tai Chi devotions, of student demonstrations and Sunday flea markets. She carefully chews brown rice and vegetables, then tops the dish off with the impiety of a chocolate mousse. Luna has told her that down at the Andes retreat, where Selena has never ventured, seekers would often drive into town for chocolate malted milks, throwing their purification diet to the wind.

Luna often jogs Selena's memory, which has become a source of pleasure to her recently. She hopes that Luna can find a way of creating some pleasant memories out of her sexual tumult. She is struck suddenly by the difference between memories and the making of them. Her apartment happens to have a lot of memorabilia in it, not because she is attached to the *things* or even to the people who brought them into her life, but simply because they have appeared, like pebbles on a beach. On her window sill is a fancy jar, gold-glazed. Luna's troubles take her to the source of the jar, as if she were falling into one of Carrie's nicks.

Her first husband bought two such jars, which he kept by her bedside, one in a drawer and the other on the night table. Whenever they made love, he would put a bean in the jar. The bean jar was their counting system, a little like the old Mayan way of time-keeping, putting kernels of corn in a bag to keep track of days. Selena and her man were not sophisticated enough then to count orgasms, as Luna may now, just occasions. He called them jumping beans. He'd say, "Well, in goes another jumping bean." Selena remembers that he nearly filled the jar during their first year together. About a two-quart jar. At the beginning of the second year, his program was to reverse the process, to take a bean *out* of the jar every time and place it in the jar below. You were supposed to see if you could empty the jar or not. The third year, you reversed the process again. Selena remembers that that year he had to go and buy another bag of beans!

But how different the jar is in memory, where it uplifts and delights her spirit, while in the *experience* of it, the jar was nothing more than an expression of good-humored sensuousness. Even the boy with whom she engaged in those simple pastimes now touches her mind with a tenderness that is quite different from the physical pleasures they enjoyed, because of the other textures memory brings to it.

Selena's memories ride with her as she takes her Raleigh back up to the Claremont for the afternoon's ceremony, the Immersions. She thinks now of Carrie and Harrison and slips a phrase into her ticker-tape machine for the ride up to the Claremont: "Harrison is handsome," which clicks and shreds, and her mantra goes to work.

As she moves along, Selena's life too moves along on either sidewalk, it seems, like a revue, a vaudeville show, and she again says to herself that today is the last of her many acts, an ultimate blackout skit.

But that thought flows along too; the mantra does not allow one to dwell upon events. The knowledge that she will die is not news to her, even if today does happen to be when. She merely watches the vaudeville revue and its absurdities.

Folly has more often than not been the theme of Selena's skits in time. Why not? she has often asked herself. For instance, she doesn't mind that her life and style are used as metaphor by Carrie. She knows she is a fool and has at times rehearsed and refined the role, walking on the edge of an abyss, at times slipping and hanging by her fingernails. It became a comfortable position for her early in life, and lately, since DU, even a serviceable one, she believes.

The revue glides in backward sequence, starting with a no-fool-like-an-old-fool theme and regressing to "youthful folly." Selena, the star of the fool's revue, always a fool about loving, giving, being involved with others, letting herself be used. At the other end of the spectrum from Luna, Selena has always let her heart rule her head. The only condition she has made is that her heart is reserved for questers.

The scenes flash back through the pre-DU days, when her questers were writers. Those were clownish times, North Beach coffeehouses, her lovers' quests maintained by alcohol, then dope, then booze again, then both. She smiles as a book of poems flicks through her mantra: *Oreos*, dedicated "to the divine Crum" by a married poet who hoped his wife wouldn't relate his corny tribute to Selena. Of all her lovers, none were more self-deceived than the writers, or more earnest in their will to undeceive others. In images from further back, she recognizes the gentler artists, the one who painted her image in silver on his floor in Sausalito, the one whose sailboat ran aground in Baja and whom she left there spellbound by vivid birds. And faster now, images flow along from further back—there goes the boy Jim Smith in the Mexican garden with the Chac Mol. There goes the bean jar filled by her husband, being interred at Selena's insistence in Golden Gate Military Cemetery, where rows of identical postwar housing are being built above it like a cemetery hill, rows of tombs for the living. "These are the soldier's remains," Selena is telling the attendant, insisting he inter the bean jar. And there, the boy himself, her wedding to him—she kisses his apricot cheek. And there, her adolescent sweethearts, dancers in the Berkeley hills, dancers who slept under the stars, visited in their sleep by tame deer from Tilden Park, dancers who by day moved from their solar plexus, faces turned toward the sun.

You might be led to think, because of Selena's mantra "Harrison is handsome," because of her escapade with Jim Smith, that Selena has always been drawn to men younger than herself. You might also be misled into imagining because of her natural inclination to repel the advances of Peter Delgado in the rose garden, that Selena is a woman who, because of some remarkable sexual desirability, has developed skill at avoiding sexual encounter. But Selena, like any other woman of her years, is sexually shelved, shunned and ignored by men her own age for those common reasons set forth by Peter Delgado. There is one notable exception which she will confide today to Carrie and Luna, but generally men of all ages regard Selena affectionately but no longer as a sex partner. Her follies revue turns round in time and brings itself back to DU as she approaches the Claremont, and she sees that although there now is little sexual content, those who love her have just as strong a tug of passion.

A retreat up in the Northern mountains attracts her, not crowded with eager novices like Mamacita's, but a place of repose and solitary contemplation where one might pass a few elevated declining years. But Selena reserves it for another life.

Surrounded by a great deal of confused and inoperative love, she remains here among her lovers of all sexes and ages. DU affords a broad spectrum: a computer programmer who has made a computer portrait of her; an astronaut who wrote a poem called "Queen Selene," a topless dancer who has had a sex-change operation, a sociology student whose dissertation is about suicides who survived their leap from the Golden Gate Bridge, with the zippy title of *Joy of Jumping*.

Selena remains here among the devotees of Bubba Burr's fold, responding to their confusions great and small, because of something over which she wants no control, possibly some unresolvable confusion in herself, for the sake of another gesture of love she may yet make, one last fool's errand. Among novice and initiate alike, Selena is there in answer to the prevailing hunger evident everywhere, not just within such structures as DU, a craving to believe someone, to hear a trustworthy voice. Starvation for the credible holds her there, among the credulous.

Selena chains her Raleigh to the bicycle stand at the pool gate. The Immersions ceremony will have to be short, for the hotel has obligingly barred its club members from pool use for half an hour. Some members are standing outside, already impatient. They lounge around smoking, some leaning on the green trash barrels outside the gate, which are absurdly stenciled: "Ecology Units." Next to one of them, a plump woman sits in her Cadillac; Selena makes a note to tell Harrison about that, since he believes the Cadillac one of the most ecologically unsound units ever developed.

As she goes through the gate, Selena pauses, puzzled. There is a flicker of movement, scarcely more than a shadow on the water. But for a second she thinks she has seen the sunlit glimmer of deer antlers. She shakes her head, surprised at a surge of feeling. Her husband had been a hunter long ago, had once brought home a set of graceful antlers. She thinks of him again, and of dying, and of those young nights in the hills near Tilden Park, waking in the dew to find deer tracks. And for the first time that day her heart swells with tenderness and love for the world, its mystery. Never is it so dear as at the time of leaving it.

Since you and I are aware of what Selena has just envisaged (if not its real identity), I can also tell you that when Selena sees the antlers, at the same moment Luna is grieving over the stag of the golden antlers bleeding in the snow like a deity murdered by her own youthful arrogance, and at the same moment Carrie in her garden is pleading for renewal of life: "Let us live!" Selena, Luna and Carrie are united in a momentary glimpse that shimmers, gleams and is gone.

And then Selena sees Elkhart in the chair beside the pool, looking sick, moaning, and apparently talking to himself. His pale face, washed with sweat, betrays a deep anxiety. "Death . . . that is the gift," he says with a groan. Then, in almost another voice, he lets out a deep, rolling laugh and speaks fiercely, "You will lose your following, because you have ignored my first rule—" Elkhart sucks air between his teeth, thrashing in the chair as if trying to awaken from a dreadful dream.

Selena imagines that Elkhart has been ignoring Mamacita's no-drug rule, but something about him stirs her compassion as never before. He begins to sob: "People need me, believe me. But this isn't what . . . I thought I'd find—" He sits on the edge of his chair, his head in his hands, groaning. "My God, I've told too much . . . the first rule—obedience . . . silence."

Until it happens, Selena could not have imagined she would ever reach out to Elkhart with any warmth, but she does reach to him now and says, "Let me help you!" using the very words Harrison speaks to Carrie.

Elkhart gazes at her wildly, scarcely seeming to recognize her, but then he addresses her by name. "Selena, I have a confession. I must tell someone. It will bring me back to life. Otherwise—the gift . . ." He sobs violently.

This behavior is so unlikely, coming from the composed and contemptuous Elkhart, that Selena sees she must set aside his apparent problems with her and possibly deal with his real ones. But it is the hour of the Immersions, and the kind of Fix Elkhart seems to need takes time.

Suddenly, Selena senses another presence at the pool. She has not been the only witness to Elkhart's dialogue with himself. There sits Tsinghai Yana, whom she has invited this morning, off to the side by the Jacuzzi whirlpool, its steam rising beside him. He is still and motionless in his American suit. Both his hands rest upon his knees, the forefinger and thumb making a circle, a gesture of peace.

Has Elkhart seen him? She cannot tell.

"My confession!" Elkhart cries. "Selena, will you hear it?" But without waiting for a reply he blurts everything out, his words tumbling over one another.

"I started this quest for the CIA. I know Bubba suspected that. There he was, down in Peru. The agency knew of his campus background here—radical politics, crazy stuff like the Free Speech Movement. Then he goes down to Latin America. What is the CIA going to think? That DU is a cover for some Latin revolution. He might be instigating it! They knew I was having legal problems, so I was the logical man to go. Got me out of the country while the heat was on. Okay—everything's clear-cut to start off. But down there— my God! Selena, down there, it became something else. It became a different ball game."

"What do you mean, Elkhart?"

"Good Lord, Selena. I didn't find a revolution. Instead, I stumbled on—" He gropes. "Well, it is more world-changing than any revolutionist ever dreamed." He laughs wildly. "*Evolution*, an evolutionary process more violent in its overthrow—"

Selena glances at the gate, fearful that there is not time enough for Elkhart's mind to focus.

He flings himself on his knees beside her. "That's what happens on these assignments, Selena. All the time. We find something other than what we were looking for." Another uncontrolled outburst of laughter. "Just as the sages say! It's true, what the sages say! It's just fantastic what my search became."

"First, what *is* it, Elkhart?"

"This need we have to *know*, this quest—"

"And what did it become?"

"Something for all of us, you, DU, the CIA. Good Lord, Selena, it's the eternal search—for God!"

"*You were searching for God for the CIA?*"

"Yes!"

"I see."

"I mean, no . . . yes! Wait a minute, Selena. My head! They didn't *send* me for God, but what I found—now, that's going to interest us. We are interested in everything, you know."

"Who is?"

"*I* am. You see, when the agency starts working for ICH—you may not have the vision to see it, Selena, but we have a very useful structure for search of any kind in the agency. We've kept pretty quiet about one area of activity, but"—his voice falls to a conspiratorial whisper—"do you think we're lagging in the psychic research race? Listen. We've almost got God cornered!"

"Elkhart!"

"My organization has to be tight with the deity. Otherwise, the wrong kind of God could get in there—mess up . . ." He falters. "Internal security." He goes blank and cannot remember what he was confessing. Then his staggering imagination crumbles. "Selena, I don't know if I have found God or not. Not really. What I—I didn't think he'd look the way he does or talk—what I found—I don't think

· 159 ·

I—Selena, it's all blowing wide open; I don't know *what* I discovered, but it's—" He breaks into sobs again. "It's too much for me. I don't know what to do!"

Selena casts a silent appeal to Tsinghai Yana, who has told her she would need him this afternoon! She receives his thought pattern once again. Words form in her mind, which she speaks to Elkhart without understanding them completely.

She says, "Sometimes a teacher will give elaborate instructions to a pupil, Elkhart, and because obedience is the first rule, we have to follow them. You may build a house for the teacher, or even a whole city, and then he may tell you to tear it down. The teacher will say it doesn't please him or just give no reason at all. The labor of your life can be thrown away just like that. In the twinkling of an eye. But if you are told to do it, you must. Isn't it so, Elkhart?"

Then she says something she has no understanding of at all, but she trusts Tsinghai completely and knows that what passes between them is not subject to her judgment. She recalls that Tsinghai surrendered his rod of power to Elkhart. Selena doesn't understand what she says, yet as the words form on her lips, Tsinghai looks directly at *me*, and I realize that in his way he is cooperating with *my* larger mission. Selena says, "Elkhart, you must destroy your plans."

A terrible twitching occurs in the corner of Elkhart's mouth, and his eyes undergo a series of spasms. But there is nothing more that may be said, for now here comes the Little Mother and her retinue, followed by Bubba Burr and the initiates of DU in a solemn procession.

"Selena!" Elkhart whispers pathetically. "Help me. Let me take part in the Immersions. After a confession, penance, which I promise you I shall do somehow. Then baptism. It will be as if I have died and am born again!"

She can only assent numbly to his dramatic plea, and goes to make a quick change in the dressing room to her baptismal robes while the procession reaches the pool arena.

As the Little Mother enters, Elkhart causes the entire party to pause while he kneels before her, murmuring something unintelligible to everyone about the Altacama Desert.

What he says is particularly unintelligible to Mamacita. She does not, as we know, speak English, but also she is apparently in a state of trance. She has not eaten for several days, and the sisters who have taken on themselves the task of following her about to see that she *does* eat (otherwise she might never bother) bear small trays of tempting Incan morsels for her. Her distant smile, however, indicates that she is nowhere within sight of food or within earshot of Elkhart's murmurings either. Though he tugs at the hem of her blue chiffon skirt, she does not notice him, and Bubba is eventually obliged to help Elkhart to his feet so that the procession may proceed.

Two young women bring poolside cushions for the Little Mother and her sisters. One of them whispers to the other: "She's Plussed-out of this world."

Tsinghai Yana moves over agreeably, and the Little Mother is safely settled, surrounded by her sisters. Tsinghai places his own porcelain cup (which contains Black Velvet bourbon) on the table next to the Little Mother's Incan morsels, and throughout the ceremony he takes frequent sips.

And now Selena takes her place at the head of the whirlpool, opposite the Little Mother, and the Immersions are ready to begin.

A pipe sounds in the sunlit air, a wooden flute coming from the women's bathhouse. The two attendants pass straw reeds from a tray among the initiates. The purpose of these reeds is soon clear to the Little Mother's audience (even to the club members peering through the gate to see what is going on). Mamacita herself still betrays no awareness of her whereabouts.

Two by two the initiates enter the whirlpool until all twelve—fourteen counting Elkhart and Bubba, who enter together—are inside the hot, steamy water. It is a trifle crowded, but they are all intimates.

Selena watches Elkhart, concerned that the temperature may be too much for him, if he has indeed been on some drug, but he has assumed a look of sublime devotion, and she cannot catch his eye.

Resonating across the water from some source comes a taped Murma: "Water fire water fire water fire water . . ."

Selena instructs the initiates to fix upon the Murma, bring their straws to their lips and to submerge. At the sound of the flute, a few notes of which mingle with the Murma, they are to reappear. She gives an open-armed signal, and all heads go under.

It is her intent to hold that gesture for the two-minute interval during which the initiates are under the water, but such is not to be the case. No sooner are the heads out of sight than someone tugs frantically at her sleeve, whispering in a voice possessed of such cosmic terror as she has not heard since—well, since she became aware of cosmic terror.

"I've got to show you this—right now! Hurry!"

"What is it, Evi?" she whispers. The girl is stark white, and her entire frame is trembling. She is carrying that portfolio of drawings she found in Elkhart's room, and she pulls Selena over behind a palm tree and sets the drawings on a table.

"Where is Elk?" asks Evi.

Selena gestures to the water.

"Oh, my God!" Evi starts to dash away, gesturing helplessly toward the drawings. "Look at them—decide."

But Selena hangs on to her. "What's wrong with you, dear?"

"He'll kill me," she cries. "He'll kill us all!"

She motions speechlessly to the portfolio lying on the table. Selena opens it.

The portfolio bears a finely printed heading: EARTH RESTORATION PROJECT (E.R.P.)

Inside are elaborate blueprints and mechanical drawings on graphic overlays of plastic and paper transparencies. On the top layer is the legend BACK TO THE SOIL, for some reason repeated in Latin and Modern German, and three finely drawn symbols known to everyone, as old as symbol-making: a double cross, ancient sign of the sun; an elaboration of the cross with rectangles at each of the ends—a mandala of some sort, Selena thinks; and the crux ansata, a cross closed at the top. And so the top overlay, in no way alarming, persuades Selena only that the ceremony has been interrupted for no good cause. She closes the portfolio and tells Evi to wait.

Evi gasps, "Selena, help me! You know how many points I have to earn. This is my chance to make up for Atlantis!"

Evi has forgotten the *Sayso*: "Personal reward is no reward." Selena advances toward the pool.

"Fire water fire water fire . . ." goes the Murma.

The two minutes of the Initial Immersion have passed and the fourteen bodies are steaming in the whirlpool. Selena lifts her hands to signal the flute player, and at the sound all fourteen heads come up, quite pink-cheeked, furnishing full evidence of a marked increase in circulation. Selena instructs everyone to close their eyes and turn their faces to the sun.

". . . water fire water fire water . . ."

After a minute passes, another signal from the flute instructs the initiates to reinsert their straws, fix upon the Murma again and sink their heads below the surface.

Evi, who has hidden behind the palm tree out of sight of Elkhart, again takes Selena's hand, pulls her back to the open portfolio. Convinced that Selena's wisdom and her own instinctive grasp of things are the just and proper combination for combating the menace she has uncovered, and mostly fearful of her life, she now flips the pages quickly for Selena, pointing out certain intentions in the sketches, noting that there are dates set for the execution of Elkhart's plans, obliging Selena to realize the probable meaning of the E.R.P. That first page, which might appear to a casual observer as innocent as any of the thousands of books available down the street at the Shambhala Bookstore, gives place to a second which outlines, Selena realizes, sites for the construction and installation of the complex machinery on the subsequent pages.

She reads quickly:

> Thar Desert—serving India and Southern Asia
> Gobi Desert—serving China and Russia
> Kalahari Desert—serving Africa
> Death Valley—serving North America
> Altacama Desert—serving South America

When she comes to Altacama, she gives a start, remembering Elkhart's peculiar mutterings. She reads on, realizing the full potentiality of an Elkhart reconstructed. More than two minutes have passed, and the reeds in the whirlpool are beginning to bobble among the less advanced of the initiates. She folds up the portfolio, motions Evi to disappear with it into the bathhouse to await the final Immersion.

And then she signals the flute to play again.

The initiates come up gasping, their boiled faces wincing at the sun. Bubba speaks to Selena: "This is hotter than the water up at Calistoga." He appears to be supporting Strong Elkhart, whose head topples against Bubba's shoulder. But Selena nevertheless beckons Bubba to join her at the poolside and gives the final cue to the flute player for the last Immersion.

Everyone goes under except Bubba and Elkhart, who also responds to Selena's summons because he cannot let go of Bubba.

Selena stands at the bathhouse door and is gesturing Bubba to join her inside. But Elkhart has pulled Bubba down to his knees in a tribute to the Little Mother, and the two red bodies prostrate themselves before the Mamacita.

This gives Evi a chance to bolt. Waving hastily to Selena, she flees past the steaming Jacuzzi bath with its dozen trembling reeds, past the gate where the club members are beginning to raise their voices impatiently.

Evi disappears, not to make her way back into our story until later in the evening when she will keep her appointment in that very Jacuzzi whirlpool with the bellboy. Evi is a woman of her word and has never known herself to go back on a bargain or to fail in a service she commits herself to. Let us now take a look at the extent of the service she has just performed, while Selena awaits the confrontation she must have with Elkhart and Bubba, while the reeds waver in the hot pool.

In kneeling before Mamacita, Elkhart is searching for a sign. He still believes she sent him into the desert to discover his Other Teacher. Having been overcome by doubt, having cried out that he wants to be born again, he would now give anything to learn that what he has schemed to bring about was Mamacita's doing, possibly so that he may fix blame somewhere outside himself. Here are some details of his scheme for us to examine while he and Bubba are on their knees.

The blueprints and mechanical drawings are most artistically presented, and the graphic overlays number thirteen. There are, however, three major drawings in the portfolio; overlays and transparencies clarify the utility and unity of the work and also detail relevant parts of those basic designs, the star, the double cross, and that powerful cruciform rattle of Isis, the crux ansata.

Throughout the pages that translation pattern mentioned before, with minute notations and numberings, suggests there is a master key or legend of the plan which Evi did not find. Possibly the master key would be of only academic interest. What she has discovered is sufficient to show us Elkhart's intention—to replenish the earth from those remote desert regions, and to use for the purpose human bodies.

Not just any human form will serve—Elkhart primarily intends to offer the fertile daughters of Isis themselves. Selena has realized from her brief examination of the drawings that Elkhart means to solve the overpopulation of the earth by extermination measures far more sophisticated than any ever used before. And that he also believes women (and some incompetent males, homosexuals and racial inferiors—determinants not here stated) will be the most favorable ingredient.

His resentment of mothering impulses in women like Selena is here carried to its ultimate end. Elkhart expects to curb, control and, indeed, eliminate those reckless producers, who out of an irresponsible maternal appetite to breed, out of a craving for more and more creatures to nurture, out of their demented lust for more and more mouths to invade with their full, relentless breasts, have wrecked his world. In a total contradiction of the argument with which he has persuaded Bubba Burr to merge ICH and DU, Elkhart imagines in his dreams, Mothers first, Mothers first.

A transparency of the eight-pointed star is headed R.I.P. Beneath it, a colorful mechanical drawing indicates the star is a design of eight metal corridors, closed and windowless, with a center dome for an elaborate computer. Notations below this dome and corridor apparatus suggest that it is the central headquarters to be built in each of the desert locations. The master key would doubtless reveal that the computer has complete demographic reference to the geography of the world and could locate any female with reproductive organs intact anywhere in its control range.

The next underlayer is also headed R.I.P., but here there are several translations, one in English, saying Restoration Input Portable.

This portable is a closed aluminum room with a trap-door floor. The R.I.P. unit can be removed and replaced at the end of each corridor in the star unit. It can be lifted from an enormous metal eye, looped with a metal cable and removed from a coupling unit, rather like an airport jetway. Each room's weight capacity is twenty tons.

The next drawing shows that the twenty-ton capacity will be filled with the FFV, of whom Elkhart spoke to Bielbog in the desert, the Female Finalist Volunteers. Their tonnage is indicated by the female biological symbol, itself based upon the cross of Isis. Each aluminum unit will contain twenty tons of human flesh.

You will recall the enticement conceived by Bielbog, the necklaces of Knuckle Root. One of them still hangs about Evi's neck, yellow, deceptively precious-looking. One bead, and she would be ready to become "the first sacrifice."

An underlayer clarifies the use of that basic mandala, the star corridor, in which eight of these aluminum rooms are attached to their coupling unit, a Ferris wheel on a flat plane. This drawing bears the gruesome heading *Circus Ultimus*, which is variously translated.

The transparency that follows reveals how the R.I.P. units are removed. Here are drawings of two multibladed rotors of a super helicopter, and the copter is gripping in powerful airlift claws an aluminum R.I.P. unit.

The detailed plans for the helicopter bear the heading SOLV (Ship of Last Voyage), also variously translated. This helicopter of enormous power, already developed by the U.S. Air Force for Asian wars, has a capacity for lifting much more than the twenty-ton weight of Elkhart's aluminum rooms.

The plans that follow are the critical ones and reveal the full workings of the entire scheme. The transparency of the crux ansata is headed HOG: Anointing Unit. No translations are offered for the three letters, an apparent acronym, which would doubtless be clarified by the master key, but which to those who know Elkhart cannot help but call up the memory of his now hopelessly insane wife Piggy.

The cruciform sistrum of Isis is the root of Elkhart's plans. Its design is the basic chassis of a machine whose scale references show it to be of enormous size. In an overview of great suspension axles, for rubber tires with heavy traction tread, the kind huge earth-movers use, the crux is outlined insistently in red.

Next comes an overview of a cockpit, like a ship's helm, provided with a center aisle and labeled NAVE (Navus), which separates personnel living quarters from the propelling instrumentation. Then follows a full side view of the machine, and we see that it is a tanklike structure, its cockpit an armored dome. Painted on its side, after the fashion of World War II pilots, are the letters HOG.

The next overview and drawing (in perfect registration with the others) shows the mouth of a funnel at the top of the machine behind the cockpit.

And then comes a more detailed drawing of the base of the funnel, with a surface like a cheese grater. Anyone familiar with equipment in the lumber mills of the northwestern United States will recognize this multibladed machine, actually called the Hog. In the lumber industry, log butts and other wooden debris are sent down a chute into this machine and are instantly reduced to fine chips. Incidentally, certain workers who have labored long with its fascinations have been known to offer themselves in accidental or suicidal plunges down the chute, in which their bodies, softer and lighter than logs, were even more quickly demolished.

The last two drawings make the entire works abundantly clear. In one, a helicopter with an R.I.P. unit hovers over the funnel mouth of the Hog, ready to release its trap-door floor. The twenty tons of volunteers will then be received by the whirling, grinding teeth of the Hog.

The last drawing reveals a depository unit attached to the crux chassis, showing that the helicopter contents are injected into that depository and spewed out from a broad exhaust to the rear.

Elkhart has told Evi that he has had an experimental Hog built, that it is ready to be tested, and he has taken advantage of the prior existence of aspects of this machinery. Elkhart has adapted other existent material and has made expedient purchases. From lumber-mill machinists he has bought the Hog bearings, its driving motor and thick metal shroud. He has also purchased parts for the crux body, the broad rear exhaust and funnel. This last is from a small-scale land reclamation project in Illinois, where sludge is used as fertilizer sprayed out onto the ground from such an exhaust. Sludge is of course partially composed of human waste; Elkhart's plan merely reverses that term, after the usage of warriors in Vietnam who brought into the American language the daring concept of "wasting humans."

So it is that Elkhart's giant machine can create a paste of bright red (the color of his aura), vivid matter which will be quickly desiccated by the desert sun. The Anointing Unit, the anterior rear exhaust, is to spread its carpet of finely slithered bones and shredded flesh across the deserts, covering them with inches of matter which, with proper irrigation and agricultural techniques, will regenerate, restore and fecundate the world.

At this moment the Little Mother comes out of her trance and gives a signal, which all choose to interpret variously. She falls to the right, into the arms of Tsinghai Yana. Before she becomes completely unconscious, she murmurs what many believe to be one of her famous one-word *Saysos*. Elkhart looks up with a fixed decisiveness. He has heard her say: "Altacama."

Then the four Sisters lift her in their arms and rush her out the gate, past the many club members who have been waiting to enter with mounting impatience. Seizing this opportunity to get through the gate, many members push their way inside, some of them entering the Jacuzzi whirlpool and encountering the submerged bodies there and nudging them out of the way.

This makes the initiates imagine that perhaps they have missed the final cue from the flute, and they come up eagerly. They flop onto the sides of the pool, some of them grabbing towels, wrapping up their bodies, shivering. Two of the girls faint dead away.

Meanwhile, Selena has induced Bubba to bring Elkhart into the bathhouse, where Elkhart, seeing that Selena has his portfolio, begins to ramble about his studies with Bielbog, telling everything, swearing that Mamacita has put him up to it. Hadn't she just admitted it in saying "Altacama"? (And wasn't so disgusting a plan just like a woman after all!) He holds onto Selena's white baptismal robes, upon which ICH and DU have been interwoven in embroidery by a solicitous novice. He kisses her robe, kisses the words, swears she is the Divine Mother, Isis, not human, no, not an insatiable human woman, but Selena, goddess of the moon, Mother of all. "You have given me rebirth today!"

Bubba, meanwhile, has been gazing at the portfolio and now looks at Selena dejectedly. Selena asks, "Bubba, did you *know?*," to which Bubba replies in a lapse into political jargon: "I knew he needed help. But, Selena, we're all one team, and well—I think I can cover for him . . . We're in too deep—Selena, what can I do?" For he has realized Selena is not going to support a cover story. She has at last risen to the occasion I have been preparing her for, is ready to assert her full strength in the realm of (dare I say it again?) the female principle.

She tells Bubba exactly what to do, to gather up the portfolio and have it placed in the hotel safe. And to take Elkhart away to some quiet, confining place. In short, she is now empowered to use those qualities of resourcefulness in peacekeeping and responsibility toward the natural order, restraints so badly needed among ruling men.

However, lest some factions celebrate prematurely, devotion to my task obliges me to report another incident. And we might also remember Luna's remark that the best of four men she knew might add up to one good man, and recognize that I have had to use a number of my resources of the female principle for this modest achievement. As a *Sayso* says, Don't expect a miracle.

No sooner is female virtue employed than one of the worst examples of female aggressiveness invades the woman's bathhouse. Two very insistent women who have paid their dues in the Pool and Tennis Club, and who feel the natural order of their lives has been disagreeably disrupted, burst in and shout: "Women only!"

One of the women, who is old enough to know better, manages to kick Elkhart in the shins in an apparent accident. When he cries out, she says, "Get out of here, will you?"

Elkhart takes advantage of this order to withdraw, and he vanishes before Bubba can follow Selena's instructions.

And then another woman comes in and begins to shout her indignation over Bubba's presence in the women's dressing room. Just then, the flute player, deciding he has missed his cue, bursts into the final notes of the Immersions rite.

Everyone has been gone for twenty minutes before a pool attendant is able to discover and disconnect the source of the tape-loop Murma. "Water fire water . . ."

Black Soul

"But what do you suppose the Little Mother *did* mean?" Carrie asks. Selena has come back to her garden and has been telling her of the events at the Claremont pool. Carrie, so disturbed herself by what she has been witness to, is even more deeply troubled to hear of how Elkhart has broken down after that strange visitation.

Selena sighs. "One of the sisters clarified the Altacama business. She only meant she wanted to go to sleep after the long plane trip and change of altitude. What she really said was '*A la cama,*' to bed. Even '*Alta cama,*' 'high bed,' would have made some sense," Selena says. "Everybody thought she was Plussed out; she was really just pooped out."

As Selena is herself. She is now stretched upon a canvas chair in Carrie's garden, resting. And Carrie is filled with a foreboding of what may yet come to complicate the cryptic events of that day. She takes out a sketch pad, but although she starts to sketch Selena, she finds she stops and stares into space. "Where is Elkhart now?" she asks.

"Vanished. Bubba took the drawings to the hotel manager and had them placed in the vault. Then he and I talked it over with Emil Jewels, and I insisted we ask Tsinghai to be there, too.

"We decided to go ahead with the wedding. Emil even tried to laugh off the possibility of Elkhart's scheme ever coming about. It couldn't happen, he said. And *he* was a refugee!"

Actually Selena would not have consented to go on with the wedding had Tsinghai presented any objection, but he seemed willing for reasons not yet clear to have the ceremony go according to plan. She muses, "In a way, I can see how Emil might treat it lightly. His own attitude toward women—notoriously bad, you know. He might not go as far as extermination. Enjoys contention too much. Rape is more his line. *I* know," she gestures to the center of her chest.

At the word "rape," Carrie looks up in consternation. It is not surprising that the bizarre story of Elkhart's master plan should call up associations of violence, and besides everything that has happened today, her conversation with Harrison, her own visions, even her cat's luncheon feast of the finch, has been tinged with violence. She is not yet used to having her thoughts run concurrently with another person's. And when Selena mentions rape in connection with Emil Jewels, a memory is at that very moment flashing through her mind, of being raped when she herself was seventeen. Another insistent feeling presses in on her, that a rape is at that moment occurring. She cannot ignore the notion that it is happening to someone close to her.

Then suddenly she remembers the warning given Luna by the psychic Jim Smith. She sets down her pencil and closes her eyes. "Oh, dear, Selena! Luna is down by the waterfront, and she's not with Jim Smith. I wonder if I should call the police."

Selena opens her eyes to see Carrie shake her head. "This is too much," Carrie says. "I must be seeing things again."

Something very curious *is* happening down in the Emeryville Mudflats, and although the signals Luna originally sends out, and which Carrie intercepts, are of alarm, dismay and horror, as the happening follows its course, the signals become mixed and quite confused.

The man who has accosted her after her speeding-ticket incident, the man with the knuckle-size ring, has thrust Luna inside the Elephant, one of the large wooden sculptures on the beach. He has deftly reached up under her Bedouin skirt and yanked down her underpants and is attempting through the tangle of dark-blue hand-woven fabric to do violence to Luna's body.

You can imagine with what speed her mind begins to race, with what jolting suddenness the imagery of life riots throughout her being. Rape! Precisely what Jim Smith must have first warned her against. Was it her own fault? Forewarned, not only by Jim but by her own uneasy sense that he was right, that here was another self-styled drama, one which could even throw a cloud over her future. Is it one she has brought on herself, first speeding in a state of rage, brought on by her frantic search for—what? Self-realization through sex? But she has known for ages, better than any of her friends, as well perhaps as Carrie, that *sex is a cop-out!*

She must have spoken those words aloud, because the rapist, thrusting his way further into the body of the elephant, clawing at the billowing skirt, grunts, "So what else is new, baby?"

He has jammed her into a corner from which escape seems unlikely. Inside this driftwood sculpture made of boards and chicken wire, she cannot easily elude him or take the attack. The man is amber-colored, all amber, though his kinky Afro suggests he passes for a black. He paws at her dress, cursing it, squinting into her face with amber eyes. Everything about him matches the glow of late afternoon, the hovering yellow sunset over the smoggy bay. Amber, a stone from mountain streams, swept into the sea. He smells of resin, in fact. This not unpleasant imagery, her billowing, ballooning skirt—and the treasure of her life suddenly becomes rich, like a basketful of cakes, flowers, wine, waltzes, concertos, that and the sudden flight overhead of cormorants, traveling in a triangular formation, warm-blooded, red-eyed, purposeful—all these signs call up Jim Smith's image of her as a balloon whose basket safeguards her life's treasure.

I decide that I must help her, if not to find her life, at least to retrieve her body. I flick into her mind a skill she has learned down in the Andes at Mamacita's retreat. As she considers what to do, she hears another exchange between herself and the grunting, panting assailant.

"Why are you doing this?" she asks.

He answers without pausing in his purpose. "I like to catch chicks down here where the freaks put up these statues. It knocks me out."

The Emeryville marina statues are famous, a frequently photographed spot where hippies have created from the flotsam of the bay an array of creatures (a dinosaur, a giraffe, a lion, a drummer with a complete set of drums) separated by a cyclone fence from the freeway, where occupants of passing cars traveling at least fifty-five miles an hour would not believe a rape was occurring inside the driftwood elephant if they noticed.

Luna asks, "You like the danger—is that it?"

He snorts, showing teeth ambered by nicotine. "The patrols never see me. I fuck em inside this elephant and the patrols never look. They never think to look at the animals."

"It'd be a hell of a place to get caught," says Luna. "Right now, for instance, they'd have to pull you out of here by your ass! What if I were to scream?"

He shrugs, thrusting her further into the elephant, still tangled in the Bedouin dress. "Chicks don't scream when I do it to them."

"But *here*? It's sheer exhibitionism," she says, but he only bares his amber teeth again.

She glances at a nearby sculpture, an enormous hand, possibly either the Black Power fist or the Hand of God, depending on your persuasion. It is hard to say whether the tall planks of which the hand's fingers are made are intended to be a fist or to hark further back to that Egyptian god Amon who took himself in hand and masturbated forth Geb and Nut, heaven and earth. Her knee knocks against the inside of the elephant, and she suddenly remembers Carrie's dream. The triangle is the key, she tells herself, to her strongbox! This thought impels her to the use of the occult Peruvian skill. She listens for a moment as I speak to her in Selena Crum's voice, instantly ascends into her most successful DeFix.

In the Andes, Luna has been competent only in elementary DeFixes. However, in the pressure of crisis, she makes a leap into an UpFix that the most practiced and devoted of Mamacita's followers would envy.

In that space, she flies among some kites which have drifted over from the favored marina kite-flying site, and almost tangles in the silvery gleam of a mylar tail. She ducks, forgetting for the moment that to the kite she is invisible. Below her the San Francisco skyline steams across the bay; the freeway traffic streaks past the statuary of Emeryville. She can observe from this perspective the bodies below, struggling like two beetles on the beach.

The first thing she notices is that she is not being stabbed or brained with an axe, is not running down the road aflame with napalm, is not being eaten alive by the jaws of the San Andreas Fault or by a nest of red ants, is not even in danger of her life. Lucky Luna. From where she floats up among the kites, it is obvious that her assailant will not kill her. But then, among rape victims, Luna is unusual.

The next thing she sees is that she does not even know, despite her unusual visual power, whether the man has made entry! Can that be because Jim Smith was right, that only flimsy ropes connect her head and body?

Concentrating on her body's predicament, she sees herself below, thrashing at some of the rape-resistance techniques she has learned at a Rape Rap Session (kick at shins hard as you can, grab at eyes, cut at neck with fingernails, etc.), along with a few poorly remembered attitudes from that Oriental art of self-defense HoHo. Once again this shows her how scattered her existence is, how unconcentrated upon her various pursuits she has been, how feeble her tenacity. But she is also enabled to see into the heart and spine of the criminal, a gift few victims have. In fact she sees something that Jim Smith might see if he were doing a reading of the rapist. If she can see through to her flimsy ropes, she realizes, she is looking through the man's body! In its transparent state, right in its center there is a bowl—and what is that inside? A bowl of corn-meal mush! A soft spot. Butter melts in the center.

Brutalized, he is accessible, and Luna sends a message down to her body to stop thrashing. She sends another message, which initiates the following discourse.

"You're not all black, you know," her body says. "There is a yellow spot in you."

"High yella, baby," says the rapist, thrusting. This spark of wit encourages Luna's body.

"You'll get caught, you know."

"I been caught. Three-time loser. I'm in analysis now on parole. But that doan stop me. I'm dedicated."

"What do you get out of it?"

The man grimaces, pursuing his calling, pushing, sweating, but what he says next shows Luna that her view from the kite, one on which she has now rested in weightlessness, is one of the finest she has ever had into her own resentment, straight through this other body. For she can see that point at which it connects in the two of them, herself and this miserable man, and causes them to switch engines.

He is still thrusting, but he says, "You mean, what's a nice guy like me doing in this line of work?" And warming to this theme, he bursts out with the bitterest irony, breaking it up rhythmically with little gasps and rutting grins. "Well, you see—I have this idea—I might meet me—some nice rich girl some day—who'd take me away—from all this sin."

Luna seems to cringe at his heavy-handed play on the old cliché, or to cringe away from something else—she's still not sure he's in.

Her body says, "I'm rich."

"No shit," he says, with no let-up.

Luna's body presses the point. In fact, it begins to speak under my inspiration. She sends down a thought about the psychic reality wedding, where two thousand souls will this evening commit mass matrimony. She asks, "How would you like to get married?"

His voice sinks to a ferocious whisper. "Married! You bitch!"

"No, but I mean it! I'll marry you. I *will*."

He bares his yellow teeth again, gripping her hair in a fury. "You cunt, you filthy cunt!"

"But I mean it," the body cries sincerely.

"Taunts, lies, cheating bitches. You're all alike. Just poking—poking—poking—"

He, of course, is the one doing the poking, but he can't seem to finish what he is trying to say. Luna, from the tail of a kite, seems to have worked a spell upon him. Surprise and amazement mingle with the contempt and hurt raging in his face, and he finishes his business, while Luna still peers down from the kite, unsure of whether it has even started. He jerks away, stuttering, "Poking—poking—" until at last he can sob out, "Fun at me!" And to his own amazement, he flings himself away from Luna's body, curling up at her feet, still inside the elephant. Her body is able to recollect itself, to adjust her skirts and untangle her legs, even though one of her arms is still thrust down into the elephant's trunk, and escape is blocked by the man's huddled form.

It is clearly safe now for Luna to go down for a reentry into her body. I decide to issue a warning to her, in my own voice, to put a scare into her.

I say, "This is the last rescue from such unbecoming incidents, Luna." She goes flashing all over the kite looking for me, as I haven't made myself visible. "Philomen!" she cries, both in and out of her body.

And then she makes a full reentry and is staring at her disspirited assailant. She is promising me that she will be more careful of her anger in the future, and begins at once.

"Help me out of here," she says commandingly, calmly.

But the rapist is wrenched and cannot move. He sets up a wail as if he has been stabbed. Luna looks around, thinking someone might come to his aid. But he was right, no one has heard his cries. He sobs out, "Promises, promises! You're all alike!"

"This is absurd," Luna says. Confident now of her superior strength, she shoves his shoulder resolutely with one of her heels, tossing him out of the elephant altogether. She scrambles out, standing above the man, who has fallen flat on his face.

"Stop blubbering," she says, "and listen."

Her authority causes him to subside, and so she asks, "What's your name?"

Between two short breaths, he says, "Black Soul."

Luna sighs. "Oh, brother." But Black Soul doesn't hear. His name is the least of what weighs on his soul. He is shaking his head in humiliation. How has he lost his self-possession in front of a victim? Never before has this happened! He brushes off his clothing, scarcely able to look at her, yet aroused by an intense curiosity. Something extraordinary has caused him to crack.

"How you do that?" he asks.

Luna, aware now that she has unwittingly OverFixed him (a skill very few in the Andes ever master), yet not inflated in that she realizes she has had unusual help, is more concerned now about the inner workings of *his* mind. Is it true, she wonders, that a rapist is just a disappointed romantic? Hoping like an old-fashioned fallen woman for a hand-out to the Good Life?

She says, "I can show you what I did. But first tell me about yourself. You're not ordinary."

Black Soul begins to regather self-esteem as he gets into the subject of himself. "No, I'm not ordinary. It's just that this shrink I got, she puts me down." *She!* Luna can't help wondering how a woman therapist copes with a rapist during their solitary sessions.

"She knows every time I slip it in an threatens to send me back to the slams."

Black Soul's language is typical of Berkeley High graduates, even among many whites. He speaks a fair general American, reserved for the public. But among his fellow blacks he enjoys dropping his copulative—thus his "How you do that?" But then again with white intimates, which we must agree Luna has just become, there is another word play—a Sambo parody, in which the tongue is thickened to a deliberate but boiling Brer Rabbit stew. Luna has no problem with it, being aware of it as a way of discharging aggression. Black Soul has plenty of that to discharge.

"I remin her," he goes on, the speech becoming thicker, "they goan stick my brain in Vacaville if she send me back. They said las stretch, I show up one mo time I get the psychosurgery. This shrink, she mean, but she doan dig that psychosurgery. So she say well, you get a job, Black Soul. An I say I goan get me a ho an not work no mo. All I got to do is get over in the city and get set up. They some badass chicks all over greedy to work for me. Get me somebody with meat on her an clothes an style. I say I goan get me a fool for my tool. And she say that jive, pimpin just as bad as rape, an to get me some decent job. An I remin her how I learn a decent line of work an cain get a job at it. How many certified psychopaths you know learn a print-shop trade while doin time? Huh? How many learn letterin besides? You could look all over this town an not find somebody like me."

A sly look comes over him at this point, and Luna can see he has completely forgotten his earlier shame. A crazy pride possesses him. He says, "Single-handed, I change most the 'Meet the Turk' Camel signs in town."

Luna shakes her head. She has seen some student graffiti artists at work on the sign in her own neighborhood. And the person I noticed earlier on my way to the Claremont was definitely not Black Soul.

He lowers his voice as he reveals more confidences, unaware that Luna has her doubts. He tells her in a conspiratorial tone that he felt a murderous urge start up in him when the first Turk appeared in town. "My chest feel like I been hit by a ton of nicotine." Clearly Black Soul is a smoker, as evidenced by his nicotine-stained teeth and fingers, and so Luna knows it isn't the tobacco itself he is against. He explains it: "It's the fuckers who goan fall for that macho appeal who want to be like Hairy-chest with the white shirt unbutton to his navel and the white chick in the background and the beaked birds and the priceless artifacts, and the thousand-dollar bills in his pocket." And here Black Soul slips Luna a look of paranoic glee, as he tells of his raids on the billboards, when he started modestly with "Meet the Turk-ey," and then moved on to alter the signs more outlandishly. "My 'd' on 'Meet the Turd,' that was a masterpiece—you must have seen it." He gives her arm a little nudge. "Even after you looked twice you couldn't tell it didn't come that way." He changed the slogan showing the Turk with blue sky behind him to "Meet the Bird," then came "Meat the Jerk," then "Meet the Junkie." Then he moved on to "Beef Jerky," and to tampering with the second line: "He smokes for pleasure," which under his furtive and professional hand became "He strokes for pleasure" and "He farts at leasure." If time permitted he would blot the sign out altogether and write in his own lettering: "He sucks," for example—literally true of any smoker.

Luna is soon won over by the idea of Black Soul at work, always late at night, when, even so, prowl cars might spot him. She cannot doubt it when he states that single-handedly he must have cost the

Reynolds Tobacco Company close to twenty thousand dollars. She imagines him always working against time, enjoying the challenge of risking his parole. She appreciates the heroism he draws from the high-tension risk on top of the Liberty Building downtown when he dared to blot out and reprint an entire line: "Two humps are better than one." She cannot help expressing a measure of admiration.

Black Soul merely nods, telling her, "My shrink dug that one, too. This one thing she wouldn't rat on. Saw it as progress. Claimed I'd soon forget about rape." But then the ads stopped, and Black Soul, at a loss, has returned to his daily rape. He has tried for a while working over the Winston ads: "If it wasn't for Winston I wouldn't—" Well, "smoke" having five letters, he started off with "wouldn't snore," then "belch," then tried a few with only four letters, but it was too easy, and all at once the thing went sour. "It just seemed childish," he complains. "A waste of my skill.

"You know, good as I am at letterin, you think I can get me a job?" He cannot join the union because of the nature of his record; no one will knowingly hire a rapist even in an all-male print shop, his theory being people fear that one sex offense leads to any other kind.

"You might try a DeFix on them," Luna says.

Absorbed in his story, Black Soul has temporarily forgotten his interest in how Luna has disarmed him. But this remark brings his attention back to what has passed between them. "Tell me how you broke me down just now."

Luna looks at him carefully, coming to a decision. She has always been able to find in people the redeeming qualities that might be overlooked in the heat of the moment, this despite the welter of emotion in which her own life swarms, and that is of course one of the qualities in Luna that makes us keep watch over her. She knows it is risky to teach a "certified psychopath" any of the Mamacita techniques, but she also suspects that there is a reason why she has been rewarded with success (if success it was—she's still not sure). She takes the plunge, reminding him that she has told him she will marry him, telling him what can be explained about the Psychic Reality wedding ceremony, telling him to come to it at the Claremont Hotel, and saying that with a little help she has zapped him with a trick of the mind. "You might find it useful if you really want to get a job," she says.

His sly look grips his face, and then he looks tempted, churlish, filled with hideous, confused, indistinguishable longings. "A trap," he says. "The cops be there for sure. You ain the first tried to get me that way."

She stands up, brushing her skirts, telling him to think it over. "It's up to you."

And just at that moment, a patrol car pulls up beside the cyclone fence, and two Berkeley policemen, one of them black, run out with their pistols drawn. Black Soul, jerking up as if to flee, intercepts a look from Luna that stops him. The black cop says, "We got a call to come down here. Some woman said there was trouble. This fellow hassling you?"

Luna shakes her head with the utmost composure. "I'm okay. Who phoned?"

The cop sighs. He and his buddy put away their weapons. "Somebody claiming she was having a psychic experience. You know, the town is full of nuts."

They drive away, and Black Soul gives Luna an admiring gaze. Something new has entered the tormented inner regions of his emotional life.

Rape! The three women are moved by a compassion never yet aroused to such a depth among them. For who has not feared it; nor trembled at the creak of a stair; nor cringed at a sinister hiss or whistle; nor crossed the street with the hair of her body rising, to avoid a strolling insolent gang. Who has not fantasied her own helpless shrieks, even at the sight of a truckdriver spitting crudely out of his cab window; or speculated about how to defend herself or whether to seek revenge, to undergo the ordeal of police inquisition, to confront publicly one who has invaded her inmost privacy.

And who has not been prey also to the dizziness of ambiguity, in which adolescents are summoned up, of being carried away by some intriguing stranger, an outlaw, a gypsy, knowledgeable of arcane powers; also a violator to the heart of her life's matter, furnishing a final affirmation of what has been told her in daily insidious secrecy all her life, that she is not held dear, that she is cheaply and easily had, rent, cast aside—a cipher, a nothing, a woman.

"I saw it all," Luna says to Carrie and Selena, explaining how from the advantage of height in her DeFix she was able to see into herself, into the *bottom layer*, as she says, of her problem as a woman, and received this view miraculously through the body of her very attacker, Black Soul, for first she must look through his muddy, brackish self-loathing, then through that bowl of golden mush into her own thrashing ropes, which kept her head and body separate from one another in a hating, despising, loathing attempt to deal with the resentment of being born physically equipped to have this experience available to her!

"Resentment of being a woman," she says, "must be the last thing women let go of before it doesn't matter what sex we are. But I had to see the resentment in Black Soul to understand my own!"

And so Carrie and Selena, having always appreciated what I most enjoy in Luna, that virtue of seeing merit where others quail, are now moved, touched and stimulated by this further value she is displaying, of turning what might be a traumatic, painful ordeal into an occasion for seeing things about herself she has previously overlooked.

Here I would enter a brief defense of gossip. Clearly this is an example of what I meant early in my report, gossip as a form of experience-sharing that may lead to keener insights. My fondness for these three entities aside, they do strengthen one another.

Luna says to Selena, "I saw you sitting in the lap of the Mayan god," remembering the snapshot from Jim's atlas. Selena smiles, realizing she has briefly remembered that incident herself today. Luna makes use of another rap group technique; confront the woman you envy with its counterpart, your admiration of her. She asks, "How did you ever get rid of resentment, Selena? Did you resent Jim back in those days?"

Selena reflects. "Lord, no. It was about then I started using my strength and stopped wasting energy. In that case it was simple primate grooming, though I imagine he needs something more complex now. The trouble with strength is that it's easy to misuse or apply at the right time. Today was challenging," she says, thinking of Elkhart. "So was my rape, come to think of it."

"*You've* been raped?" from both Carrie and Luna.

A shrug. Selena imagines that the initial rape occurs when the mere thought of it is fixed in a little girl's mind, for she believes that thoughts are things and deeds.

"My rapist is Emil Jewels," she says, and Carrie remembers Selena's earlier allusion, and her own remembrance of being raped at seventeen.

The three women are sitting in the wrought-iron chairs as the evening dusk gathers. As usual at this hour in the Bay cities, there is a cool breeze, not yet unpleasant. Carrie picks up her sketchbook and begins to draw Selena's face as she tells her story.

Selena was in Calistoga Hot Springs, where, you will remember, she found Harrison down the road from the DU Retreat, and where, on another occasion, Luna has gone with the Sisters of the Tantric Arts to consult Emil Jewels. The evening of Selena's story, she went alone into the baths, where seminarists withdraw, after insightful experiences in their meetings, for sometimes solitary, sometimes group bathing without restraint of separation of the sexes. It was a lovely night. There was no ceiling in the bathhouse, and Selena could see the Western moon, the same moon Jack London rode under in nearby Sonoma, in country where the grapes shone like moonstones and garnets in their vineyards below a velvet field of stars. She opened the wide spigot that filled her tub, not a traditional porcelain tub like the one next to it, but a large square Roman tub, a pool where group bathing and other more immoderate activities occasionally went on. A sulfurous waterfall filled it for her, and she sat cross-legged enjoying the steam, which was not (as Bubba has said this afternoon) as hot as the artificial mineral pool at the Claremont Hotel.

"I notice some bubbles rising next to me and imagine somebody submerged inside, but I pay no attention until I hear this voice," she says.

"A vision of earthly delight," says the voice, and it is Emil Jewels. "I assume he thinks some young girl has come into the baths, because Emil's eyes are failing, especially at night, so I sink into the water, opening my eyes to the full moon above me. Then he goes: 'Daughter of the Moon, how like a virgin you look under the element, Selena.' So I know he knows it's me. 'Your own element,' he goes on poetically, 'which erases lines and lifts breasts, so that under the water every woman is nubile like a nymph. Selena, goddess!'

"I look up, and there he stands with a full erection in the moonlight, and before I can object he splashes down on top of me splattering me with his wet white beard and shouting that dumb *Sayso* of his: 'Wake up and come!' And he grabs me by the underwater hair—both ends—and says insultingly, 'How long has it been for you, Selena?'

"And he actually gets it *in*," Selena says, "but I've got a weapon right within reach and it is going full blast in a moment. I turn the cold-water hose on his ass, which cools him down right away, and I slide out from under as he's turning over, in time to squirt the hose in his face, making sure he gets a mouthful of cold sulfur water. 'Good for your insides, Emil,' I say, 'Cleans you right out.'

"Then the damned old buzzard makes me feel sorry for him. He scrambles out of the tub, shaking with shame. And he says, 'Selena, don't you ever mind getting old?'

"But I'm merciless. I say, 'Go to your room, Emil.'

"He grabs a towel and whimpers pathetically. 'I'll go bang it in a dresser drawer,' he says."

Luna and Carrie smile at one another, for they know that at some later time Selena and Emil actually have become lovers, possibly after Emil has tried another approach than assault. Their smile is not lost upon Selena, who says generously, "Unlike you, Luna, I didn't immediately see the virtue of my assailant."

"Nor did I," Carrie says. And she realizes she has not yet forgiven Jack Kulish, who has thrust her up under a steering wheel when she was only seventeen. She tells them about it, probably the most commonplace form of rape, remembering that Jack, a war hero recently returned from Anzio, used to violence, was surprised, horrified, that she was a virgin. He had escorted her to a country club party, bought her a corsage, and to further betray his conventional turn of mind had assumed a conventional end to the evening, petting at the lake and maybe "going further . . ." So carried away had Jack been that he had pierced the thin membrane that can never be repaired, ignoring Carrie's protests. Then he sat bolt upright, stupefied with realization, leaving Carrie to struggle in confusion with her displaced clothing.

"He lapsed into a grinding, guilty silence, and sucked his cheeks and bit down so hard I thought blood would gush out of his mouth. And he went round behind the car and threw up, poor boy." Carrie recalls hearing, through the crickets and the frogs at the lake, the sound of his convulsive vomiting. "And I wondered what was the matter with him." For so frightened was she by the abruptness with which their physical contact had begun and ended that she couldn't give it a name and thought perhaps Jack Kulish had merely had too much to drink or had maybe bitten his tongue.

"He got back into the car, slumping before the steering wheel, shaking his head, a ghastly expression on his face. 'A virgin,' he muttered. 'I never did a thing like that before,' he said, and then he turned to me fiercely, as if I were to blame, and commanded, 'Don't ever let anybody do that to you again!'

"I didn't realize until much later that nobody ever could!" Carrie says.

The event had brought into focus Carrie's extreme ignorance of biology. Not only had it escaped her that she had been deflowered, but by coincidence her period began the next day, further intimidating her grasp of the experience. And being a teenager uninstructed in the gestation process, she wondered for a while in utter confusion if she were pregnant!

Carrie's rape had been, on the face of it, the most ordinary of the three, and yet perhaps her reaction was the strongest. For she has never learned to drive a car and still prefers any other mode of transportation. She says, "I didn't feel anything when it happened. Only the next day, I was scared to death, and apparently for years after."

That remark brings to Luna's mind her own tendency to delayed reaction. Her face goes to her hand, her bracelets jangling. She is still not sure Black Soul has actually achieved what he set out to do. He had turned into such a crybaby. She gasps, "I was trying to get pregnant today! I may not be able to tell who the father is!"

While everyone is trying to imagine the consequences of this insight, Carrie glances down at her sketch pad. She seems to have strayed somewhat from her subject. Instead of a sketch of Selena Crum, she has drawn a set of antlers with many tines.

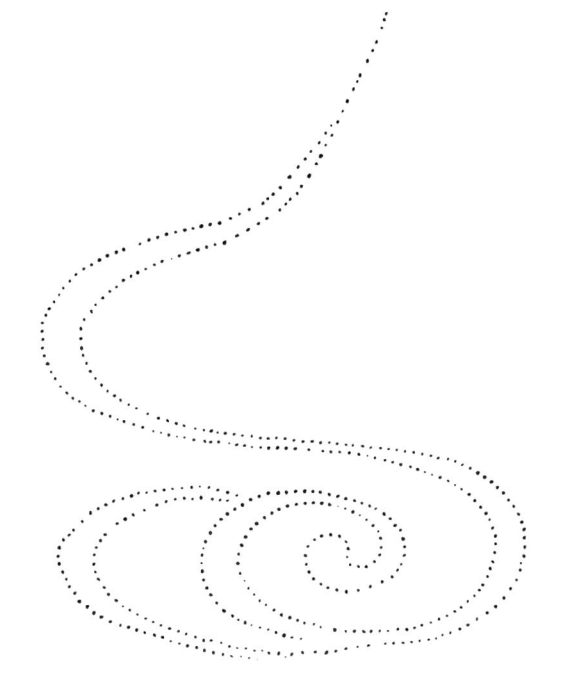

Wedding Rings

And now, the high event into which so much preparation by all of us has gone may be revealed.

It is a joyous meeting, and for that I am glad. I would not like to devote the end of my report to some of the sorrier spectacles I have witnessed lately, where the pain of longing is at times unbearable, where the young who cannot sit still and yet who long for the discipline of belief come to incense-smogged rooms to chant in a minor key, logy with the love of searching. I do not want to get into that sadness of the young, who crave to find something to believe in. I will not have to treat here their frustration, futility, their longing, longing . . . Yet can this report be complete without it? It is the very thing to which Selena has devoted her strength for many years.

Oh, yes, we guides feel it all. We are not free from that work that holds them, in windowless rooms, faces fixed upon some figure they hope will have no ego, some picture, some image, some visitor they imagine to be free of the restraints they suffer. How many I have seen at Elkhart's meeting, when he has brought his latest Eastern discovery to show them, for them to bow before, to revere, to question! ("Why do you wear sunglasses, Master? May I see your eyes, your face? May I see your feet upon the mountain? Are you God?")

They gaze earnestly into the face of the new guru; they wear ponchos from Peru, huipils from Honduras, saris from India. They bear relics, icons, thonkas, prayer beads, tokens by the thousand, in the feeble gestures humans have always made to the channel, to the path, to the hope there may be a Way, out.

If they cannot sit still, they can sit cross-legged and barefoot, for they have not had to change to the stiff clothes and the pews of their parents. They find more sincerity in the guru business than the church business, and they can move about, lift their arms, chant, sing. When I listen to them, I hear an echo from the newly converted slaves of a hundred years ago, who struggled in the rhythms of foreign sounds, foreign prophets, and who created a strangely moving religion out of a forced conversion and homesickness. Costumes then were casual too, for slaveholders do not provide church clothes. But they also cannot inhibit those plaintive, eerie chants from the heart: Oh, Jericho, oh, Jordan, oh, Shiva, oh, Shakti, oh, Krishna, Allah! Oh, Moses, oh, Shadrach, Meshach, Abednego!

Will this homesickness never end? And will we who guide these humans never bring a light clear enough to burn the longing out?

The Claremont ballroom is astir with special effects. Electricians are installing the lighting at the dais, where the Little Mother will be seated with the Three Wise Men. They will be able to provide circles of white light, which will materially represent the white-light circles attained by advanced members of the wedding, and will also symbolize the many wedding rings that will here be joined. An audio expert is setting up the sound system which will be in use throughout the evening, and which in the intervals between live music will play tapes for the wedding festivities.

Bubba Burr, rested after the afternoon ordeal, is overseeing the preparations with meditative calm. He has concluded, perhaps prematurely, that Elkhart has left town. Occasionally he calls upon one of the young new initiates of DU, cooled off from the Immersions, to run an errand to obtain some necessity. Evi is nowhere in evidence. Luna, however, is setting up her video equipment.

Bubba observes her with amused indulgence as she places her video camera at what she considers the most strategic location, next to the dais and facing the ballroom entrance. She also places a number of microphones throughout the ballroom, linking the mikes to her triple audio deck, which she will edit later on. She links the camera by cable to her Sony videotape recorder, which together with the audio deck is concealed behind the dais, and is prepared to create the tape which will (although she does not yet know it) launch her as a promising young expert in Meaningful work.

Bubba says, "You've acquired a professional air, Claire de Lune," harking back to the nickname he has given her in the Andes. He is not merely making conversation but toying with the idea of Luna's reentry into his life. For now he has more than ample indication of Evi's dyadic cooperation with Elkhart and remembers Luna's indignant refusal to be passed around at Bubba's whim. He has to concede to himself that instinctively Luna has been a step ahead of him as far as Elkhart is concerned.

He goes to her and slips his arm around her waist. "I've missed seeing you, Claire de Lune," he murmurs.

Luna extricates herself, screwing a coupling of two cable loops together. "Thanks for telling Selena I could tape your scene," she says briskly.

Bubba smiles. He has yielded to this request believing that Selena will make sure that only decorous publicity will result. He does not know that events will make decorum a near impossibility.

"You may no longer be a DU-by, Luna, but we think of you as one of us." Luna merely raises her eyebrows, adjusting her camera, and peers at him through her lens. She goes back and turns on the Record switch just as Bubba speaks again, this time right into the mike she happens to have in her hand.

He says, "Every wedding should have its family album." And Luna knows her tape is off to a good start.

Bubba, reassured by the quiet way in which the final preparations are being made, does not know that downstairs in the lobby the management is having a crisis. The Claremont did not imagine, in renting their main ballroom to the eminent psychologist, Dr. Burr, of whose organization they have never read anything unpleasant and of which they have heard only respectable reports, that the occasion would bring forth complaints from the swimming and tennis club patrons. And now, an even more unfortunate stir has begun down in front of the plate-glass doors. The hotel is being picketed, apparently by groups in opposition to Dr. Burr's convention.

Aloof on its hilltop, the Claremont has never had to take account of any of the city's radical activities. Probably its most audacious involvement was that of serving alcohol back in the days before campus repeal. Then, because it was less than a mile from the World's Greatest University, the hotel was zoned into Oakland, causing a waviness in that line Selena was cycling earlier between the two cities. Although for a time the Claremont was the fashionable place to go for an entire Bay Area of boozers, it has now reached its dowager years, and whole floors have been turned over to apartments for the aged, and its ballrooms to proms and tea dances. Its marquee offers forgotten-name bands or such enduring ragtime groups as Turk Murphy from their San Francisco base, Earthquake McGoon's.

All this was in Bubba's mind in choosing the Claremont for the Psychic Reality wedding. The hotel, he believed, was far enough removed from the usual centers of foment to be peacefully ignored except for the participants. In this, however, he has overlooked two factors. One, Berkeley demonstrators may lapse into periods of indolence but they never die, and two, the publicity-conditioned followers of ICH, having heard in the afternoon of their leader's disappearance, were confused, touchy, defiant. When the first of the Berkeley picketers appeared, half a dozen ICH members went into private caucus, unknown to Bubba, to decide upon counteractivity. The result is a profusion of sign-bearers blocking the entrance to the hotel.

The picketers who have first arrived are classic Berkeleyites, amateur protesters whose signs even betray an unevenness of intent, a confusion as to what DU and ICH are about, what the psychic reality wedding is designed to do for its participants. All they seem to know is that there is some kind of spiritual trip going on.

GOD IS A COP-OUT.
BERKELEY MEANS REVOLUTION—LOVE IT OR LEAVE IT.
LOSERS UNITE—YOU HAVE NOTHING TO WORK BUT YOUR SOULS.
REINCARNATION SUCKS.

Evi, whose fate it seems today is to be the bearer of ill-tidings, spots the pickets from her room. She has decided to stay there, maybe even throughout the wedding, at least until time to rendezvous with the elevator boy. But she decides after a glance at the pickets that they call for interpretation by Bubba, and she phones him down in the ballroom.

The ICH caucus has already taken action. They have, in fact, induced several DU members, who after all have come up through Berkeley radical politics and have not yet overcome the deep-seated tendency to proselytize, to join them in creating a counter picket line. By the time Bubba gets downstairs, he is dismayed to see that some of his very own initiates are engaged in this vulgar display.

Their signs read like this:

MEDITATION SAVES.
DON'T HATE, MEDITATE.
GIVE YOURSELF ANOTHER CHANCE: REINCARNATE.
ATLANTIS OR BUST.

Bubba takes a dismayed look at the scene. He scarcely knows where to begin. Inasmuch as many of the opposing pickets know each other, there are no firm lines drawn between them. As the basic garments, blue Levis and dresses made of Indian bedspreads, have undergone no transformation in trading radical politics for psychic reality, and as many old friends are seeing one another for the first time in some months, it is a difficult scene to disperse. Moreover, one of the Claremont patrons has called the police, who are at this moment arriving, with gas masks and pepper gas!

The cops are very like those same police who came to Luna's rescue at the marina, despite being more heavily armed, and are disinclined to disrupt a peaceable, indeed friendly display. One of the cops remarks that it looks more like a class reunion than a real demonstration. "It's as cool as Sproul Plaza these days," he tells the manager, who is not interested in this barometric reading of the campus.

It is small wonder that the Berkeley policemen have this attitude. They spend most of their days responding to eccentric calls, many of which are valid enough, and therefore they move with promptness, if an occasional lack of thoroughness. In Luna's case, for instance, they had scarcely glanced at the figure of Black Soul, or they might have recognized him. But among the many borderline cases they examine every day in this unaccountable city, they are seldom surprised, though often amused.

Even though many of the 120,000 souls may be engaged in the routine industries that occupy Middle America, such as buying, consuming, repairing, depleting and depreciating, the ones the police are called upon to observe include the many who have come there because of Berkeley's reputation for permissiveness, and so there are thousands doing a thing which is uniquely theirs—writing, photographing, tap-dancing, miming, sketching monarch butterflies, sculpting elephants out of driftwood, thieving, conning, pushing, mugging or raping. There is even a burgeoning middle class of people under thirty whose education is less than that of their parents and who are so engaged with their street life of poverty they have no time even to appreciate with more than a passing "Wow" the inventiveness of their neighbors, such as carving of yarrow stalks, learning how to Rolf, boff, Bahf, rap, meditate; to read signs, tea leaves, divining rods; to bioenergize, psychosynthesize, bonsai, or gather expertise in knives from the bowie to the samurai sword, and catalog the whole earth.

It is small wonder that the city's creative energies erupt into bizarre situations that make frequent demands upon the police force. We can imagine how much time Black Soul's whimsical pursuit of the dogged Camel alone must have cost the cops, yet such is their good humor that they enjoy his wit.

The manager of the Claremont obliges one of the policemen to get out of the police car. "My plate-glass door," he says. He has only recently installed it, and if the cops can't disperse the scruffy crowd, they can at least protect the door.

Luna has followed Bubba downstairs with her porta-pack camera, and just as he begins to mingle with the pickets, whispering to those he knows to be members of DU, she focuses upon him. Later her narration will describe his years as a campus activist, which led him to the Path of New Beings, some of whom are beginning to arrive in time for Luna to show flash examples of them on her tape.

Bubba is making an appeal to the conscience of DU members when an incident occurs that affects many pickets in their future lives.

Tsinghai Yana makes his arrival and is obliged to cross the picket line.

Tsinghai is not entirely sober. His enemies (even a silent monk has enemies) are inclined to say that his vow of silence has been taken because he is incapable of speaking a sober word. His defenders (among whom there are many) are quick to point out that his order is a drinking order who finds lucidity in the Wine of Life, and that in the days when he did speak, the words, however slurred, flowed like liquid gold. The gold of his silence is more solid (say his enemies, with satirical reference to the offerings he demands from his followers). Whatever the truth of the matter, Tsinghai Yana has never given any explanation for his vow.

He is carrying a brown paper bag, handed out of his car to him by the chauffeur. It contains a white porcelain cup and a bottle of Black Velvet. Approaching the hotel door, he takes small careful steps in his Oriental slippers.

A picketer comes up to him waving his sign at him in a threatening manner. Tsinghai Yana, who has never shunned a communication despite his silence, pauses and peers at the sign in an effort to read it.

It says: NEW BEINGS BALL.

The picketer waves the sign around as if he doesn't want Tsinghai to read it. He says, "Don't go in there, they'll make a monk-ee out of you!" He laughs uproariously and nudges his neighbor. Tsinghai Yana titters a silent appreciation of this wit, however hostile.

Bubba Burr catches sight of the monk and rushes to his side, taking him by the elbow.

"Speak, damn you!" screams the young man with the sign rudely.

"It's Tsinghai the Silent!" cries another member of the crowd. His identity is quickly taken in, and he and Bubba are surrounded.

"Come on, let's hear it from you. Is it true you're drunk? Are you the Atavar? Can you sing high C?" These and other typically astute Berkeley questions are thrown at him ruthlessly. Bubba tries to take the brown paper bag from him to keep the crowd from detecting what is in it, but the gesture is a giveaway, particularly as Tsinghai hangs on. "He *is* drunk! Look at him." Tsinghai bows his head and seems to reflect. Then he lifts his head and a light bursts upon his face. He smiles with an inspired friendliness, and before anyone can react, he disappears behind the plate-glass door, in a sudden spirited move. The crowd is stopped by the cop guarding the doors.

"Magic! Did you see that? He got away from us by magic!" people in the crowd mutter. But others protest, "No, he just took us by surprise. He's just a jerk-off capitalistic monk." Bubba sighs and follows him inside. His experience with Tsinghai Yana leads him to suspect that Tsinghai will reappear to communicate further with the crowd if he possibly can. Bubba intends to try to persuade him not to go back outside.

Luna has meanwhile taped the entire encounter. Now she returns to the ballroom.

The sound system has started as the guests begin to appear and is playing strains of *The Barber of Seville*. Luna wonders who could have chosen that. Anyhow, she tapes it onto her audio reel as the invited New Beings enter the ballroom.

A number of Uninvited Beings are hovering outside the door to watch the arrival of the sages and the Little Mother. The sages pass through one by one, each arriving rather like a premier star, despite the absence of the usual trappings of publicity. Teenage girls, some of whom have been outside among the pickets, some whose parents are Pool and Tennis Club members, have been drawn during the afternoon Immersions to learn more. Emil Jewels has his own following, and some curiosity-seekers have simply come for a glimpse of him, as one would think of taking a look, say, at any fabled prince who happened to be passing your dining room or country club.

Emil Jewels passes into the ballroom before Luna's lens. His alert, active body is covered with a flowing caftan, the color of his aura, pale green. He dances lightly to the Rossini, which causes the person on the tape deck to become aware of the music and to silence it. Something more sober and processional takes its place.

Emil sits down and folds his caftan about him with mock dignity. He is soon followed by Bubba Burr, escorting (propping up, some say) Tsinghai Yana, whom he has overtaken in the hallway. Bubba carefully places Tsinghai in his white robes on his cushion in the lotus position and refills his porcelain cup for him from the brown paper bag.

Next comes Ali Pshaw. He is very erect and is the only member of the wedding to wear an ordinary English-cut business suit. He has declined to commit himself to an auric color, and a debate about the meaning of this is beginning to rage in one corner among members of ICH. A shunner of panoply, Ali Pshaw has been the most difficult of the sages to persuade to participate in the event. He has finally been convinced of its suitability by Bubba's promise that everyone who attends must purchase all twenty of his books. A member of DU is exacting payment for the books before the invited guests may enter. Ali Pshaw believes that perhaps the most important contribution he can make to higher consciousness is the dissemination of secrets, and his books are his way of doing it.

Excitement of the onlookers rises in pitch as Mamacita approaches the ballroom door, followed by the entourage of her Sisterhood. An inquisitive murmur goes through the crowd.

The Little Mother is alight, just as she frequently was in the Andes, with her halo. This afternoon her fatigue has been so great she has not made the halo visible, but now as she proceeds down the hotel hallway and pauses at the entrance, the golden glow above her head may be seen by all, above her robes of auric blue.

Luna, having photographed the three Wise Men on the dais awaiting Mamacita, turns her camera to the doorway, just in time to see Mamacita stop alertly. She looks directly into the eyes of a teenage girl who is lounging at the entranceway.

Were we to see with the eyes of the Little Mother, we might understand what auric light emanating from that girl in particular has given her pause. Her quick glance darts about her at several other girls, but she comes back to this one, who wears a Guatemalan shirt over Levis and who, taller than the rest, is easing a hand up to a gold snake bracelet and detaching it from her upper arm.

The Little Mother speaks to the girl distinctly in Spanish: *"No me molestas, hija"* (Don't you touch me, baby), but before the words are out completely, the entire ballroom is swarming with alarm. People are climbing upon one another's shoulders to see. Luna has fortunately gotten very close and is rolling her videotape, as two of the Little Mother's Sisters quickly disarm the teenage girl with a HoHo neck pinch, so that she lies in what is apparently a lifeless heap on the ballroom floor.

Linked in her snake bracelet on the floor is the Little Mother's golden halo. And it appears to be a battery-operated neon hoop, lying there being flashed upon by Luna and a photographer from the Berkeley *Gazette*, who is that moment arriving with the reporter Ms. Barnes. The Sisters encircle the teenager, nudging Luna and the photographer away.

The Little Mother, smiling as if nothing has happened, enters the ballroom without the circle of light above her head. There is a radiance to her being, however, as she takes the seat assigned to her at the center of the dais. She sits, whispering to one of the Sisters, who bends over her, and who sends a signal to another Sister at the ballroom door. Instantly, the lights throughout the room are extinguished.

The guests whisper in expectancy and apprehension. Then Mamacita's unmistakable voice sounds through the amplifying system. A soft, lovely voice full of mystery and love speaks, saying the word "miracle" in Spanish so that the sound itself takes on a light and spreads a glow: "Mir-a-glo," says her voice, "mir-a-glo . . ." A pause, and then one of the Sisters offers an interpretation of this one-word koan, transmitted to the Sister by thought transference.

Everyone gathered there, she says, is persuaded by miracles. She is happy because now the occasion has arisen for Mamacita to perform a miracle. She does it not in the spirit of offering proof of her divine power, for that is never good reason for using power, but because she wishes to teach, has come out of her Andean home for that single purpose.

Then in the void of that quiet room, in the hushed darkness, there appears in the place just above the Little Mother's head, a golden glow, unattached so far as anyone can see to any part of the known physical world. The Little Mother has grown another halo.

The halo's light spreads downward gently, creating its miraculous glow, lighting the benign face of Mamacita. Slowly the lights in the ballroom rise again, to reveal the company. Many faces are streaming with tears. Many fall to their knees before the dais. The teenage girl, upheld by two sisters, stands just in front of Mamacita, holding both her snake bracelet and the halo, two rings. She bows her head and is sobbing uncontrollably. She falls at Mamacita's feet. Her voice babbles her incoherent thoughts.

The rest of the company in the ballroom go to their knees or further prostrate themselves, depending on their stage of development. A murmur of her name spreads and rises through the room: "Mamacita, Mamacita," like a mantra.

The chant goes on and on, reminiscent to Bubba of those days in the Andes when they surrendered themselves to tape loops: "Mother marry mother marry mother marry . . ."

Tsinghai Yana at that moment commits another miracle. He levitates from his lotus posture, floats to the feet of Mamacita and without apparently settling to the floor, bends to kiss the hem of her chiffon garment and the nail of her large toe. He silently floats back to his own cushion and lifts his porcelain cup.

The chanting of the crowd now changes, swelling into a great, resonating OM. Emil Jewels rises to his feet. He holds his hands over the Little Mother's halo and says: "This is the ring by which we all are wed, in eternal marriage. Though we may break the circle, we may never undo it."

And at that rather long-ish *Sayso* the wedding party leaps up; music, joyous music, spreads through the ballroom, and the wedding dance begins.

Scarcely anyone present remains in a neuter state, Bubba observes. Everyone is Plussed out, up and over, even those who have had no DU training; even overly commercialized ICH members have seen the Halo's inner light and are in a deeper state of Plus than Elkhart has ever led them to.

Luna takes the arm of the teenage girl (who, lacking a tissue, is wiping her tears on her Levi pants), guides her to one side of the room. The girl, still dazed, is unaware at first that Luna's camera is focused upon her, nor would it matter, so lost in insight is she.

"What is your name?" asks Luna gently.

"Duzy Maccoby," she says dazedly. "I've never—never—"

"Would you mind describing the halo for me?"

"It was light. Very lightweight." She clears her throat and tries to pull herself together, realizing she is speaking into a microphone. She smooths her shoulder-length hair and picks a thread from her Guatemalan blouse. "It yielded after a slight jog and slipped from the back of Mamacita's neck as if it were attached by some hook."

"Ms. Maccoby, did you see a hook?" asks Luna.

"No, I don't believe there *was* any hook now, after what we've seen. Don't you know, it's a miracle!"

"Do you think some sort of mass spell may be happening here?" Luna inquires. "Hypnosis?"

Duzy Maccoby shakes her head emphatically. "I don't, no! I think it's a simple miracle. I've never seen anything like this."

"But why the neon effect?" Luna persists.

"Well, you know in underdeveloped countries they have a fascination for American technology, gimmicks. Oh, you mustn't use that. I mean I don't want it interpreted as an ethnic slur upon the Divine Mother."

"Thank you, Ms. Maccoby," Luna says and moves on, turning her camera now upon the ecstatic dance taking place among all the wedding members.

However, the golden moment of miracles is not over. The two Sisters who have been guarding (so it seems) the young woman named Duzy Maccoby now lead her again to the dais. Before the feet of Mamacita there is a large cushion with an indentation in its center. Duzy suddenly sees what she is meant to do.

She bends and releases the golden snake bracelet onto the cushion, also surrendering the damaged halo. Tsinghai Yana lifts his hands to his lips and bows deeply to the cushion. That is like a signal.

Tibetans, like the Inca, hold gold sacred. The witnesses come forward then, moving in their dance one by one past the platform, to place upon the cushion whatever gold they have brought with them next to the bracelet and the damaged halo. There is a musical clink as necklaces, bracelets, anklets, and many rings, some of them wedding rings, fall upon the pillow, gold ringing upon gold. One man, a physician who owns a world-famous collection of Dutch gold pieces from a single minting discovered in an eighteenth-century wreck off the Scilly Isles, takes a handful of these coins which he has made into medallions and places them among the glowing heap.

The reporter from the Berkeley *Gazette*, Ms. Barnes, undergoes an overwhelming transformation. The girl, who has come there wearing orange (an auric color she has been told is most undesirable), suddenly turns to the photographer, grabs his camera and smashes it on the ballroom floor, whereupon the photographer leaves in disgust, and Ms. Barnes falls at the feet of Mamacita murmuring: "This is it, this is it, this is it!" over and over, as if she has received by Multiplex Transmission her very own Murma. She tears from her neck a gold necklace she purchased in Greece for a whole month's salary and flings it on the pillow.

The crowd, freed of its metal encumbrances, becomes even more light-footed. Joy thrusts dancers up into the tenderest Plus-plus places, where one must move carefully if at all.

Ali Pshaw has been speaking to the DU collector of funds from his books and has received from her a rather large metal strongbox containing the take. He now holds a whispered conference with one of the Sisters. In a swift yet delicate movement, he gathers the collection of gold, holding the pillow, together with his strongbox, against his chest, and walks with dignity out of the ballroom.

So Plussed out is Bubba Burr that he does not notice this inconspicuous departure. This is something of a misfortune, for he might have accompanied him. Ali Pshaw is heading straight to the hotel manager, whom he momentarily disengages from fretting over the demonstrators at the hotel door, and asks to be taken to the hotel vault. In his confusion, the manager asks, "Do you want the package now?" Ali Pshaw, sensing a secret, merely nods, murmuring that he also wishes to leave some other valuables in the vault. He therefore exchanges the gold and his royalties for the drawings of the Hog, after carefully exacting a signed receipt for his own treasure, and disappears into the elevator with the secrets of Strong Elkhart.

Bubba, for all the work and expectation he has placed in the evening, and despite his disappointing setback with Elkhart that afternoon, is beyond delight. He could not have foreseen the good fortune that miracles would occur, and in fact, living as he does in a world of omens, he has expected the worst. Never before has he seen so many people—many of whom never before left a simple neuter state—in a state of Plus-plus.

As the guests mingle, Bubba distinguishes many old friends; everyone seems familiar, of the same family, in fact. Carrie and Harrison arrive and begin to speak with Luna and Selena. Then it is that Bubba has his Depth Insight.

The three women are One! he tells himself. Come together there to show him female completion in three stages. He remembers the insights of his Fix with Elkhart in the Andes, in which he conceived the true dialectic with the divine and its ensuing celebration of the emergence of the Female Principle in Man. And here it is manifested! Luna has come to show all that she, Woman, can accomplish, no matter how many lifetimes it may take. Bubba sees that he will now write a book expounding this original conception of his, that Womanhood will bring Humanhood to the future!

Bubba, Plussed out of his mind, peaks higher than he ever has in his entire life.

Here I must allude to my own difficulties again. I have been moving in the wedding structure cautiously because there is so much going on, such active imaginings, so many open souls that any spirit guide may be in danger of falling permanently into one of them and getting locked up in its eventual closure. This may have just occurred with Ms. Barnes, in fact; she could have taken some lost guide into captivity. I must maintain some distance, and so it is somewhat a relief to me to follow Harrison's mind as the thought of escaping the wedding crosses it.

Emil Jewels has just descended from the dais and asked Selena Crum to dance. They comment on the dance of life itself, and Emil says to Selena that one of his favorite Zen masters has said, "It would be too cruel not to dance with them," and he and Selena waltz away. Harrison takes Carrie by the elbow and pulls her to the ballroom door.

I follow them in some relief. But I know I shall not be able to stay with them for long, because two things occur just as we are leaving.

Tsinghai Yana rises from his lotus posture and walks carefully out of the ballroom door, heading for the plate-glass doors in front where demonstrators still are chatting together.

And another figure slinks into the ballroom, catching sight of Luna behind her video camera. She focuses the lens on his face before he can lift his arm to hide it. It is the man who has cause to hide his face from public record, Black Soul. Luna rushes up to him pleasantly, taking his hands, saying, "Soul! Now I can keep my promise to teach you DeFixing. Sit down cross-leggged right here. Go on!" My parting glimpse is of Luna sitting in the middle of the ballroom floor linking little fingers with the man who has raped her that afternoon and whom she now calls only "Soul," as if to emphasize the likeness she sees between them.

Harrison has not been able to relate to Psychic Reality at all, but on his way into the Claremont he has noticed on the marquee that an old favorite of his, Turk Murphy of Earthquake McGoon's and his ragtime band, are playing in another part of the hotel. He tells Carrie about it, who in her way is not making it at the wedding either. Like many sensitives, Carrie, as we've seen, is easily overstimulated, by a glance at a rock with ladybugs on it, for example, and cannot readily tolerate so much input as is available in this excited scene. She leaves with Harrison, nodding to Selena. Selena has danced off with Emil Jewels, who will soon have to call an ambulance for Selena to deliver her, too late (or just on schedule, depending on your point of view), to Alpha-Omega Hospital; she waves goodbye to them knowing they have to escape this—to Harrison—farce, and find their own way. She waves farewell to them.

"I used to go and dance at Earthquake McGoon's in the fifties, Turk Murphy's heyday," Harrison tells Carrie as they are seated by a window. "When the Saints Go Marching In" is playing in fox-trot rhythm, while in another part of the hotel the saints of ICH and DU march to their different drum.

Behind Harrison, Carrie has a full view of the bay. She can see the bridge and part of the freeway with its gently moving flow of night traffic lights. She can also see on the dance floor one couple in particular, who look as if they fell early under the spell of the Duke and Duchess of Windsor. Harrison remarks upon their similarity as they fox-trot past their table. They wear clothes of the thirties, the woman in tiny 4B white pumps, with a swirling crepe de Chine skirt; the man is in a white linen suit and spectator shoes, which he skillfully glides in between the tiptoe pumps of his lady. Harrison is oddly touched by them, yet he is unreconciled to the tug at his emotions.

His afternoon with the men from Detroit has been a frustration, and he has begun to doubt that he can bring off his plan. He now thinks that the industrialists may simply buy him up and shelve his additive. It has been done to others. He sighs, clasps his hands on the table, orders a drink for himself and one for Carrie. Harrison doesn't like to drink.

Carrie is staring now at the San Francisco Bay Bridge in astonishment and growing understanding, appreciation, wonder. Unexpectedly she has entered another *nick*.

She reaches out and touches Harrison's folded hands, lets one of her own lie there, while her gaze seems to draw the bridge closer to her.

Her gesture is like a signal to Harrison, and he cannot help himself. He opens his hands, cups her small one in them and looks at it helplessly. He loves her.

Carrie, still fixed on the bridge, murmurs something Harrison doesn't understand. Even if it had been loud enough its meaning could not have gone through the tumult of his emotion—he is at once engaged in a renewal of his resistance to her. *He*, hermit, farmer, crazed inventor—how could he have been pulled down here by that madwoman Selena Crum, to find himself taken up with the size and force of a small woman's hand? Did it signal a loss of grip of his own, that he should want the support of such a hand? And what on earth could he do about it? Take her up to his farm and ask her to grow vegetables? She has her own gardener and no apparent inclination to leave this inexplicable territory she lives in. And if she did, would she bring that incomparable mess she works with, surpassed in the space it consumes only by his own laboratory? Would he have to clear out one of his own rooms for her? Sacrifice some of his machinery? Oh it was all too damned much trouble! (Here he puts down her hand, runs his own through his hair and stares at the Duke and Duchess of Windsor. The Duke sacrificed a kingdom for the woman he loved. The Duchess—had she come equipped with paints, clay, easels, cats, daughters? Harrison hasn't even met Carrie's daughters!) He begins to sweat. It is really a lot for him to bear. And then he looks at her and sees that she must be having one of her peculiar spells! What *was* she staring at?

He focuses on her hand again. Should he close up his farm, his own laboratory, bring his current projects down here, set up in a loft, bring his work to this poisoned edge of earthquake country? Here Turk Murphy breaks into a shrill trumpet solo of "The Saints," for the sake of all who will perish when the San Andreas Fault gives way again. Should he sacrifice clean air, his own little kingdom for the sake of a Woman? Would she even consider coming up to Calistoga Hot Springs? It wasn't any Bermuda. And besides, he would probably have to do the cooking! She has given him two meals now, and they were disasters. Harrison is a good cook. He doesn't like her style at all—a kind of Berkeley Creole, everything overseasoned. It was too much!

Turk Murphy lets out a vocal chorus: "Oh, Lord, I want to be in that number . . ."

Carrie's hands, both of them now, are gripping Harrison's, but she is still not looking at him, being rapt, seemingly, in what may be going on outside the window.

What Carrie is seeing will astound and involve beyond extrication Harrison's will and imagination. She says, "Oh, Harrison, they're backed up at every freeway exit and entrance for miles."

Her words stun him. He can only stare at her.

"They've been stopped on the freeways for more than an hour. People are beginning to get out and walk home."

They are holding one another's hands, looking at one another. Harrison doesn't know what to say. It is as if someone, *she*, has looked inside his mind. He has never written down his Master Plan, and so she would have to be seeing his own vision, or the fulfillment of it, there outside the window, where the lights are glittering on the bridge and traffic to his eye flicks along at its steady pace.

"Harrison," Carrie says solemnly, "I see now why you were insisting everybody put the additive in their cars and start using it all on the same day."

"What are you seeing?"

She shakes her head. "You are crazier than *I* am."

"Don't romanticize me," he says. "What are you seeing?"

She tells him that she is seeing cars backed up outside the Claremont half a mile from a freeway entrance, drivers getting out, questioning one another, and that she knows it is because of his additive, that the "kink" he has been working on is a slow erosive factor that will gradually but completely destroy the engine of every car in America, though there may be enough unadded-to fuel left to haul them all away eventually to be pressed into junk for making some new form of transportation. And as she is explaining these insights to him, she recollects her own aversion to the automobile and its stemming from that personal encounter back in her adolescence, that rape and humiliation, which makes Harrison all the more appealing to her in his dramatic and impossible scheme. It does not matter to either of them now that Harrison's plan may come short of its fantastic vision, for they are both sunk in that special wonder that pair-bonding tends to create in humans.

Carrie says, "Come on, Harrison, come home with me." And that is all they say about the immense churning going on inside them, and they leave their drinks and walk out into the night, where Carrie tells him she sees automobile drivers backed up from a nearby freeway exit calling upon the policemen parked by the pickets, drivers who are trying to get the police to leave the pickets and come down and get things moving again. All this Harrison does not see, of course, but now he believes she does. And Carrie, under the inspiration of her nick, is understanding that at a time when many are giving up on the world, she is fortunate to enjoy her peculiarity, these nicks of time, and that even if they are nothing more than messages to herself she can in no way miss the meaning of this one for her, that things may yet be mended, and through the only way humanly possible, by love, and that love must by definition involve a measure of sacrifice, however irritating, demanding, enraging the sacrifice may be on a personal level, and that she is fortunate, yes, to have someone like crazy Harrison to make that sacrifice *with*, she understands, not *for*, because what one gives up for the sake of intimacy and continuity, *two* also give up, surrender together, in imitation of and tribute to that which is most lacking there on the fragmented earth.

And I am not yet able to disclose whether in Carrie and Harrison we have the combined force needed for the uncompromising reconstruction they both envisage, for the true marriage of art and technology foreseen early in the day by Jim Smith, even though Harrison's is the kind of adaptive imagination needed by those who think the human race is salvageable. With her record of failure and divorce, her shortness of temper, her perfectionism, even though springing from devotion to art, or indeed with Harrison's shortcomings, his querulousness, his incapacity to survive in the city, his temperamental gloom, we have a considerable human factor weighing against total success. We may as well, however, decide with a certain arbitrary élan to place our confidence in them. After all, no one knows better than I that they are subject to proper guidance.

And now they are about to enter through the gate leading to Carrie's garden, where Harrison has stashed his pile of machinery, where he will pause to explain further details to her, and where they will finally yield to the readiness of their bodies to get undressed and get as close together as is humanly possible in order to find out the exact details of the trouble they have decided to take on in one another.

We may also leave them there at the garden gate, not needing to follow them into Carrie's house, which is an old brown shingle, or into her bedroom, where she has windows with small Tudor frames, which when it rains make bell-like sounds of differing ranges, where it is most pleasant *not* to lie alone, in spite of her long defense of it, and where when it is not raining two can as easily as one look out those tiny frames and glimpse the uncertain stars of the Western sky and the vast Sapphic spaces of night after the moon is down. But we already know, thanks to Luna and many male and female novelists who have more than adequately explored the subject, that sex is the easiest part of the human problem, and so I will end this part of my task without following Harrison and Carrie inside.

We now return to the Psychic Reality wedding. I am braced by the knowledge that Harrison and Carrie are mending the badly damaged etheric plane, and so I now can cooperate with the completion of the events at the Claremont Hotel.

During the Immersions ceremony that afternoon, Tsinghai Yana has noticed a pile of firewood near the swimming pool. Carrying a small blanket, he goes through the hotel door and strolls unattended toward that pile of wood. He gathers a sizeable load of it and ties it in his blanket. Then he carefully pads back to the front of the hotel and to the crowd of demonstrators with whom he intends to make communication.

Tsinghai Yana in his lifetime of silence has studied practically every known means of communication other than the verbal. Because he knows the Berkeley demonstrators are so various and, at this moment, distractable, he has decided against the mode of thought transfer. He believes he can reach all of them at one moment in a more appealing, though perhaps a bit showy, manner. Berkeley demonstrators are always favorably in tune with any Third World sign, and he believes someone among them will know how to read smoke signals. He himself has learned them from a Paiute chief at Pyramid Lake, Nevada, where Elkhart took him on a mistaken hunch about the origin of his own pyramid.

I cannot linger at the moment over Tsinghai Yana because of the immense psychic tug up in the ballroom, where Luna is engaged in DeFixing Black Soul. She has left him momentarily in his sitting posture, drawn irresistibly to the desire to put him on tape as he goes into a primary DeFix, for such a lesson has never, so far as she knows, been taped before. She starts her camera rolling.

And when Black Soul tunes in, my entire project of reporting this high event goes under threat in a most surprising way. As I have often said, we guides do not know everything, and the unexpected overtakes me here.

Black Soul is quick to learn, but being the black soul that he is, having led such a life of paranoia and pain, he can tune in only to a Minus state, which Luna has had little experience with. He begins to grin diabolically, like one possessed. And he attacks her, fortunately only verbally.

"You fuckin bitch," he says. "You puttin this on tape. Miz Whitey's tokenism, thas what this is!" With a glance around the room, confirming he is the only black guest, he lapses into his exaggerated soul dialect. "You gots to get some skin onto yo flick, you honky."

Luna, greatly disturbed, says, "I'll turn the camera off, Soul. I don't want to hurt you."

Black Soul is not easily pacified in this state. "Miz Whitey think she got me by the balls. She think if she report some tough talk, some revolutionary jive about how black folk goan take over an how we already got a footholt in in*dus*try and is on our ways up, then she's got us socked into the Amerikan scene." Black Soul clearly has no concept of Luna's tape. The sight of the camera has simply caused all of his social consciousness to surface in a deluge. "You cunt, you jes cut dis man outa yo tape. If I could run the Reynolds Tobacco Company out of this ole town, what you think I goan do to some white trash stickin me in a videotape?"

Luna is greatly disturbed but still believes she can handle him, after her success earlier in the day. She maintains her cool. "Can't we work this thing out?"

"Go suck. You think now you goan show the folks a real-life brutalized creep, doan you? But you doan know the half of it, baby. I had that paper shoved at me in Vacaville a dozen times to give them a release to stick me in the brain, an I shoved it back an told them what to do with it. But I tell you, even if you showed them gougin an stickin them wires in my head, givin their psychosurgery to somebody like me, dat ain enough. I doan wanna be part of this crappy tape."

"I don't want to give you a lobotomy, Black Soul," she says. "I want to keep you interesting."

"See dere, thas what I mean—ethos! Thas all you care about. *Use* the ethos of us folks."

"What *do* you want, Black Soul?" she begs earnestly. "Tell me, I'll try to give it to you."

"Give, bullcrap. It's too late for brotherhood, it's too late for tokenism, baby, it's too late for reconciliation, too late even for the Weathermen. So take all this jive and shove it. It's just too late!"

Now Black Soul, whom we already know as a cryer, is beginning to sob. Luna cries too. They are sitting on the ballroom floor and the tears come down.

"Jesus, Black Soul," she says, "can't we do *something*? You're strong. So am I." Here she suffers a momentary lapse into DU jargon. "Can't we take some Prodigious Leap over it all?"

Still sobbing, he says, "Oh, Luna lady, it's too late. I ain goan on no Dharma path. I ain part of no Psychic Reality weddin. Doan you know when you bring me here among all these white chicks, doan you *know* what'll happen?"

Luna is crying more now. "I thought we could try it and see, Soul," she says, forgetting, as she has before, the Black, which makes him grimace, a faceful of double, triple messages, a face distorted by surges, layers of resentment, gratitude, love, rage. "Jesus, is there no way for you to get on top of this heap of emotion?" she cries.

"I'll jes start grabbin ass. I hadda pass some cops at the hotel door. You know I'll get stuck back in the joint."

"I *don't* know that. Listen. The Fix I want to teach you is magic, like arrows from the blue, weaponry from the beyond." Here she is making a somewhat sneak appeal to his criminal mind. "What have you got to lose?"

"My *brain*, lady. This time they'll stick it to me. What chance has a lifer against the kind of pressure they can bring to bear?"

"You're going to get caught anyway if you keep on the way you've been going, making out at the marina in broad open daylight."

Luna is still holding Black Soul by the fingertips. At this moment, he grips her fingers more tightly, suddenly struck by her term, "weaponry from the beyond." He looks a bit more deeply into his situation than he has before, gazes out as over a sea of footlights, in *my* direction. He peers, squinting a bit as if in a glare.

"She-*it*!" he declares slowly, looking straight through Luna's physical body. "You ain nothin but—"

"That's right, Black Soul," I say, coming through to him.

"She-*it*!" He shakes his head, obliged at the same time to leap mentally from an involuntary atavistic awe to the contempt he voices. "If dat doan fuck-all."

"Go on, Black Soul, say it. I ain nothin but—"

"You ain nothin but—" He stops again, lets go of Luna's hands and slaps his thighs Sambo-fashion.

"Is that Philomen?" Luna asks, unable to see me herself.

"A ghost!" I say.

But Black Soul recovers his sense of humor. "A ghost-*writer*, you mean!" he cries. "Ripped off by a cheap two-bit ghost-writer. Dat do beat all!"

Then an even fuller understanding of himself and his seeing potential reaches him, and he swings in an awesome balance. He knows that having seen through Luna, then into the beyond she has been trying to ask him to consider, that he now has a choice. He can come closer and maybe see through *me*, even fall into whatever lies behind me and escape the fate he is so strongly protesting. He can decide to consider the meaning of creation itself, and the nature of reality, to come closer to me yet and suffer the terror of such questions as have plagued philosophers on both sides of time forever. I make all that available to him in a flash. He could choose to place himself completely beyond those racial temporalities of the body politic which prey upon him, which indeed form the shape and utility of his days. Or he can—and instantly he conceives it, he is anxiously *doing* it—scramble back, thrust his mind down into the ballroom at the Claremont. He hangs onto Luna, trembling. "Luna, what kinda Fix you gimmie? This is too far out!"

Luna, realizing that she needs help, grips his shoulder. "I'll get a more experienced teacher, Soul. Hang on in there."

She rushes over to Selena, pulling her away from Emil Jewels, and brings her to Black Soul. Selena knows at once what to do. She places both her hands upon Black Soul's brow, to pull him out of the Minus state he is in. "We need to find a simple neuter," she says. "You went a bit too far."

But again, life is never completely in our control. Black Soul is simply not yet ready for neuter. One day he will be, but of that later. At the moment he is capable only of the Minus states, and unfortunately he slips into an XX-Minus, the state known almost exclusively to such people as are possessed by demons. And at that moment, as fortune would have it, Strong Elkhart enters the ballroom door and in a booming voice demands, "Where are my plans? Who here has them?"

And no sooner are the words out than, on that XX-Minus plane, where only he and Black Soul can perceive things, the plans are materialized.

It happens this way. Having looked the plans over very carefully in his room, Ali Pshaw believes that he has been duped by Bubba Burr into taking part in a grotesque publicity stunt, and having complete command of all known states, Plus and Minus, and being as competent at mind tricks as any Hindu guru, he is aware of what may possibly take place between Black Soul and Elkhart and makes a quick decision to enable that realm of possibility. The plans appear under Black Soul's eyes, as if on a table before him. Since he and Elkhart are alone together in an XX-Minus state, they feel themselves to be completely apart, not in the ballroom but rather in a private cell-like room, the plans spread out on a table.

Since the Immersions, Elkhart's volatile mind has gone through another change. As we know, seeking has been his work for many years and has been so compelling to him that he has created his pyramid structure. However, seeking is one thing; finding apparently is quite another. He had never in his search imagined so overwhelming a find as the being his teacher has become that afternoon. He is now struggling to regain his balance, lost for a time after the appearance of that dazzling being. He knows he was not "born again," that the Immersions were merely a tactical play (however sincere he felt at the time), that he must retrench and gather together his ICH strength, beginning first with the recovery of his plans.

And that decision made, here was his first Recruitment Officer, together with the plans! What better omen could be given him that he is on the right path. He had imagined before that the Recruitment Officers would logically be sent him from already existent colleagues of the CIA. But as he learned this afternoon, logic is not a concern of the One who moves in mysterious ways. And Elkhart himself has accordingly abandoned it altogether.

"I have been expecting you," he says to Black Soul in a choked voice.

Black Soul is convinced that he has been transported into this small dark room to be confronted with a plainclothesman. He says grimly, "Yeah. Well, now what?"

"Now we can begin!"

The anticipatory delight in Elkhart's voice confirms the worst for Black Soul. This tall white man lifts a pen and starts pointing with it, pointing to what Black Soul construes to be the most elaborate release for brain surgery he has ever seen.

"What you want me to do?" He cringes from examining the papers.

"Just share this great experience with me," Elkhart says in a near whisper. "At last, after my long wait, someone to share the greatest adventure of the mind that man has yet conceived."

This is a new approach to Black Soul. Prison authorities have never before tried persuading him with such inflated rhetoric. It's insulting. It grates. He wants to hit this wild-eyed man. But the old woman Luna has gone for, Selena, restrains him. Her touch reminds him of the cost of resisting arrest. He cringes away from the pen, still in Selena's grip. "I ain goan do it," he tells Elkhart.

Now the fact that Black Soul is aware of Selena, however mistakenly, is a sign that he is somewhat divided, is being persuaded away by her touch from the XX-Minus state where Elkhart lives.

Elkhart points with the pen, making little stabbing gestures at his plans. "But you *must* do it," he says. "You are Chosen. There are hundreds like you. I am waiting for the others to appear. It was given!" He lapses into the language of the prophets.

He has not counted on any reluctance in Recruitment Officers, for he has believed that Bielbog would have fully indoctrinated them. "It was promised," he says, "hundreds will flock to me, hundreds to select, to bring forth the volunteers for the Hog."

Black Soul's brain is throbbing now; he twists under Selena's touch, wanting to flee. Yet something in her fingertips prevents him from moving. He feels magnetized by her. Something vibrates from her into his nervous system, creating confusion. "No," he groans, "I ain no volunteer."

Elkhart looks at him closely, nodding with fresh insight. In his own neuter state, Elkhart would have seen his own error at once and Black Soul himself would be an immediate candidate for the Hog, not a Recruitment Officer. Yet something about Black Soul's accent is a persuasive factor. Elkhart looks at the list of desert locations and points again. "The Kalahari, of course!" he cries. "That would be *your* installation. The African officer would naturally have a wide range of dialects at his disposal." He laughs, a diabolical roll in imitation of his desert mentor. "Ingenious! Bielbog has thought of everything!" He points now to the picture of the helicopter labeled SOLV, Ship of Last Voyage. "Think of it, this ship—it will transport our volunteers in twenty-ton weights. It will enable our metapyramid to be an unimaginable success."

Black Soul looks now at the SOLV drawing and imagines himself being transported along with other lobotomized prisoners, transported by helicopter, thousands of them. Hadn't this man said so? Taken to Africa. He always knew somebody would find a way to send the black man back to Africa, and this is it, a fiendish slave trade to—Great God Amighty—build a pyramid! This scheme was worse than his most terrible fantasies, to think that prison authorities had designated this man sitting with him, pen in hand, to become a new Pharaoh, to undertake a pyramid built with the sweat of victims he is enrolling as so-called volunteers from prison yards around the world and transporting them in this hideous giant helicopter called the SOLV. It was worse than he had ever dreamed. And worse yet, Black Soul can see that he himself has chosen it by falling back—no, creeping back—into the Claremont ballroom. He has surrendered his chance, he thinks, to get out, to let go of it—how well he remembers now the glimpse of me, the space beyond. He could have gotten out altogether, explored those now vastly lovely and appealing ranges on this side of time, but fear has driven him back to find this monstrous plan, in which he and all other such victims would be returned to the most abject and grisly slavery ever devised, worse than in the ancestral Pharaoh's day.

Black Soul, having been brought back partly into his own normal state and out of XX-Minus by Selena's touch, now looks about him in utter disorientation. He rises from the ballroom floor, or from the prison room chair, from both, and casts about him a look of helpless confusion.

"Let me outta here!" he cries.

This violent reaction in his Recruitment Officer unsettles Elkhart, who rises and makes an appeal to his aide. "Don't leave me!" His voice quivers with alarm.

In this moment of tension, I understand something about these two men. Here Black Soul stands with Elkhart, engaged in a debate nobody can win. Both of them want to commit a heroic act and can find no earthly way to do it. The greatest act of heroism Black Soul has ever found is to deface advertising posters, and his support is being demanded by a man crazed by the confusion of money and spiritual power, whose basis for heroic action springs from no earthly ground.

A soberer kind of heroism is available for the human race than either of these two can seriously consider. It may be the only option left, but Elkhart has been able to see it only as a way of manipulating Bubba Burr to his "team." The real thing is beyond his grasp, I am afraid.

"Don't go, I need you!" Elkhart cries to Black Soul.

But that need gives Black Soul an edge of superiority; he bolts. "Luna, if they catch me," he calls over his shoulder, "don't let em stick me with the wires!"

Elkhart staggers, falls to his knees. "Oh, he's gone. And I am alone," he says. He reaches out toward Selena. She places her hands on his temples now, allowing Elkhart to lean against her as he murmurs about his shattering hopes. He points woefully to the floor, helpless with dismay. The plans of the Earth Restoration Project are disintegrating before his eyes.

The plans are, in fact, dematerializing in the ballroom and reappearing upstairs in the room of Ali Pshaw, who is closing them back up in their briefcase.

Elkhart receives Selena's touch with a despairing gratitude, shaking his head. In the absence of heroic capacity, he may yet find uses for a gesture of kindness, help in small measure, response to great confusions.

Bubba Burr comes up and helps Elkhart to his feet. He leads him outside, but discomposed by the hush that has fallen in the ballroom, Bubba turns to the door briefly to give a signal to the girl at the music control so that the wedding party may resume. This is a mistake. When he turns back, Elkhart has disappeared from the hotel corridor.

The music starts up. The electricians flash white-light wedding rings upon the floor, splashes of rings upon the guests.

Now the Sisters of Mamacita begin the Dance of the Daughters of Mara. The dance is one that starts with a slow, even spiral, and then the women begin to whirl, spinning in even circles, passing one another in concentric circles, whirling faster and faster, dervish-inspired.

Luna goes to check her audio deck to make sure she has gotten Elkhart on tape, and gazes quizzically at the girl in charge of the music. Somehow during the Daughters of Mara dance, the *Barber of Seville* overture has begun to play again.

In the hall, Black Soul has decided to avoid the front door and goes to the back in the hope of finding some darkened escape passage not covered by the cops. They are still out front overseeing that Berkeley crowd, and he believes he'd never get through. He finds a door that opens onto the swimming pool.

In actual fact, Black Soul might simply have walked out the front. The crowd and the police are now completely taken up with Tsinghai Yana.

The monk has set down his pile of wood and neatly stacked it, with paper and kindling under it, before anybody notices him.

Then he shakes out his blanket, and having reflected carefully on the smoke signal he wishes to send out, he takes a match from his suit pocket.

He sits in a lotus posture before his woodpile, and touches the match to the paper.

As his fire springs up, the crowd rushes up to him, shouting and confused. When he lowers the blanket to make his first signal, they seem to grow hysterical. A girl shrieks: "Does he have kerosene?" Another: "What's in that brown paper bag?" She is of course pointing to the bag containing Black Velvet, which he always takes with him. "Oh, God!" moan several others.

Reluctantly, as Tsinghai releases the blanket and flames shoot up again, the police amble over. As soon as they see Tsinghai Yana, however, they spring into action. They know that he is a Buddhist and an Oriental, and they have seen on television what Buddhists do with fire. But they never thought it could happen right there at the Claremont Hotel. It has to be a crime, a misdemeanor, exhibitionism, disturbing the peace—something.

Quickly they seize Tsinghai, who of course remains silent, grasping him under the armpits.

"To the pool!" one of the demonstrators shouts. "He may have soaked himself. He may have other matches."

Another says, "If it's Tsinghai, you can count on it, he's soaked."

And so the cops, taking no chances, bear Tsinghai Yana around to the back of the hotel. The message from his fire goes up in smoke—for the time being.

Lolling on his back in the Jacuzzi whirlpool, we find Rupert Oaks, Boy Scout patrol leader, who feels as if he has just made Eagle rank, and he is stroking the soft silk hair of Evi. "Wow!" Rupert sighs. "I never knew it would be like this."

Evi has fortunately been a little early for her appointment with Rupert, so that by now Rupert is quite happy with its outcome. As far as Evi is concerned, it has only just begun. She strokes his cheek and says, "Oh, you're cute, so cute."

As it happens, Rupert is satisfied enough to end their communion at this point, feeling warmed throughout his being, and so in a sense what occurs next is like a rescue to him.

Black Soul, upon letting himself out the back door, trips the burglary alarm, which frightens Rupert, who thinks of his mother in a momentary confusion. "Could *she* have set an alarm?" he asks out loud as he leaps up and grabs a towel and runs into the bathhouse.

Hearing a scuffle in the pathway as the police and demonstrators approach the pool bearing the monk, Black Soul makes a snap decision. There is really nothing else for him to do. He leaps into the Jacuzzi whirlpool just as the police reach the Olympic-size pool and begin to dunk the monk.

Black Soul sees Evi at once, of course, and his old vice comes instantly to mind. How has this happened? he wonders. What a peculiar run of luck! He reaches out and grabs her, bent, of course, upon rape.

However, he doesn't know Evi as we do. There is no rape, only such a reception as would unman the most determined rapists. Black Soul *is* determined and tries hard, telling her to pinch it, squeeze it, pump it, thump it, as the water whirls about them.

Meanwhile, the crowd at the large pool are dunking what they honestly believe would have become in seconds a flaming Buddhist. "Can you smell the kerosene?"

"Naw, that's just incense or alcohol." Tsinghai Yana, having left his body as soon as the police laid hands upon him, having another errand, makes no move, but merely continues sitting in the lotus posture he has assumed when he struck the match. The police dip him in and out, holding him by his robes.

A few of the protesters think the dunking is going on too long, and they jump into the pool, laying hands on the police. A terrible tumble commences, police and protesters splashing the entire arena. Signs of protest are soaked and float face down in the water, drowned. Clothing is ripped off.

Other police arrive and begin to make arrests. In the spirit of the occasion, Tsinghai Yana is nearly forgotten. His body sinks slowly like a Buddha statue dropped in honey, eyes open, serene, still in its lotus posture.

The first young man who has spoken unpleasantly to Tsinghai, saying "Speak, damn you!" now is overcome with remorse. He dives in and begins to search around on the bottom of the pool. Frantic, he comes up without having found him, only to see him floating on the surface, as if he rests on a lotus pad. The young man drags Tsinghai from the pool, finds that he is breathing, lifts him onto one of the vinyl flowered sunchairs, smooths his face and clothing and kneels before him.

The monk is beginning to reenter his body, and now he shakes his head, smiling down at the prostrate protester, who is sobbing, begging forgiveness, begging a blessing, swearing to become a mendicant, a meditator—anything, if the monk will only become his teacher. The boy sinks onto the concrete before his master, who at last reaches out his hands and lays them on the young man's head, silencing his outpouring.

Over in the Jacuzzi pool, Evi and Black Soul go unnoticed. We shall leave them there, in a labor worthy of them both, through which they both may find a means of making that Prodigious Leap Evi has been dreaming of for so long.

Ali Pshaw goes down in the elevator and searches out the manager, who is beside himself over what is going on in the swimming pool. He remembers now that the portfolio of drawings was entrusted to him by Bubba Burr and not this man, whom he decides, in his nervous, distracted state, is an impostor.

He gives a signal to the policeman who is still guarding his plateglass door, and within a matter of minutes Ali Pshaw is in a patrol car and will be taken to spend the night in jail for stealing valuable documents. As the car pulls out from the hotel, the wail of an ambulance siren sounds approaching.

Even though Pshaw will be apologetically released the next day, bailed out by his protégé, Bubba Burr, and begged forgiveness of, Ali Pshaw is not reluctant to pass a night incarcerated, as he will wryly put it, for he is fortunately endowed with a sense of humor and tells himself he needs the time for reflection upon the frailty of ambition in some of his disciples if not in himself.

Emil Jewels is in the ambulance taking Selena Crum to Alpha-Omega Hospital. He is holding her hand, as the siren screams, and during the trip of a few short blocks he speaks to her about the wedding.

He says, "I'll be along soon too, Selena." And because he is aware that she feels little need for words and that he still has use for them, he goes on. "When I was growing up, there were rituals. Seders, bar mitzvahs, weddings. Weddings were to bring together the patriarch and sons, the mother and daughters, the grandparents, and always we knew those enactments we made were a gesture to some higher event, to create a higher consciousness in us all. A wedding has its psychic reality elsewhere, wherever the prayers went, but it was a wedding." He strokes her hand almost absently, but Selena is paying attention to him, to something in his voice she recognizes as being close to despair. "But now we do not marry. We have mock weddings, imitation families, nonevents called group-ins, sleeping consciousness, the phony high."

Selena stirs on the narrow mattress of the ambulance. They have stopped for a red light at College Avenue. "Emil," she says, "you sound—homesick."

"What a woman you are, you always know. I'm homesick, all right. For the God I used to know, relentless, ruthless, not into these pain-free deceptions. Look at you, Selena, you're going to die. My old God tells me that's nothing to get high on. But rather to despair of not having you here." A silver tear slides down into his beard.

Selena smiles, presses his hand. "Thank you, Emil," she says. "I'll repay those tears by haunting you long enough to lift you from this little fit of grief."

He presses her hand and loses his voice. She goes on, however. "Listen, Emil, do me a favor. I know this sounds ridiculous, but there I am. Don't let them leave my casket open. I had a dream a few days ago in which I was dead and they'd left the damned box open. I was afraid to look at my face. I still don't want to look at a dead face. I had imagined that by now it wouldn't matter. A body is only fertilizer, after all. Funny that in one way Elkhart is right."

"Maybe you need to look, Selena."

"Damn it, Emil, you do this. My box is all paid for at the New Life Chapel. But tell them I forgot to instruct them to close it up for good as soon as I am in it."

He pats her hand. "All right, Selena." He nods.

She frets, unhappy with his acquiescence somehow. "You could say I don't have the courage to believe in death. But the fact is, I *don't* believe in it. So I don't want to see it." She sighs. "I suppose this worry means I'll have to incarnate again!"

"Maybe if they left it open, Selena, you wouldn't see anybody there. Think it over."

They look at one another for a moment. Selena smiles. "Emil Jewels," she says, "you old toad. Leave it open. Let me see."

He bends over and kisses her on the forehead.

And with the kiss of her last lover of this life, there appears in the corner of the ambulance beside the door her lover of five hundred years in his etheric body (his present incarnation still being at the pool).

"Tsinghai!" she exclaims in what Emil Jewels has to assume is delirium. "I knew you'd come!" It has been my idea to reunite them, to have Tsinghai Yana stand in for me as guide in this inexplicable passage from one state to another. After he appears, however, the reunion goes out of my control.

She also says, "Philomen, are you there, too?"

I tell her yes. Then she amazes me by saying, "Well, you know what to do now, don't you?"

Wondering if after all she *is* delirious, I inquire, "What do you mean, Selena?"

"Your next move, Phil."

"I am awaiting instructions, Selena."

Then she says to me, "You know, you have far to go."

"True," I say a bit uneasily.

Selena murmurs. "It's simply time for you to reincarnate, old dear."

It's a shocker. I haven't thought of that, but she is right. Her last act proves it to me.

She speaks her last words: "There is just one thing I don't understand," she says to Tsinghai. "Why did you ever give Elkhart the rod of power?"

Almost at once, her face undergoes a total change. All that Emil Jewels and I can see is that she is released from her inquiring look of intense concern and seems to receive a satisfactory answer. Her forehead relaxes; her face is lit from within as if with the taper of the saints. Then she slips away from *me*, fleeting past me and Emil with her lover of five hundred years. So swiftly do they go, into regions I have never traveled, that I do not hear the monk's answer which must have brought about this change in her face. She has taken a Prodigious Leap right over me and beyond.

And as I linger here with Emil Jewels, I feel the planet's gravitational tug. He is looking at Selena's earthly form as if she is still there, while he considers her question. Emil momentarily has forgotten the perspective of multiple lifetimes from which Selena made any inquiry into motives, such as the monk's gift of power to a man who would abuse it. Her question has reached him within the more narrow confines of this one life and reverberates with all the other riddles in his troubled, only human heart. Yes, why, why?

". . . a closed aluminum room with a trap-door floor."

"Listen! We've almost got God cornered."

"... the first Asian President of the United States."

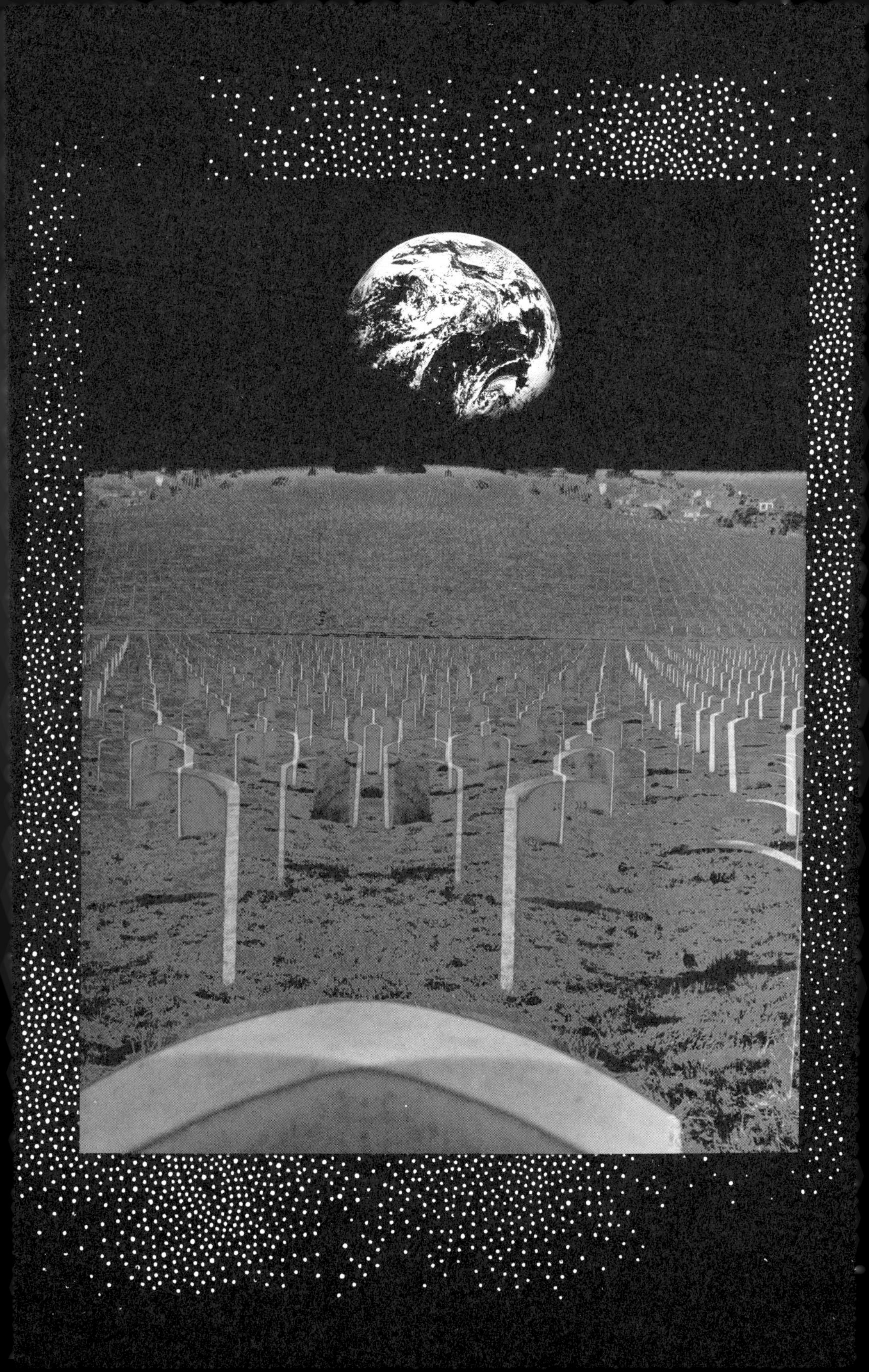

Foretellings

Many reports of this kind deal with future existences, such as Elkhart has projected in his new Atlantis. As I said at the outset, my assignment is limited to earthly happenings. Nevertheless, I shall yield to a final self-indulgence by setting down here a few forecasts about those of whom I have written. Over a hundred years ago, I was incarnated as a novelist, and in those days epilogues explained the workings of fate and the faithful received rewards and evil was not allowed to go unpunished. Because the orderliness of such epilogues suggests a Karmic patterning, I feel some poetic justice, if not literal truth, in these prophecies.

Ginseng (or Goliath) will give up his job on Alcatraz Island and become a ferryman, bearing visitors to the Island, for he will learn that Gautama himself was once such a boatman. Ginseng will begin to speak in parables to the visitors he bears across. Moreover, he will be able to join the longshoreman's union, earning more as a ferryman than he has as either a tour guide or a gardener. Occasionally he will visit Carrie's garden, to dig up the roots he has left there.

Peter Delgado will try to change his life two ways. He will go into a Trappist monastery, in order to detach himself from subjectivity and disengage from the terror of old age. However, he will still own a Porsche, and quite without warning he will occasionally leave the monastery and bolt to Mexico for his rejuvenating injections. There he is to meet and fall for a woman also visiting the German doctor's fountain of youth clinic. Peter will later discover that she is two hundred years older than he, but they will already be so involved he will have to surrender his last old-age tremor. It is not given me to know how long their adventure will last—in centuries, that is.

The Little Mother will start her own film company and will star the Sisters, using techniques introduced some years ago by Busby Berkeley but developing them in a way that will nearly burst the collective mind of the San Francisco Bay Area, but which I cannot here divulge.

Ali Pshaw will eventually make his own secret known to the world. We will learn that he leads a double life, the least of which is that of a collector of royalties for revealing the secrets of others. Word will spread that he goes about doing good as a nameless nobody, but none will ever discover who he is. He will come to be considered an imbecile.

Emil Jewels will have a small monument erected for Selena Crum, which Carrie will design. It will be in the shape of a pyramid and will contain one of Carrie's sculptures, not of Selena but of a symbol chosen by Emil, the rattle of Isis, the crux ansata, with which the goddess of wisdom offered renewal to the earth, and whose eternal emblem Selena has, probably with the help of Isis, preserved from corrupt usage.

The Boy Scout from Troup Number 7, Rupert Oaks, will go far. Following his bracing encounter with Evi, he will rendezvous all summer long at the hot whirlpool with older women who cannot resist his charm and wish to mother him. He will eventually join the company of those who have taken down a piece of the astral plane and are living on it in Grant's Pass, Oregon.

Evi's fourth chakra will become centered and balanced. Also Evi's craving to find her Soul Mate will be attained, as reward for giving up her fascination with evil.

Black Soul and Evi will not remain in the whirlpool much past midnight after the wedding celebrating subsides. However, they will reach a decision next week to marry, for Evi is even more fascinated with Black Soul's mind than she has been with Elkhart's lore.

This will mark the end of Black Soul's life as an irresponsible inseminator. His capacity for sexual activity will for a time exceed Evi's, but as Soul Mates, they will attain a nearly perfect balance, as Black Soul's progesterone goes into a slight decline in coming years. It is at such a point they may be expected to awaken to the larger world.

Then Black Soul will enter the elitist middle class and start his own business, which will be highly successful, proving there is surviving vitality in the free enterprise system. It will be a print shop, which will grow into a publishing house called Soulbooks, which specializes in the writings of prisoners, protesters and ex-profs fired by the University of California. After its political successes, Soulbooks will bring about a revival of letters never before enjoyed on this continent. As previously mentioned, Berkeley is not Paris. However, its Sylvia Beach (a black) will soon proclaim the emergence of the Berkeley school of fiction, and this generation's incarnation of Gertrude Stein will remain at home to guide the novice connoisseur to the thousand crash pads of its artists. The muses of foresight tell me that the Berkeley School will be instructed by androgynous guides.

Occasional regressions will cause Black Soul to steal out into the night to vandalize a cigarette ad, but never to violate a woman again.

The long silence of Tsinghai Yana will never be broken in this Karma. He will return from his etheric escort of Selena to find that the water cult he foresaw has started, called *Surfacing*, in which adepts will learn to sit upon the water. Tsinghai will officiate at a memorial service at Hai Phong Harbor, where this Karma will end for him. The drowning of the revered monk will occur there, where in a velvety absent-mindedness his body will sink, never to be found despite insistent draggings of the Bay. Some cultists will report that he later came ashore in the dark, having been submerged but suspended, and walked for months overland, to disappear in the Gobi Desert. Sightings of Tsinghai are frequently reported in Shambhala of the Seven Gates, a city visible only to visitors of the etheric plane. The message of the silent monk will be disputed for a thousand years by Surfacers, people who will devote their lives to silence and who will conduct their raging debate by telepathy. They will try to determine whether Tsinghai actually surfaced at the Claremont pool and sat in the lotus, or whether the entire surfacing was a metaphor. This schism will be demonstrated in paintings by those who say he was a god showing him seated in full lotus upon the water with eyes closed, and by those who think him a mortal, representing him as standing open-eyed, waist deep. These painters and other Surfacers will demonstrate that great lessons can be absorbed by the persons for whom they are intended, in this case, prisoners of speech—a story few saints can rival for success.

As for Luna's child, it will be neither white nor black, but will have eyes with a decided epicanthic fold. This will surprise everyone, and Black Soul, Jim Smith and Luna all will try to look into their backgrounds for some Asian influence, but to no avail. Luna will never unearth the facts of her own parentage. Black Soul's mother will be incensed at being questioned, will tell her son she has nothing to hide unless it goes back to some slaveholder she knows nothing about. As the slaves in Black Soul's background lived on an island off the Georgia coast where it is doubtful Asians were even allowed, the likelihood of his having contributed the fold is narrow. However, he cannot be excluded as father, because of Luna's own genetic vacuum. The only possible clue is in Jim Smith's family, which prided itself in once tracing its ancestry back to Captain John Smith, and that may throw a cloud of suspicion over the purity of the great Pocahontas legend.

What may be of stronger interest is how Luna will fare as a mother. It may be safe to say that she will be a much finer mother than she ever knew herself. But then, as you recall, she was an orphan. It will also be truthful to state that motherhood will have so favorable, so softening an effect upon her that Jim Smith will lose all his resistance to her and beg her to take part in a classic marriage with an ordinary legal license and perhaps even a minister. She, however, will refuse. Jim will not overcome his tendency to tell her all the unhappy imagery she arouses, and she prefers to keep him at a distance. However, whenever her meaningful work obliges her to travel (frequently), Jim will stay with his daughter and enjoy that latent gift for mothering Luna perceived in him on the houseboat.

Thanks to Luna's prompt and effective chelating, the child will be perfect and adorable. She will be called Onesum. She will not do psychic readings from her crib as Luna imagined, nor be at all sympathetic to psychic matters. Onesum will grow up to become the first Asian-American President of the United States, though not the first woman President.

A thunderbolt informs me that this remarkable child will be the last incarnation of the spirit of Selena Crum, in which she will enjoy a broader theater for the use of strength which she began to practice in the lifetime we have examined.

As for the sinister Elkhart, his disappearance is to be a prolonged mystery. Rumors will become rife. He will be thought to be in Grant's Pass, again trying to master the unknown on a piece of the astral plane, or to have discovered another such space in the Grand Tetons. Some will say he has been arrested, tried and sentenced for molesting a minor and committed to jail under an alias, Elkton Stronghold, and there given psychosurgery, so dreaded by Black Soul, and to have become a simpering vegetable. However, all that is probably so much wish fulfillment, for signs will begin to appear from time to time, graffiti; the first will be in Ghiradelli Square and will say simply ELKHART LIVES. But in Berkeley, where slogans abound, such as ABOLISH MONEY; SLA, HERE TO STAY: FREAKS UNITE, etc., signs will appear saying simply:

♀
ELKHART

Sometimes, the sinister design of his double-cross R.I.P. unit will be drawn underneath the name. Perhaps the most plausible explanation of Elkhart's whereabouts is that he merely slipped back into his CIA activities and will live out this incarnation doing what he knows best. But another speculation will insist that he becomes the murderous Mafia hood named Bull Bogg, who after being tried, convicted and having appeals denied, will receive, along with forty-six other hoods, the usual Presidential pardon.

And the legend, the key to Elkhart's design containing the entire nomenclature of the machine, may be discovered at some later time. Labeled "farm equipment," the component machinery will be found stored in potato cellars in Dorris, California, in sacks and boxes having such trade names as International Harvester and John Deere. The entire HOG will never be assembled, and the components will be left to rust in their sacks. The splendid chassis, however—that great ambulatory crux ansata—will be discovered in Boise, Idaho, and will be brought to Berkeley (perhaps encouraging the graffiti). It will be purchased by a new and eager curator of the University Art Museum, and will be placed on view in the rear garden. This precisely executed object lesson (all parts being metric, very special, with welded seams, welds of such expert quality that they contribute to a compelling artistic whole), this work will be praised and disputed as a product of a modern-day da Vinci, so fascinating in its detail that the entire art world will search in vain for the artist who executed Elkhart's plans.

The blueprints themselves will find a secure place in the University of California Bancroft Library of rare books, which will purchase them for a sum the governor will find outrageous. They will be stored in a vault of special documents, such as the working drawings of the Dolbe steam car and other local oddities.

Books of new psychology will continue to find their source in California. Bubba Burr will publish innumerable volumes explaining the meaning of everything. His annotated text and commentary on this report of mine, a book of more than two thousand pages, illustrated with Elkhart's drawings and an "interpreted legend" will eventually appear posthumously as the crowning achievement of his lifetime.

I must report that Harrison's attempt to correct one of man's errors, in terms of the automobile, will meet with failure. Carrie's vision of the freeway dead stop will not take place. However, an enormous sum will be paid Harrison by the men from Detroit, evidence of Harrison's own psychic foresight that they would buy him off and shelve his additive. Still in the front rank of men who foster the human activities that place endurance before exhilaration, he will next team up with a nuclear scientist in creating first an electrostatic precipitator, a simple installation which will have the capacity to wipe out industrial atmospheric contamination. Whether self-interest and corporate greed will permit its use is not given me to know. But as there is possibly no other planet being readied for the people of this earth, Harrison and all others like him will continue to receive what encouragement we can send, until they are proved wrong.

Carrie's way of seeing things will become fairly commonplace, the *déjà vu* will yield to the *toujours vu*. Once her moon-change difficulties are over, she will begin to *hear* things in a new way. She will go on living and working in Berkeley until the fault gives way. As the catastrophic downfall of the cities is already widely predicted elsewhere, there is no need to catalogue details here, but only to say that Carrie and Harrison, with other worthy survivors, will enjoy renewed life in the hills. And it is there, in those distant landscapes, where the earth yields little bright green patches of staghorn moss, that she will begin to hear things, such as the stamping of cloven hoofs and a quiet, low belling in the night.

As for me, Philomen, lover of men and women, bearer of omens, I have considered the sage advice of my friend Selena Crum to reincarnate. I see that there is still much to overcome, that though I have worked diligently at this report, it too clearly reveals that I am riddled with human flaws and fascinated by the spell of Karma. And so I shall make reentry, this time perhaps as a . . . as a male entity. One, however, who has completely integrated his female principle.

ABOUT THE AUTHOR
. . . .

CHARLOTTE PAINTER, the author of three previous books, teaches and writes in the San Francisco Bay Area. In 1966 she was a fellow at the Radcliffe Institute, and in 1973 she won the National Endowment for the Arts award for fiction. In 1974 she co-edited with Mary Jane Moffat *Revelations: Diaries of Women*.

Lloyd Patrick Baker, who took the photographs, is a painter and photographer now living in Oregon.

PS
3566
.A346
S43
1976